Hillcity Press

Edited by Monica Wanat

Cover art by Damián V.

Cover design by Mibl Art

Map by Maarten de Wekker

CROWN

OF

DUST

• SCEPTER AND CROWN BOOK TWO •

**HILLCITY
PRESS**

To Mom, for everything

Sign up for my VIP reader newsletter and get exclusive access to free stories, giveaways, first looks at covers, and sneak peeks of new projects.

Vip.cfeblack.com/join

1

ALY

A ly snatched the bullet out of the air without opening her eyes. She groaned as she twisted the hot, smooth metal in her hand. She dropped the small shell from her outstretched hand, where it lodged in the wet grass beside eight other expended rounds.

Nine bullets, and not one of them had transformed into anything remotely *un*-bulletlike.

With a wave of her arms, she pushed away a cocoon of warm, sea-storm mist swirling about her in the lawn adjacent to Refere's royal palace. To the left, below a row of neatly trimmed hedges, Vona's rocky shores broke the waves tossed up by an oncoming squall.

"Again," Aly demanded.

A few steps away, Red sighed. "Let's take a break."

Distant thunder punctuated his last word. A nearby game of croquet paused, and the players began to collect their balls and shuffle toward the palace.

"We have to be able to replicate it," Aly said, her words not carrying beyond the barrier of her magical shroud that also conveniently hid them from watching eyes. She pressed her

1

palms to her face and tried to think of *something* she hadn't tried. "We agreed to do ten."

Sliding one more cartridge into the pistol, Red shook his head gently. "Last one, Aly."

"Aim for my head."

Red's mouth worked for several seconds. He lifted his pistol, then lowered it. "Come on. This isn't working."

Aly bit her lip. "I can do it. I made that," she said, indicating his ash blade in its sheath at Red's waist. "I think the reason this isn't working is that I need to feel afraid in order for my magic to —" she waved her hands in little circles, "—do whatever it did that night."

Red wiped sweat from his forehead with the back of his hand. "Then let me at least say that, for the record, I hate this."

He lifted his arm, took aim, and fired.

The quickness of his movement, the unexpectedness of it, made Aly flinch. Her heart tripped and restarted, and in her hand, instead of a bullet, rested a large, white peony, half-crushed from her grip.

"A-ha!" she screamed, jumping up and down. "It worked!"

Red rushed to her side, peering down at the crumpled flower. "A rose?"

She tossed the bloom at his chest, where it flumped sadly and dropped to the grass. "A peony, actually. A *flower*, Red! That was a bullet you shot at me." She pointed at the dead bloom.

Eyes wide with curiosity, he stared down at the petals. "That's not even made of metal."

She smiled. "A complete transformation."

"Should we keep it?" asked Red, bending down to pick up the flower, which fell apart, scattering its petals on the lawn.

Aly took it gingerly from his hand. "Strange," she murmured.

"What is?"

"This flower has a Well." She met his gaze with lifted brows. "It's small, but it's bright." Her mind pressed into the tiny Truthwell sparkling inside of the flower. *This feels familiar…* Aly tilted her head, brows pinching. "Bizarre," she muttered. "The flower's Well has the exact same pattern as yours."

Ignoring Red's questions, she cut her eyes to the hilt of the ash blade at his hip. She'd examined it many times, mostly not wanting to hold the blade that had killed her father, but drawn to its curiosities all the same. It had no Well, of course, like most manmade items, but the blade, which crackled and glowed like true embers, seemed as if it contained light within that she simply couldn't access.

Red abandoned his questions about the flower and lifted his coronet to run a hand through his curls. "Can you tell what you did differently with this one? Did you figure out the secret? Because I really don't want to shoot you again."

Her concentration on the small, star-like Well of the peony made her nearly miss his words. "And here I was thinking you were enjoying it." The corner of her lips curled up.

He tucked the pistol back in its holster. "So, are peonies your favorite?"

Aly blinked at him, surprised by the sudden new inquiry. "I think so, why?"

"You think so? You don't know what your favorite flower is? I though all women knew that."

Aly smirked. "Oh, right, we just sit around contemplating our favorite blooms so that we can be swept away when a man magically gifts us the one type of flower we love most." She batted her eyelashes. "Then we'll know it's meant to be."

Shaking his head, Red let out an exasperated sigh. "I was only curious." A look crossed his face that spoke of embarrassment or possibly regret.

Aly froze. Maybe he *was* trying to figure out her favorite flower because he wanted to give her a bouquet of them. Her stomach twisted at this possibility and threatened to break the concentration she needed to maintain the Pull from his Truthwell

3

that fueled her magic. She couldn't look at him as this thought flooded her mind, so she poured her attention onto the mostly petal-less peony.

The memory of his hand resting against hers on the train had replayed in her head a thousand times. As it flashed in her mind again, the hot blush that always accompanied these thoughts burst up her neck and face. She'd been an idiot to say anything to him—to give him any reason to look at her the way he now did when no one was watching.

She kept her eyes averted, but his gaze washed over her like the breaking waves below, and her shroud flickered as she fought the desire to look back at him with matching intensity.

Growing up a poor girl from a small town, she'd never imagined she'd garner the affection of the king—or want it.

But now that he'd shown her what it felt like to be seen, she knew she could never go back to the life of shadows that she'd endured for so long.

With a courageous inhale, she turned her eyes up to meet his. For a moment, neither looked away. His expression held admiration, respect, and something buried beneath those feelings that she wasn't yet ready to admit. Using the energy from his Truthwell, she kept up a half-dozen spells—her shroud to hide them from watching eyes, the constant swirling of her new Master's ring comprised of white mist, and protective enchantments on Red, Elise, Sebastian, and Lord Weston Grey, who were all inside Vona's palace awaiting dinner with King Lordan.

The energy burning inside Red's Well called to her mind like food to the starving man, but another appetite had surfaced of late that was proving even stronger: the desire to drink in his gaze.

She heaved a sigh, always mentally reprimanding herself for these slips of duty—these moments when she cherished his glance. "Don't distract me," she quipped, pretending his playful grin was entirely unwanted. He frowned, his expression snagging inside Aly's chest.

"Ah, here she comes," Red said.

Aly's eyes snapped up. Princess Elise strode toward them, already in her dinner attire. Her golden gown flowed out to meet the fading rays of a sunset cut short by the oncoming storm. Ever since arriving in Vona days ago, Red's sister's entire demeanor had shifted. On the train ride, she'd been tense, flittering, wringing her hands more than a princess ought. Now that they were here and she was facing the man who'd broken her heart, King Lucien's son, Lordan, she stood taller, her cheeks hard as marble, her eyes sharp as a chisel about to shape stone.

Aly smiled at her as she extended her shroud around the older of Red's two sisters. "Thank you for meeting us out here," she said after the women exchanged polite curtseys. It warmed Aly's chest to accept these acknowledgments from Elise. She'd dreamed for years of a friendship with the two princesses.

Elise looked around at the thickening clouds. "I do not mind the fresh air, but do not expect me to dally out here in the rain." She smirked at her brother. "Why are you out here, anyway?"

"Shooting Aly," he said with a sly grin.

Elise's face jolted in surprise. She peered between Red and Aly then said, "Oh, you are serious." Her eyebrows pinched. "What an odd relationship you two have."

Aly's attention dropped to the grass.

Red coughed away a quick laugh and said, "I've changed my mind. We need you to speak to Lordan."

Elise tossed her chin up and gave the most proper chuckle Aly had ever heard. "I knew you would see reason, brother. What is it you wish me to say, for I imagine you still do not want me to slap him?"

"While I'd very much like you to slap him, I don't think slapping the new King of Refere would have an advantageous effect

5

on our nations' alliance. But we think King Lordan would be more likely to tell you the truth than us."

"But you have magic," Elise replied.

"But he was in love with you once," Red said.

Aly cringed in unison with Elise's scowl. Red often meant well, but sometimes his words came out as blunt and rough as splintered wood.

"What he means," Aly interjected, "is that King Lordan owes you the truth. He knows you better than he knows us. He will expect *you* to think he is lying, which means he will not be surprised if you demand a Reckoner—and you should."

Red nodded at Aly's words. "Yes. Make sure to find out the truth. Ask as many questions as necessary." At Elise's sigh, he added, "You wanted to help; we're letting you. We must find out if we can trust Lordan."

Elise examined her gloved hands. "Anything else?"

Red and Aly shared a glance. He replied, "No. Nothing else. You may go before it rains."

Elise spun and marched back toward the palace.

Once Aly had released the princess from her shroud, she said to Red, "She's still in love with him."

Red laughed in disbelief, shaking his head. "No way."

Aly's gaze narrowed. "She wouldn't be putting up this much of a front of *not* liking him anymore if she truly didn't."

"Should we be worried?"

Aly stepped through the wet grass toward the footpath that led back to Vona's mesmerizing palace. "Your sister is not to be trifled with. No, I don't think we have to worry about her."

The swiftly moving storm blotted out the sunset, speeding up night's arrival. Glancing at the sky, Aly said, "We should go inside."

"I thought you said *it's just rain*?"

"I don't mean the rain. I mean the beasts."

With that, they bolted for the palace.

Since leaving Bulvarna, stories of escaped Canyon beasts had trickled across the continent, spreading tales of horror in their wake. The soldiers stationed at Caridan had been overwhelmed as the beasts, emboldened by some unknown force, had begun rising from the Deep in waves. And now that Kassia had fled her country and no sovereign had yet taken her place, the few soldiers stationed along the Bulvarnan side of the Canyon had abandoned their posts, leaving that side of the Canyon unprotected. Staying out of doors in the dark was a risk no king should take, not when visibility was limited and Canyon beasts preferred to hunt at night.

"Think Lordan will come to our aid?" asked Red, for the dozenth time, as they raced the rain shower to the palace entrance.

The new Referen king had agreed to meet with Red tomorrow, amid the influx of well-wishers, mourners, noble families, and opportunity seekers coming to Vona for the former king's funeral and Lordan's coronation. In Refere, there was no Accession ceremony, no period of trial for the new sovereign in which the throne was considered temporary before the official coronation months later. Refere only held one ceremony, which happened as soon as possible after a monarch died. Lordan's coronation would happen before Red's, which was set for summer's end.

"Yes, I think he will aid us," she replied again, as she had each time her king had asked. Lordan's father had fought with them in Bulvarna. Refere was an ally they could count on.

Aly did not use magic to keep herself dry; instead, she relished the coolness of the rain soaking her clothes. As a child living in the small cabin outside of Kitrel, when she was discovering her magic, she had tried to stop the rain over her head. Since she'd mastered the simple magic of diverting the water droplets, she'd rarely let herself feel the rain. But today, there was something refreshing, painfully nostalgic even, in the scent of it on her skin, the pressure of it on her hair.

At the portico to the guest entrance, they stopped and flung water off their hands and wiped it from their faces.

"Will you not dine with us?" asked Red as he scuffed some sticky grass off his boots.

He'd taken to wanting her visible all the time. A part of her yearned for this—a life of being *seen*, of being part of reality—yet there were advantages in invisibility, and a king should recognize that. "You don't always show your enemies your greatest weapon," she retorted.

A wry grin flickered on his face. "*You* said Lordan was on our side. Wear the cloak and mask. Please come."

Warmth flooded Aly's cheeks. The way he'd looked at her these past weeks had awoken in her a magic she'd never known, not even when she'd trained with Grey. It threatened to muddle her own intentions.

She stiffened. "I must walk the parade route, cast my enchantments for tomorrow's procession. We can't take any risks."

Referens took celebrations to a new level, and Lordan had ordered a parade for the following day, and the day after that, and the one after that. *In memory of my father,* he'd said, but really these parades were a way to show himself at the head of the line, as the head of state. As another young king, Lordan would face many of the same obstacles that Red faced. He needed to prove himself a strong leader from day one. People loved to celebrate, and Lordan was giving them what they wanted. Not a dumb move.

Red's smile vanished. "Very well." His tone switched back to business. They were, after all, under a Binding agreement, much like business partners. He was to rule. She was to keep him alive and well enough to fulfill this destiny. Her vows bid her to serve the sovereign, not laugh with him at dinners or dance with him in foreign palaces. He unhooked the buckle holding the holster for the ash blade, then he passed belt, holster, and blade to her. "See you in the morning, then." He turned and departed into the palace.

She looped the belt around her own waist, as she had done every night, per his request—as though giving a blade to a sorcerer meant much. Nonetheless, she was grateful for the hope he held that somehow this strange blade she'd crafted with her magic could somehow accomplish more than an average dagger and that by giving it to her for her nightly walks, he was in a small way adding to her protection. She tightened her invisibility shroud around herself, no longer needing to hide another person. She slipped back into the rain, her mind reaching into the darkness for threats and fiends.

Vona's cobblestone streets were already decorated with all manner of flowers, banners, and even magical enchantments placed by Protectors. Aly spotted a cloaked figure conjuring two leaping dolphins made of glinting shards of glass; these would make a dazzling display in the sunlight of tomorrow's parade. As she passed, the other sorcerer shot her a narrow gaze, his magic enabling him to sense her presence even when no one else could.

Per their new king's edict, all Vonans were under a loose curfew, which meant no nighttime excursions without an express excuse. Naturally, the people did not obey. As Aly turned down one particularly tavern-dense street, the noise of bustling pedestrians greeted her ears.

"He should have made it an order," she grumbled to herself as she weaved, unseen and unheard, through the loud throng of people. These revelers had no idea the havoc a foxblood or pack of woodwolves could wreak if it happened upon this happy crowd. Aly shuddered at the thought.

Her job was to protect Red, but she couldn't resist tossing up an enchantment that diverted any prowling foxbloods or wood-wolves from this street. Perhaps elsewhere in the city people were more sensible and had gone indoors. She could only hope.

She walked the parade route as quickly as possible, not feeling the need to fly and not feeling the need to dawdle. Much like the magical decorations, her enchantments would remain until tomorrow. As she walked, she scanned the Truthwells around her for signs of lyths or people corrupted by Canyon magic.

The rain had stopped, and the sound of the waves drew Aly toward the shore. She elected to walk back to the palace along the seaside, using this time to think.

On the road overlooking the Gulf of Eseda, Aly twirled the ash blade in her fingers, mesmerized by its amber glow, perplexed by the way the light danced within the weapon she'd made. She inhaled sea air, convinced she would never tire of the salty scent. Her hair, on the other hand, battled with the humid breeze, and Aly tired of continuously swatting her curls off her face and neck. A quick spell glued her hair to her head.

When this blade had killed her father, she'd given it to Red so she wouldn't need to hold it or think about what it had done, but as they'd traveled farther from Bulvarna, her curiosity and attraction to the blade had grown.

Somehow, this weapon was the key to understanding the power behind a Beacon and Beholder.

All she knew so far was that this blade had pierced her father's magic shield—a shield not breakable by any other spell she'd attempted. The Master's ring she'd worn for years, the one that she'd also crafted to remind herself she'd one day face her father, had fueled her idea for the dagger now in her hands. Magic obeyed the truth. In that moment when she had faced her father, the truth inside of Aly, guided by the *Verad* and powered by Red's bright Well, had created the very weapon she'd needed.

It was almost like the magic acted on its own, driven by a stronger hand than mine.

Her mind rolled through everything she'd studied about Beacons during her six years of serving the late King Gevar. The *Canticles of Magic*, poetic episodes penned by sorcerers over the millennia, spoke of the beauty of Beacons, but they rarely described *how* the Beholder managed to draw more power from the Beacon or how the sorcerer was to wield this kind of energy. If anything, a Beacon was more dangerous than any other creature alive; to hold the energy to change the world was a terrifying thing.

"Maker, guide us," Aly mumbled, scared at her own thoughts and worried she'd muddy her chance at improving the world and, instead, wander into magic she didn't understand and ignite unforeseen consequences.

The sea smell turned bitter, laced with the stench of rotting fish, but as she glanced down the to waters splashing the seawall below, Aly's stomach churned. The waves seemed to reach up, angry at her presence. *Or are they merely agitated from the storm?*

Stop it, she told herself. The sea was not the Black River. The sea was lovely. It sparkled despite the darkness. It teemed with life-giving fish. The Black River's oily waters offered only death.

Her memories of that night were fuzzy. She'd never felt pain like the agony of the death curse raging through her. The water of the Black River had held onto her, gripping her as the curse funneled back into its source. She shivered at the memory, despite the warm summer breeze.

To keep from falling into those dark memories again, she closed her eyes and focused on the light swarming all around her. The ocean's warm, bright depths soothed her agitated mind. Behind her, safe within their homes, human Truthwells glowed like bonfires.

A few Truthwells, however, roamed the streets.

Aly yawned and spread her arms wide. Her cloak barely fluttered in the dying post-storm breeze. She'd spent the past two nights keeping watch over her travelling companions, barely allowing herself any sleep as they reposed in the palace of a man who could quite possibly be involved in the scheme meant to kill Red through the gift of a cursed handkerchief. She needed a burst of energy if she wished to stay awake. Words whispered from her mouth. The breeze obeyed.

A violent rush of sea air pushed against her, nearly toppling her balance. She smiled. Her cloak snapped in the otherwise quiet space.

Then she thought she heard a suctioning sound in the water. With a command, the breeze ceased.

Her senses exploded outward, exploring the area. Among the many flickering Truthwells, there were none dark enough to be a threat to the people she protected. None that disappeared.

Not a lyth, then. She exhaled.

She heard the noise again, then a splash. It came from directly below her.

Squatting down, Aly peered over the stone wall. The disturbed waters swirled. With her mind, she probed the depths, seeking out the Truthwells in the watery world below, those Wells that suffused the entire bay with a golden glow. The Wells of fish drifted about. Even the seaweed danced with its own dim light.

A shadow darted among the pale light, a shadow only her mind could see.

Aly recoiled, nearly losing her balance atop the wall. To keep from toppling backward, she gripped one of the decorative stone pineapples dotting the seawall, then lost track of the swimming shadow. All her concentration diverted to the water, to locating that dark shape.

Her eyes roved the surface, looking for more ripples. The sea was so full of life and light that finding one shadow was like looking for one particular leaf on a windy fall day.

"Didn't take you for the drinking type," said a voice behind her.

Aly hopped up so fast she actually *did* lose her balance. Toppling over the side of the wall, she let out a small scream, not of fear, but of surprise. A man's voice hollered with her.

Within seconds, she rose over the wall and touched down on the flat road, ankles barely wet from her almost plunge.

Sebastian Thorin had both hands clamped over his head, his mouth hanging open. She smirked, and he snapped to attention, recovering his swagger.

"Nice trick," he said.

"Not a trick. You scared me." She drew the hem of her cloak around her shirt and pants. No one but Red had seen her in these clothes. *Idiot*, she chided herself for dropping her shroud as she'd searched the water.

"You weren't hurling the evening's vintage?"

She frowned in confusion.

He raised his hands. "Fair enough. It looked like you were..." He mimed puking in a most ungentlemanly way.

Under her cloak, Aly crossed her arms. "What are you doing here?"

Seb pressed a knuckle to his mouth and heaved, stumbling forward. Aly leaped aside, only to spot the look of utter delight on Seb's face as his cackling laughter filled the night. Aly shook her head at him, appalled and annoyed that she'd fallen for his little trick.

"You dress like a man," he said, brows up. "Who knew?"

Aly hugged herself, hiding under her cloak. He'd only stated the truth, but she wanted to drop her shroud over her body once more and disappear. Aly titled her head, examining Seb. He had a bag looped around his shoulder.

"You call me out for dressing like a man, yet you carry a purse?"

Seb chuckled. "Nicely done. Red never told me his beautiful

sorcerer was funny too." He slung the bag onto the seawall beside a stone pineapple.

His statement ricocheted in her head. Seb had dropped the word *beautiful* like it was nothing, a foregone conclusion. Red had yet to use this word to describe her. A pang inside her stole her focus away, and she searched out Red's Well in the nearby palace, spotting it like a flash of light on water. A faint *clang* brought her back to the moment. "What are you doing?"

Seb had pulled a tall candlestick from his bag, setting it down on the stone. "I came here to, uh, delight a local." Another candlestick appeared, followed by a blanket.

Aly covered a snort with the back of her hand, but Seb heard it. He stood, a long, white candle in one hand and a broken, white candle in the other. "Guess I'll just have to break this one too," he said, eyeing the one still intact. "She'll never know the difference."

"And who might *she* be?" Aly had never really spoken to Seb, but she'd watched Red converse with his friend so many times she felt she could talk to Seb the same way.

Seb cocked his head back. "You are not at all what I expected."

"Heard that before."

"I bet you have." Seb smiled. He jammed the short candle in one of the elegant holders, then he snapped the taller one and added it in its place. "There. Perfect. Sort of. It's the sentiment that counts. Women like sentiment, I've found."

Aly pursed her lips. "Will this woman enjoy the sentiment of you leaving for Mardon in a few days?"

"You meddle, don't you?" he asked, a slight grin softening his words.

Most women found this man dangerously attractive. He was roguish, but he was so coarse and had as much affection for the women he wooed as he did for a nice suit. "I intervene when necessary," she retorted.

Seb unfolded the blanket. "Her name is Vittoria. And I'm not going to break her heart." When Aly scoffed, he added, "I can show her what *effort* looks like. Most men simply dance with a woman once, ask for her hand, and that's that. Where's the romance in that?"

Pushing a breeze to ruffle his blanket, she said, "You call it romantic to use women and leave them behind? I call that cruelty."

He stood up straight, his smile gone. As she dipped into a brief, dismissive curtsey, she heard a violent splash.

Together, Aly and Seb rushed to peer down at the water. A little to their right, where the seawall curved inland and vanished from sight, fast waves beat outward toward the open water. Sounds of something smacking the water rose in a sickening, off-beat pattern.

In seconds, Aly left Seb and was hurtling toward the disturbance, cloak billowing, her entire body hidden under her shroud of invisibility.

By the time Aly landed on a small, rocky bit of seashore abutting the base of the palace's outer wall, all that remained of the incident were puddles among the stones and droplets dripping back toward the still-swirling water.

Aly raked the water with her mind, searching for the shadow she'd seen. The water was bright with a thousand Truthwells, but she glimpsed a large, dark shape jetting seaward, the darkness of its Well like that of a Canyon beast.

Then she noticed a small cluster of human Truthwells hovering in a place she thought was no more than rocky seashore. They stood directly below one of the massive outer walls of the palace.

Two of the Wells swarmed with the tangled darkness that indicated these people were either habitual liars or trapped unknowingly into believing many lies. Aly determined to see who conspired in such a hidden place.

After scrambling along the wet rocks below the seawall, Aly gave up and hovered above the stones, easing herself along the wall, one hand tracing the damp bricks as she neared the Truth-wells. They hadn't moved since she'd spotted them.

As she turned with the curve of the seawall, she noticed a small path, built right up against the base of the palace. It was not visible from any road or beach, and likely not noticeable from the ships in the harbor, as the path was too small and was surely under water at least twice a day. Even now the storm-tossed waves lapped at the path.

Aly stopped short when she saw who stood in this secret place.

King Lordan of Refere stood before Elise, one of his hands pressed to the stone beside Elise's shoulder. Aly darted away—certain Lordan's Protector would be able to sense her presence—and at that moment, Elise reached back and slapped the king.

2

ELISE

Acool breeze hinting at magic wafted over the tiny, cobbled path and drew a chill into the warm shadows of the coastal night, subduing the angry flush on Princess Elise's cheek. Her hand smarted from the slap, and her breath came faster than the waves.

Lordan, the new King of Refere, cupped his hand-printed cheek. The blonde hairs on his arm were almost white against his tanned skin. "I suppose I deserved that," he grumbled, flexing his jaw open and closed.

Elise stepped out of his reach, sliding her hands across the cold stone wall in this secret place where he had told her to meet. She'd heard her brother's earlier warning not to slap him, but hearing and obeying were two different things.

"Do not bother with pleasantries," she snapped. "The only reason I came to Vona was to hear you deny your hand in my brother's curse." She looked around at the high wall without windows, the narrow ledge on which they stood, the sea's rhythmic waves merely a leap away.

The king's guards stood nearby, arms clasped at their waists, chests high, as if to intimidate a princess.

17

Observing her wandering gaze, Lordan ignored her statement and said, "This is a little-known escape route from the palace. None but the royal family and the thieving crews know of it."

Elise lifted a pale brow. "Are you equating the two?"

He snickered, shifting his weight toward her. He was a slender, tall man composed of precise lines. His straight nose, jutting cheekbones, and flat eyebrows fit well above the royal cut of his suit.

Toss it, he is handsome, Elise concluded for the thousandth time. She'd wanted to marry this man.

"I suppose the police know of it, as well, but they are paid by the crews to avoid this place."

"That does not bother you?" she asked, turning her back to him, glancing down the moonlit stone path. The storm had passed, and stars peeked out from behind the clouds.

"Kings and crews are not so different," he said with a half grin. "We both have need of secrets."

"Indeed," she hissed, whirling on him. "The cursed cloth that nearly killed my brother came from you!" Stepping forward, she pinned one angry finger to his chest. "Explain yourself!"

A flicker of familiar pain crossed his face. She felt an ache in her heart at the very sight of his eyes and the grief they both experienced at the loss of their fathers, but beneath that a small, silent part of her was glad to see him suffer. The feeling was momentary, replaced immediately by regret. She remembered what it felt like the night her own father passed.

Lordan stiffened, hands behind his back. "He survived, did he not?"

So unexpected was his remark that Elise snorted in disbelief. "And do you know the only reason he is alive? Because *he entered the Canyon.*" She hurled the words at him, as if they were poison darts. "Some people think my brother is *corrupted* now. Oh yes, he is alive." She waved an arm. "But he paid a price. I cannot imagine having to go down there." She shuddered.

Lordan studied her with a measured expression. "You want me to tell you the truth?"

"How can I know it is the truth?"

His eyes challenged her for a moment. Then he flicked his wrist, and from behind the guards stepped a young woman. "One of my Reckoners, Salome."

Elise narrowed her gaze at Salome's voluminous dark curls, painted eyes, and full figure. He could have chosen *any* Reckoner, and he chose this one to bring to his meeting with Elise. The woman pulled the neckline of her dress toward her shoulder, revealing the tattoo of a Reckoner—a flaming sun. Elise cringed and looked away. *Why did her tattoo have to be there?*

Inside of Elise, rage snapped to life like kicked embers. She walked down the path a few steps, the sea breeze filling her nose with scents of seaweed and salt. "Why did I come here?" she whispered, more to herself than to Lordan. *Have I fallen into another of Lordan's schemes?*

She spun on her heel. Ignoring the way his eyes melted her insides, she sloughed off her sadness, her emotion, and envisioned a mantle of strength and calm wrapping around her shoulders. A brief image of Aly blinked through her mind. That woman wore a cloak to symbolize her power. The idea of a wardrobe that touted one's strengths wasn't such a bad idea.

"Tell me everything. Leave nothing out, no matter how terrible," she said, measuring each word. She had come here to punish him, and if that included ripping open the wound of his grief, she would do that. She would do whatever was necessary to expose the truth, to learn what really happened.

Lordan stared at her with hard eyes, his jaw working. Then he turned, leaned against the stone wall and cupped both hands behind his neck, very much at ease. "It will not sound good. Any of it."

"You almost killed my brother. He almost *died*, Lordan! Do you know what that did to me?"

"I am sorry," he muttered.

"That is not enough!" She stomped a foot. "I could not sleep. When I found out it was the handkerchief *you* had given me, I could not eat. I could not bear that I had played a role in what could have been his death! Horrors ran through my mind, all because of you!" She stopped herself again. She wanted to hear him speak, not herself. Another narrow glance at his Reckoner soured Elise's mood even further.

"I..." He cleared his throat and began again. "I did not know it was a death curse."

A tidal wave of relief mixed with anger surged inside of Elise, and she fell against the wall behind her, hands gripping the water-smoothed stones. She couldn't even bring herself to speak before he continued.

"The idea of a handkerchief as a parting gift sounded so *reasonable.*" He kicked one foot up on the wall and tilted his chin up to the receding clouds. "Mira Mirkova was the one who suggested it."

Queen Kassia's niece? Elise's stomach tightened into a knot. Then, unbidden, her heart cracked and fell like a rock from the sea wall, bouncing down into the ocean with a splash. *That little spider!*

"When she was visiting our court last fall, she suggested I give you a gift as a way to soften the—" he paused, searching for the right word. Elise lifted her brows, but he changed course. "She even provided the handkerchief." Lordan stepped away from the wall and turned to face Elise. "I gave it to you. That is all."

Elise couldn't look at him. Instead, she peered around until her eyes landed on the pretty Reckoner. Elise shook her head, breathing deeply to calm her tempestuous nerves. "You trusted the niece of our shared enemy?"

He blinked in shock at her boldness. "Elise, I truly am sorry."

She laughed. To the waiting Reckoner, she asked, "Are his words true?"

The Reckoner—if she was indeed what Lordan claimed and not another one of his rumored *temporary interests*—nodded.

"I am not at fault here," he added.

"No, only guilty of being a fool."

He tossed a hand up. "I thought it was a simple handkerchief. I assumed Mira was trying to play for my hand. All women do it."

Elise jerked her chin up. "Oh, do they?"

Suddenly, Lordan stepped forward, invading Elise's space. "Elise, I should never have ended our relationship."

The words hit her so hard she nearly fell into the water. She placed one hand on the stone. He stepped nearer, his palm reaching for the wall right above hers. The bodice of her dress was tight and she couldn't breathe deeply enough to dispel the tangle of emotion inside of her.

"Stop. Do not talk about us."

She turned away from his hand as it reached across the small space toward her. She couldn't let herself want his touch again, though her resolve was cracking even as he spoke. She'd thought herself stronger than that.

"I realize now that my actions brought harm to your family." He sighed. "In a way, it brought about the death of my own father." The pain in his voice rattled Elise. "Fool is right. I am a fool, and I must live with what I have done." Lordan slammed his fist into the rocks, his signet ring making a loud cracking sound. Though she'd wanted to see him squirm, the pain that crossed his face was more than she could bear.

Watching him, she wasn't exactly sure how to respond. His father's body had been unloaded from a train. King Lucien had travelled north to Bulvarna with Red to meet with Kassia and discuss the defenses against the Canyon's increasingly dangerous beasts. Refere had been loyal to Tandera, loyal to the death. King Lucien, Lordan's father, had died fighting Kassia and her men.

The strain in his confession meant there was truth in it, at least some.

She pressed her hand to her mouth to stop herself from saying anything more. His eyes met hers, those blue eyes that she had looked into and dreamed of a future. They were broken. She too was broken. Neither one of them, wounded as they were, could pick the other up. Humiliation ignited her cheeks.

"My father is gone and it is my fault," he finally agreed, breaking the silence. "I must live with that. Thank Theod your brother lived."

As he stared at her, the words of his confession searing like a brand, something else crossed his face, a flicker of what was either eagerness or anger. He was waiting for her response, and the longer she remained silent, the harder his expression became.

Elise glanced down at the gently lapping ocean waves, so calm despite their recent fury. He was vulnerable in this moment. She'd come here to hurt him, but she couldn't do it.

"Bulvarna is responsible," she said, the merciful words spilling out like cool water dabbed on a hot brow.

"Thank you for saying that," he said, a huskiness edging his voice. He stepped up to her, close enough that she knew what he intended.

As her body met his, he pressed her against the wall, leaning in to kiss her. She twisted her face aside, his lips colliding with her jawline. The air whooshed out of her lungs, her entire scheme of revenge, once so certain, melting away like wax.

"Wait," she breathed. "How can I trust you?" Rebelliously, everything inside her wanted to trust him again. *Where is that resolute, iron-clad will I'd brought with me?*

This close to him, her heart burst with a fire she'd thought was quenched.

After a brief yet eternal moment, he pulled away. "Elise, can you ever forgive me? Tell me what I must do to earn your trust."

For a breath, she steeled herself to change her mind. She had not come here to forgive him. In her imagination, there had been only one way this conversation would go. This was not it. When his hand slipped beneath her hair, all remaining hopes for revenge left her.

A small smile flickered on his face. "Anything, Elise."

Her mind raced. An idea struck. "Promise me," she said, forming her plan as she spoke. "Promise me you will do everything in your power to aid Tandera." Red had said they would need Lordan's help to defeat the Canyon. Here was her chance to be useful in that fight, to secure the aid of a necessary ally.

Perplexity pinched his brow, then he chuckled softly. "Tell me your brother did not put you up to this."

She frowned. "He did not." *Not this part, anyway.*

"Very well." Lordan exhaled, his breath teasing the hairs around Elise's face. "I promise." Then he leaned in and pressed his lips against hers.

In that moment, on a narrow path made for keeping secrets, she knew a secret of her own: within her shattered heart, a mending had begun. At all costs, she would defend her heart from breaking anew, because if it broke again, she would never heal.

3

RED

Afternoon light pierced through the dust-thick air in Lordan's opulent private study. The King of Refere relaxed on a plush couch, his legs crossed and his fingers brushing idly against the velvet. Aly, in her cloak and mask, stared obliquely at Refere's Royal Sorcerer, who peered out a narrow window at the sea. Small sailboats dotted the harbor and two enormous clipper ships cruised in for unloading.

Elise had told Red of the ultimatum she'd given Lordan. He'd never expected such boldness of his sister, but he smirked at the notion that she'd managed to squeeze a promise out of the Referen king. He only hoped Lordan didn't let her down.

With a *humph*, Red noted a docked steamship, no doubt staffed with a Comforter incapable of pushing air like the Protectors who guided the clippers, but who could keep the fires always burning. Those who could afford Protectors to move their cargo gained even more wealth than those who could not. The pattern had created such a disparity in the merchant and noble classes that it hardly seemed fair for a merchant to enter into international trade. The clunky steamship beside the glittering clippers was a stark reminder.

"Oh, you see the clippers?" asked Lordan, lifting his chin to glance out the window. "Brand new, both of them. Beautiful, are they not?" Lordan's blond hair was swept back and secured with a blue ribbon. His crown, unlike the plain coronet of the King of Tandera, was all gossamer silver swirls, twisting and curling about like the waters that surrounded three sides of his country. "Pity though. We had three in our harbor only last month. One sank, despite its Protector. Now, rumors of a sea monster disquiet our shores." He clicked his tongue.

"The steamship. It looks terrible."

Lordan chuckled. "That piece of *resta*. Count Birini insists on using it, but every trip it makes, the thing needs repairs."

"A count without a Protector?" Red asked. He didn't know nearly enough about the shipping industry. He hadn't really had time to learn the ins and outs of it. If Seb were here, he'd launch into some poetic discourse about how these clippers were going to change the world, pushing out even the magic-propelled train that could only travel along its track. Instead, Seb was probably lounging on the Vona beach, making some unfortunate woman fall in love with him.

"The man's not cheap. He has six Protectors in his employ. However, there are delicacies to international trade that require, as you know, certain discretion." Lordan lowered his voice. "He is the only one of my men I trust enough to import my *tigas* without altering his logs, and steamships draw much less interest from watching eyes."

Tigas? Aly asked into Red's mind.

Red cleared his throat, thinking of a way to answer Aly's question without offending the man whose allegiance he hoped to secure. "The migrant workers continue to come from Esvedara, then? Bulvarna has not cut you off?"

Lordan recrossed his legs. "Esvedara does what it wants, for the most part. It still ships me its finest. Spices, perfumes, workers, what have you." Lordan smiled. That was the smile of a man who sat at the top of the world, a man who spoke of laborers as if they were crates to be unloaded. *He used the word "import" like they are goods.*

Gevar's words filled Red's mind. *Every man is sovereign over his own home, son. Remember that and you won't become a tyrant.*

"Good to know," Red muttered. It *was* good to know that Bulvarna hadn't forced its colony, Esvedara, to cease trade with Refere after what happened in Isardra two weeks ago. Perhaps Kassia wouldn't cease trade with Tandera either, despite the fact that Red and Aly had killed her Royal Sorcerer. Or maybe that was simply another mad hope. "Perhaps Kassia's preferences lie with her finances rather than her feuds."

"Ha! Well spoken, cousin," barked Lordan. "I have something even an offended Kassia will covet."

Red's brows rose. Lordan was dangling information. He'd want a boon in return. Resigned to come up with a secret to share with this man, Red cleared his throat. "Explain."

An officious smile spread across Lordan's face. "Wheat. Developed by sorcerers and academics together. It grows faster and lives through almost all conditions. A boon considering the growing drought across the plains."

Red stared a moment out the window. *This will change the world,* he thought, aware that such an advancement in agriculture would put Lordan's kingdom at the top of trade. All other kingdoms would be begging for what he could provide, if in fact this magical wheat would grow as he said. This was a most valuable tidbit to share. Red would need to plumb the depths of his creativity to find information equally valuable to share.

"That is indeed impressive," Red finally said.

Lordan leaned forward. "But I know why you came here. We cannot talk of ships and crops all day. You fear what Kassia will do."

"Fear?" Red spat. "Now that Kassia has fled, all of her troops have withdrawn from the Canyon. One entire side of that evil place stands completely unguarded. Already the beasts grow bolder. You have heard the reports. With no resistance on the Bulvarnan side, they will creep into our world in droves."

A slow nod preceded Lordan's response. "Yes. This is of concern."

Despite Elise's words about Lordan's promise, Red did not trust this man. He'd broken his sister's heart and had given Elise the handkerchief that had triggered Red's death curse. Kassia, via an elaborate maze of players, had used Lordan like a high card tossed aside to create her winning hand. Maybe he was innocent in the matter, but Red couldn't be sure. Lies hid everywhere, most dangerously beneath the most longed-for truths.

Out of respect for Lordan's loss and Elise's desire to even the scales on her own, Red had thus far avoided discussion of the events in Bulvarna, other than to offer his condolences. But he'd evaded long enough.

"Answer me this, cousin," he asked, "did you have any knowledge of the curse you passed to me?"

"None at all," Lordan replied, eyes averted out the window. He spun his signet ring on his right hand. "You may demand a Reckoning if you wish." He beckoned his sorcerer forward. "Come, Reckon the truth for my dear cousin."

They weren't cousins, of course, but the word among sovereigns was an age-old tradition. "Your sorcerer is a Reckoner?" *A powerful combination.* Lordan offered a curt nod. "All right, then." Red eyed the masked sorcerer. His broad neck was dotted with moles; his shoulders firm and unyielding. He towered over Lordan's low couch, his massive frame an intimidating feature, aside from the fact that he could kill a man with a single spell. His dreadlocks spilled down over his back, completing his mountain-like appearance. "Did Lordan know of the death curse in the handkerchief he gave my sister?"

The Referen sorcerer inhaled, inviting a moment of tension. "No."

Everyone in the room exhaled.

"Well, *that* is definitely good to know." Reckoners, gifted in ways even most sorcerers didn't fully grasp, could extract the truth in answer to a direct, specific question. The trick was in asking the right question.

Lordan opened his hands. "Now, let's proceed to business. Kassia, for starters."

"She disappeared," Red said. He knew more, thanks to Lord Weston Grey and his network of spies, but he wasn't sure how much to share with Lordan. This was a chance to return Lordan's secret with one of his own, but he had to choose wisely. "She fled to the Candul region." If Lordan didn't know this, he would soon.

Lordan nodded and steepled his fingers. "I had heard several rumors, but the truth was less certain."

"She is a fool. Fleeing into *my* country was not a wise choice."

At this, Lordan perked up. "You consider Candul *yours*." A small, surprised chuckle left his mouth. "Perhaps that is foolishness too."

A hot spike of offense pricked inside of Red, but Lordan was not exactly wrong. "The Candul region lies within Tandera's borders."

"Yet you have never conquered it."

"No one can. It is occupied entirely by Zealots."

"Much like the Crescent Forest, which also lies within your borders. You and your tolerance for the crazies." Lordan flicked his wrist.

Red tried not to grunt. "It is not that we tolerate them. They simply *come* to my country."

"Because you are too nice."

"We cannot do much about them. Their magic is erratic, dangerous."

"Wipe them all out."

"That is easy for you to say, your country is not full of them."

At Aly's pointed cough, Red added, "And anyway, killing them all is not the answer. They stick to themselves. That is all we can ask for."

Lordan stood abruptly. "Yes. Let them destroy themselves. It is what they do best." Aly fidgeted in Red's periphery. She disliked this talk of the wild, untrained sorcerers, known for killing each other with uncontrollable bursts of magic. "But why would Kassia go to them? Will she choose her new sorcerer from among the Zealots?"

Refere's sorcerer scoffed. "Zealots hate those of us who serve," he said. "They believe it is wrong to attempt to restrain magic, to control it with careful study. No Zealot would agree to serve her." A trace of disgust sharpened his tone.

"Has Tandera sent scouts to the area?" asked Lordan.

"We have dispatched a small party from Luxler to the region. They should be arriving within a couple of days. It is difficult travel over the desert."

"Did they take a sorcerer with them?"

"Three."

"Good." Lordan glanced at his sorcerer. "What do you think?" Red thought it was interesting that Lordan was asking for the sorcerer's advice so openly.

The mountainous man nodded respectfully. "Your Majesty, if she has gone to the Candul region, I do not believe any scouts will find her." He peered at Red. "If you want to know my opinion, I believe she went there not to recruit a new Royal Sorcerer but to disappear."

A rap at the door interrupted the sorcerer's words. Lordan glanced at Red. Nobody interrupted two kings in conference.

Lordan waved a hand at his sorcerer, who stood to open the door for him, as if he were nothing more than a servant, when a moment ago the king was asking for his advice.

As the man's back was turned, Red darted a glance at Aly, whose masked face betrayed nothing other than the enigmatic

C. F. E. BLACK

flame-tipped feathers of a phoenix. The broad-shouldered man turned around with a letter in his hand.

"For you, Your Majesty." He handed it to Red.

A bit surprised, Red took the letter, slipped his finger into the small wax seal displaying the red phoenix of Tandera. A letter sent via post and not via a sorcerer's more direct means of communication meant that the sender had no access to a sorcerer. The paper made a soft scratching sound as it slid out from its envelope. "It is from General Daniels," he said, offering a small hint. As he read through the note, everyone in the room peered down at him, waiting. When Red finished reading, he sat back, hands turning clammy.

"General Daniels reports an attack at Caridan, our camp at the Canyon's edge," he added for Lordan's benefit. "Twelve men died. All three Protectors have disappeared."

Aly gasped.

Red, too distraught to remain seated, stood and paced the room. "Without the Protectors, the men will die. Daniels reports that many soldiers deserted in the hours after the attack." Red pressed a hand to his forehead. "They need help, and fast." He turned to Aly. "We must help them."

Red now stared at Lordan, thinking of his men at the Canyon. Those men were their first and strongest hope against the beasts that lurked in the depths. After what happened in Bulvarna, Red had ordered more troops sent to Caridan. The Comforters who fought alongside the men were decent soldiers, but they were not powerful enough to cast enchantments around the camp where the men slept. Undefended, the camp would become a deathtrap.

"The Master Sorcerers left?" asked Lordan, hands on his hips. He glanced out at the bay. "Those men are as good as dead." His words soured the already tense atmosphere. Here was his chance to prove whether or not he would uphold his promise to Elise. "My ships can reach your border nearest the Canyon, but it would take weeks, even on a clipper driven by magic. How fast can the trains arrive? For reinforcements?"

"Nearest train stops in Mardon. We are still completing the track to Luxler." To Aly, he asked, "How fast can we send a message to Luxler?"

"I can send a message today," Aly said. "I'll go now. What should it say?"

Lordan stared at her. "You can send a message across the entire continent?"

Red cringed. This had previously been information Lordan had not known. Sorcerers could send mental messages to anyone whose Truthwell they could identify. Most sorcerers, however, couldn't pinpoint someone across large distances. Messages were sent via a chain of sorcerers whose sole jobs were to send and receive these mental messages. Aly, on the other hand, could detect Truthwells across vast distances. Though Red wanted to trust Lordan as an ally, not all secrets were to be shared among them.

Before Red could intervene, Aly nodded. Lordan's brows rose.

"Very well," Red cut in. "Tell them every able-bodied Protector in Luxler is ordered to the Canyon."

Lordan coughed politely. "The people will not allow that. Noblemen want their Protectors, especially if they hear of the attack. They hired them. They pay them. Convincing rich men to let go of things they value is not easy, cousin. A lesson my father made sure to impress upon me. What about sending the Comforters instead?"

Red nodded, his gaze on Aly. "Tell them every able-bodied Comforter is to report to Caridan. Ask that Protectors volunteer as well. For the sake of our people." Comforters could make excellent fighters and their presence would boost morale at the camp, but without Protectors, the soldiers would eventually flee.

"Say," Lordan cut in, "do you not have a band of Protectors

somewhere that you can dip into for things like this?"

"Do you?" asked Red, incredulous at the thought. Masters were rare when it came to magical ability, and most became Protectors, the most sought-after job of a Master Sorcerer. They were paid incredibly well and enjoyed a nobility of their own among magic wielders.

Lordan said nothing, effectively answering the question with his silence. *How many secrets does this kingdom have? How many secrets does Tandera have?* Red knew there were many more state secrets for him to learn. Aly, from her time serving Gevar, knew more than he did, and surely the king's network of spies knew even more. Despite several briefings, he'd not had much time after Gevar's death to learn all that he was expected to know. He needed to plumb Grey's vault of secrets sooner rather than later.

His men needed help. The Canyon had to be contained. "I can spare the sorcerers of my councilmen." To Aly, he said, "Alexander and Wyndall will volunteer them. That's two. Grey's is here with us. There must be other men we can trust to give up their Protectors. For the sake of us all."

Aly cleared her throat as if she might disagree but said nothing. "From Mardon it will take them three days to reach the Canyon," Aly supplied. Master Sorcerers could, of course, fly.

Turning to Lordan, Red pictured Elise's face as he asked, "And what are you going to do about this?"

"Me?" The room fell silent for a moment. "It is your country."

"You cannot tell me the Canyon is not your problem. Refere has always been our brother-at-arms against the beasts of the Deep. We fight together against this enemy."

Lordan rubbed his chin. "We always have, yes." Lordan turned away from the window now, his face growing darker with his back to the sun. Red tensed, preparing to hear an answer he didn't like. "I will dispatch a company of soldiers," Lordan added with a small nod.

Red's brows lifted again. "A company?"

"It is all I can spare, now that you have so adequately described the upcoming onslaught of Canyon beasts to my country's borders."

Red's blood heated like coals under a bellows. "If we had enough manpower at the Canyon, you would not have to hoard your soldiers within your own borders." Red strained his voice to remain cordial. "Furthermore, it will take weeks for this *company* to arrive on foot. Can you not spare a sorcerer?" Red stared at Lordan, but he was never good at decoding the tension in a smile or the hesitation in a pinched brow.

Aly's voice pressed into Red's mind, soft but quick. It still startled him, but he had also grown to appreciate the subtly of silent communication. *He promised your sister he would come to Tandera's aid, but this is a pathetic excuse for sending help.*

Red glared at Lordan. If this was his way of proving his love for Elise, Red wasn't impressed.

Declarations of love should leave no doubt, no room for question.

He crossed his arms. One word came to Red's mind: *liar.*

After Lordan had broken Elise's heart the first time, Red had watched Elise come to breakfast with puffy, red eyes too many times. He'd watched her withdraw into herself, leaving behind the carefree young woman she'd been for the reserved, unflappable princess she had become.

If Lordan broke her heart again, Red feared what it would do to Elise.

"We will accept your men when they arrive at the Canyon," Red declared. *If anyone is left.* "However," he added, pushing every bit of warning into his tone that he dared, "I am not sure my sister will be impressed. She does not do anything halfway. A half-hearted effort to win her affection will not do." And an angry Elise was a dangerous thing to behold.

Lordan drew up to his full height and looked down his nose at Red. "Then she shall be the judge."

4

ALY

Lights flickered along the edges of the palace's central courtyard. Twisting flames were suspended at intervals in the air above the murmuring guests, courtesy of Refere's sorcerers. The women's swishing silks and dangling diamonds reflected the moving flames in a way that filled the evening with the twinkle of ephemeral magic.

From where she stood beside an ivy-covered column, Aly watched Red speaking to Lordan. She half-listened to a Referen Comforter discuss her employer in brisk tones. Both young kings looked resplendent in their finest suits, drawing the admiration of everyone at this gathering. Red wore the crimson of Tandera, his freckled face bathed in the warm glow of the flames above. His crown sparkled among his curls, and his smile added light to the summer evening that even the torches and the brilliance of his Truthwell couldn't match.

His eyes traveled to find her. When he spotted her, his smile relaxed, smooth and fiercely content. Beneath her mask, her cheeks warmed.

The reality was that he shouldn't look at her like that; yet every time he did, a freeing sensation swept through her chest, like barnacles being scraped off a boat too long anchored.

"My lady, what amuses you?" the woman before her asked. This woman kept her glass of champagne chilled so that it boasted a frosty glaze.

Aly blinked at the woman. "I apologize. I am quite amazed at the beauty all around me."

The woman smiled kindly. "Our king spares nothing in his celebrations. He goes to such great lengths to please his people."

You've only been his people for a couple of days, Aly quietly mused. Red needed this kind of devotion from his people. If parties would do the trick, Aly would suggest Red throw a month of celebrations. Rumors of his descent into the Canyon had tainted his reputation already. People feared the Deep, and now that people were finding out their king had gone to the Black River itself, they were dreaming up all sorts of problematic lies that Red would have to combat.

All kings faced lies. All kings had to rise above them. *Truth will rise,* she reminded herself.

"Oh, but now," the woman's words drew Aly's attention back to the present, "our handsome king must choose a wife. It is not fitting for the queen's throne to remain empty." The woman clasped her hands in delight. "And what a joyous occasion his wedding will be!"

Indeed. Aly's breath hitched in her chest as the thought of wedding bells and beaded silk filled her mind. Tandera's king would wed one day as well. Instantly, she was transported to a dream she'd been forced to put away.

No, it cannot be.

"Is something the matter, my lady?" the woman asked.

"No," Aly muttered, politely dismissing herself with a curtsey.

Aly drifted closer to Red and Lordan, who stood in the center of the courtyard beside a small fountain. Flowers hugged the sides of the fountain, filling the night with their sweet aroma.

Elise had not yet arrived. Aly understood the princess must be feeling crushed—again—by Lordan. His weak attempt to uphold her ultimatum must be dredging up all of Elise's buried pain. Aly wished she could be with Elise now, offering an ear or a shoulder or merely a kind face; however, Aly's duty was to Red and to Tandera. Since Aly and Elise shared a suite at the palace, Aly could check in on the princess before retiring to sleep.

Aly slid among the courtiers and servers, her awareness attuned to any possible threats. She caught the pattern of a familiar Truthwell in her mind.

Lord Weston Grey stepped hurriedly between two guests, even moving one aside with a polite but strong hand. He wore a grave expression, eyes on the king.

Uh oh. Aly angled her steps toward him. The man of secrets walked boldly toward Red and Lordan. The look on his face spoke of bad news.

By the time Aly snaked her way across the courtyard to where Red and Lordan conversed, Grey had taken up a place where he could stare at Red until he broke away from the Referen king. Interrupting two kings would be a discourtesy to both kingdoms, so Grey was forced to wait.

Aly stood beside Grey. He grunted to acknowledge her. "Must be bad," she whispered.

He grunted again.

Aly spoke to Red's mind. *Grey bears some news. Leave Lordan to entertain his court.* Red blinked, obviously having trouble absorbing both Lordan's words and Aly's simultaneously. After a moment, he and Lordan exchanged bows.

Red approached, placed a hand on his stomach, and nodded to Grey and then to Aly. Grey and Aly returned the proper greetings.

"Your Majesty," Grey said, voice gritty and quick. "We must speak in private."

Red eyed the party around them. "Now?"

"Yes."

Aly met Red's gaze. "If we all leave now, people will wonder why."

Grey did not look at Aly. "Your Majesty, it is of utmost importance. It cannot wait."

Aly sensed his agitation in his writhing Truthwell. As a spy, he collected truths—those unknown by many others—but the job also demanded he live many lies, and as such his Well swirled with shadows. She trusted him, as had Gevar, but the sight of his ever-darkening Well caused a twitch of pain inside her. He'd been much brighter when they'd first met, and even then he'd been working as a spy. Kings needed spies, but the job took a toll.

Red nodded. "Lead the way," he said to Grey.

Grey returned the nod. Though acting formal and composed, Aly could tell he was ruffled—and Grey didn't get *ruffled*. Grey jerked as he turned, his arms swinging like stiff canes at his sides as he trooped out of the courtyard. Aly wondered if everyone else here could see his distress.

She tossed out a few spells that sent tiny pebbles knocking against the courtyard walls on opposite sides of them. As expected, most heads turned to the sudden small sounds and away from the three of them as they exited the party.

When they'd passed through one hallway and then another, finally finding a room Aly sensed was empty, she pushed her shroud around the three of them and unlocked a door with a spell.

The room was not much bigger than a closet, but it was empty. She lit the air with a bit of magic and discovered it wasn't so much a room as a passage between two much larger chambers. There was a bench and a carpet and a pair or mirrored doors that made the room appear infinite. Aly looked away from the cascading repetitions of their faces and stared instead at the trim running along the floorboards.

"Sire," Grey began, "my network has discovered a most alarming piece of news. I fear it will be known to everyone in Refere by the morrow, if not within the hour, as messages are received. I apologize for interrupting you tonight, but I wanted you to be the first to know that Lord Alexander plans to declare himself king in your absence."

Aly sputtered and immediately covered her mouth. She peered up at Red. He wore a blank expression, his chin barely moving from side to side.

"He made proclamation to his closest friends and supporters over an hour ago." Grey never once looked at Aly, as if she weren't even present. "In the morning, he will attempt to take up residence in the palace."

Red scoffed, coming to life. "Does he think he will get away with this?"

"He has been preparing for this for years, sire." Now Red and Aly both guffawed. "He has a lineage as royal as yours, albeit not *tainted*, as he says, with commoner's blood. He served your grandfather happily enough, but when Gevar married your mother, he never approved. Since then, he's been cultivating alliances, gaining power among the nobles, maneuvering for such a time as this. I never thought he would attempt this, not while Gevar was alive. Gevar's death and your descent into the Canyon, however, provided him the opportunity he needed to call your reign into question."

"Are you saying this is my fault?"

Grey stiffened. "Everything is the king's fault, sire."

Red rubbed a hand down his face and turned away, staring at a thousand iterations of his reflection, stacked like nesting dolls. An annoyed chuckle escaped his lips. "That is what my father always said."

"Sire, what do you wish to do?"

Red stared at Grey. Eventually, he glanced over at Aly. His eyes brewed with restless energy and a desperation she hated to see. When he acted like this, he often did something rash.

"We will leave at once," Red said. "Tomorrow. We must not allow Alexander to take up residence in my house."

Aly envisioned a dozen ways this could go wrong. She wanted to caution Red against impulsive actions, but she also knew they should return to Mardon as soon as possible. Even with her magic speeding them along, it would take a week for their entire company to go around the mountains and arrive in Mardon.

Grey nodded, never questioning his sovereign. He was a good soldier, taking orders as given. But he was also a good spy, which meant he could toss aside those orders when they interfered with collecting information.

"I will begin preparations for departure."

"Very good."

"And sire," said Grey, "I must caution you that Alexander's loyal friends are more numerous than you might imagine. Tread carefully." With a nod, he turned and opened the door leading out into a mostly empty state room lined with massive paintings of battle scenes and glowing generals atop rearing steeds.

At the other end of the grand room stood Elise, arms crossed, with a look on her face hot enough to smelt steel.

ELISE

The palace Comforters, with their cool breezes wafting through every room, did little to ameliorate Elise's burning embarrassment at Lordan's rebuff. Even the thought of Lordan and his pathetic attempt to fulfill her ultimatum fanned the furnace in her blood.

How could I have been so stupid? The truth was, he didn't care *enough* about her to act usefully for Tandera. The shock of it had kept the tears at bay. His kiss had been a lie—everything about him was a smooth-talking, handsome lie.

She'd let her heart hope again, only for it to be dashed against the rocks like some poor fishing boat standing up to a storm.

No, this time, I will be the storm, she mused. Her gaze turned to the door through which Lord Weston Grey had just emerged.

"There you are," she whispered aloud.

The king's top spy had been *hiding* in some closet, making her prance all over the party to find him. When he appeared, her brother and Aly walked with him.

Grey's face was usually stoic and a bit scary, but his grave expression was made more frightful by the way it was mirrored by both Red and Aly. Elise's insides knotted even tighter. Something was amiss—something more than Lordan's stupidity.

Grey slowed his pace, allowing Red and Aly to reach Elise first. She pursed her lips, not wanting to hear whatever bad news had been disclosed in that closet but knowing she'd hear about it anyway. She eyed Grey as he slunk out of the room without so much as a nod in her direction. The man was impeccable in his execution of duty—a fact she'd learned from her father in the way he praised Grey for work she never saw him accomplish. Gevar had not once admitted Grey was a spy, but she'd observed enough odd instances to surmise his true role, and now Red was taking conference with him in discreet closets. She would need to be clever to find a way to speak with him in private.

He was the key to her next steps—the key to surviving the brokenness inside of her.

"Elise," Aly said, taking her hands.

The sinking feeling in Elise's chest felt like an anchor plummeting to the bottom of the bay. Aly glanced back at Red, who made a strange grunt and turned away.

"What is it?" asked Elise, ready to be free of this conversation to find Grey.

"Lord Alexander," Aly began, saying what was apparently too difficult for Red to relay, "wishes to depose your brother."

The words sailed right over Elise, and she couldn't now grasp them and force herself to hear them. After several moments of waiting for Elise to respond, Aly repeated herself.

"Depose," Elise muttered, fixing on one word. "*Depose?*" She shook her head.

Red stomped out of the room. Aly gazed after him, dropped Elise's hands, and with an apologetic look, stepped after Red.

"We leave tomorrow," Aly called out as she walked away.

Elise stood in stunned silence a moment until a Referen courtier brushed past her into the state room, come to admire the art or simply escape the crowded courtyard.

Depose. The word sounded vile, as if inappropriate to say aloud. Elise shivered and snapped out of her trance-like state. She spun, more determined than ever to find Lord Grey and speak to him.

In the courtyard, Elise scanned the faces for Lord Grey. He could hide almost as well as a shrouded sorcerer, mingling in a crowd without anyone noticing him. Elise *humphed* as she spotted Grey. He stood beside Sebastian Thorin, who appeared entirely engrossed in the attentions of three women, their flittering accents marking them as Viriennese, their fluttering eyes marking them as under Seb's spell.

What is it about him that charms them so?

"Hello, my lady," Seb greeted, voice low and touched with self-importance. Elise spread a false smile across her lips and bowed her head at the women, then Seb. Grey said nothing but offered a small nod.

The three Viriennese women curtsied and shook with giggles. Elise inhaled and steeled herself for another conversation she dreaded having. She eyed Lordan. He stood across the courtyard. Perhaps he wouldn't notice her. Or maybe it would be better if he did, and he'd assume she was unaffected by his actions.

"Sebastian, I see you've made some new friends," Elise drawled, careful to keep her tone proper but her expression dripping with disdain.

Seb covered a short cough with his fist before introducing the ladies. The women chattered in Viriennese. Seb responded to them.

"You speak Viriennese like it's your own tongue," Elise said, a bit surprised. The man could read ancient Edrean better than she, and his Viriennese accent was nearly flawless. Elise had never mastered their throaty *r*.

"My tongue is rather talented."

The women giggled.

Elise rolled her eyes. "And your head is rather full of itself."

To the women, she said in their language, "This man once translated an ancient poem about the Black River."

The three women paused, exchanged glances, and turned a singular, horrified stare upon Seb. Elise pressed her lips together in satisfaction. The women suddenly discovered reasons they were needed elsewhere, and with brief curtsies, they were gone.

"Poof," Elise said, gesturing at the departing women. "I can make things disappear too."

Seb groaned like a child who hadn't gotten his way. "I'm not a fan of your magic."

"You really want to break as many hearts as possible, don't you? It is rather cruel."

He turned a puzzled expression on her. "That's not my intent."

Brushing off his words with a hand, she turned to Lord Grey. "Having a fine evening?" She was not entirely sure how one spoke to this man. He turned only his eyes and gave such a small shrug she wasn't even certain he'd moved at all.

Seb leaned toward her. "He doesn't speak to women. They scare him." His breath was warm on her face. Too close.

"Hush," she hissed.

He smiled again. Seb's good looks were the kind that Elise could handle. He was *too* handsome for his own good. To other women, his presence made them tremble and blush. To Elise, his dimpled cheeks and just-pinched eyes spoke of his vanity, of the charm he *assumed* he exuded. This pulled him down from the heights, reminding her he was merely human, and a cocky one at that. He was the type of man that needed to know not all women found him irresistible.

Lordan's looks, on the other hand, stabbed her through the middle, pinning her to the spot like a butterfly on an entomologist's board. He was speaking now with her brother and gesticulating wildly, somehow managing not to spill a drop of his champagne.

Toss him. She looked away from Lordan and, mind made up, stared intently at Grey until he caught her eye again. Using the smallest movement possible, she flicked her eyes aside. A spy would know what that meant.

She hoped he would take the time to hear her proposal.

"Enjoy breaking hearts," Elise said to Seb before stepping away.

It took a quarter hour, long enough for Elise to wonder if he'd understood, but Grey finally found her beside a wall draped with bougainvillea, engrossed in reading the engraving below a statue of a horse that had belonged to one of Lordan's ancestors.

Grey moved like no one else. His presence appeared and disappeared, but he never seemed to travel. He simply appeared beside her, arms clasped at his back, when a moment ago she'd been alone.

"You wished to speak with me?" he asked, pretending to observe the statue as well.

Elise leaned forward as if to smell the hot pink flowers, and whispered, "I want to be a spy."

A laugh burst from his mouth. Elise straightened. She pressed her lips into a hard line.

"You are serious," he stated, wiping his forehead with a handkerchief.

Elise bristled at the sight of the handkerchief, recalling how her entire life had pivoted around the presence of a similar piece of cloth. Lordan's handsome face swam before her, and she gritted her teeth, shoving down the ache that accompanied it.

"Gravely," she replied. "I wish to gather intelligence to use against Lordan."

Grey's jaw worked as he studied her. Out of the corner of her eye, Elise spotted his hand flickering in an odd way. Suddenly, the world around them muted, as if covered with a blanket. He'd signaled his sorcerer, drifting among guests nearby, to shroud their voices but not their figures. A convenient tool for a spy.

"You realize," he began, extending his arm to point at the statue as if that was their topic of discussion, "that spying isn't about destroying your enemies. Rather, it is often about befriending them."

"So that one day you can betray them where it will really hurt," Elise added.

Grey paused, turning a skeptical eye on the princess. "My lady, do not do this if your sole aim is to bring suffering on Lordan." He moved them along the flower-covered wall, pointing at each statue they passed, to make it appear like he was giving the young princess a history lesson on Referen royalty.

"Why not?"

He sighed. "I have handed out enough retribution to know it does not satisfy."

"Preach to someone else." Elise stopped and faced a rose bush bursting with pale yellow blooms, her eyes cutting aside to Lord Grey's trim, haughty profile. *Who is he to play the moral guide?*

Grey picked a rose, smelled it. "You think me callous."

"The women at court say you are made of stone."

He offered her the rose. She stared at it but did not take it. For a moment, they both watched a happy bee, gathering his last pollen of the quickly dying day. "Fulfilling these duties requires a certain distance from one's emotions, and the longer you do what I do, the more you withdraw from all feeling."

A glance behind her told Elise that Lordan was all the way across the courtyard, surrounded by layers of well-wishers, among whom stood many hopeful young women.

Grey's words pricked Elise, almost as if the bee had stung her. Despite their sting, those words were exactly what she wanted to hear. "Good," she muttered. All she wanted was to sear off the pain poisoning her heart.

A few steps away stood a stone bench, moss filling its grooves. Grey stepped over to the bench and extended his hand, inviting Elise to sit. She pursed her lips and perched on the stone.

She would not leave Refere until Grey allowed her to enter into his employ. If that meant listening to his attempts to convince her otherwise, she'd oblige, but in the end she would win. No longer was she the accommodating princess who did only what she was told.

She plastered on her most agreeable face and turned to him as he sat a respectable distance away.

With a large inhale, he began. "My father never loved me." Elise blinked in surprise at this unexpected confession. "He used my body to fuel the magic of his sorcerer. He never wanted anyone diving into his own Well, but he wasn't willing to live without the magic he'd come to expect as the son of a wealthy nobleman. Children were given to him like wood for a fire, expendable as fuel for his desires for magic. My father had three Masters in his employ. Three children, you see." He leaned forward, elbows on knees, his chest expanding and contracting like he'd raced across the courtyard.

Elise busied herself with her lace gloves, shocked that Lord Weston Grey was telling her any of this—Grey, the ruthless soldier-spy known for killing beasts and fending off fortune hunters at court.

"You would think," he continued, "that after not being loved by the one person whose affection you crave, a person would give up." He gave an almost imperceptible shake of his head and bit his lips. "I always thought my father would change, that one day he would embrace me and ask my forgiveness." He glanced over at Elise. "Instead, he died."

Elise's right hand pressed to her lips. She didn't know how to respond to this.

"My point is, Elise, as long as you wish for the love of one who will not return it, you will feel pain, no matter how much you wound in return. I learned from a young age to push my feelings aside, to *not* feel at all. I was, in a sense, being prepared for this job even then. I can't say I'm thankful, but I can at least serve my king and do my job without risk of becoming emotionally compromised. You, on the other hand, are already emotionally compromised."

She leaned back, offended. He was right, of course. Her thumbs traced over the fine lace on the back of her hands. *He is testing me, even now. I have to show him I can do this.* "Lordan has broken my heart, twice. I am incapable of loving that man. It is now that I am most able to spy on him without fear of losing myself."

Grey's dark brows rose. For a man approaching thirty, he appeared much older. "I think, my lady, that you are still most vulnerable." With that, he stood and began walking away.

She hurried forward, desperation winning over decorum. "You must allow me do this. I am in a position to *help*. I have never been able to do anything useful, other than sit in the palace and wait for a man to offer me his hand. The one man I hoped would, never did. Now, I have resigned to never love again."

"You're too young to make such assertions."

"I am seventeen."

"My point exactly."

She scowled at him. "Do not deny me this. Let me help."

Grey sighed and ran a hand down his face, returning to his former, closed-off self. "You will not give up, I see. Then know this." He turned a severe expression on her. "If you do this, you are stepping into a role with lifelong ramifications. To be an informant, a good one, is to consign your life to doing whatever is required."

"I can do that."

"Elise, I'm not sure you understand. If, over the course of your employment, Lordan offers you his hand, you would have to accept." He leaned forward. "Because if you woo him, only to turn him down—as I fear is your goal—it would look most suspicious. There would have to be a good reason. You'd risk turning an important ally into an enemy, for the sake of your own vengeance. A good informant cannot risk such things."

She couldn't bear his stare or his piercing words, so she closed her eyes. Her mind raced forward with possibilities. "I am willing."

"I know that look," Grey said, walking down the path. "You want to hurt him." She caught up and he slowed, grateful that the others at the party couldn't hear their conversation. "I will let you do this, on one condition."

"Yes?" She stumbled in excitement as her shoe struck a cracked paving stone.

A heavy sigh preceded his reply. "You must prove one thing to me. Before I allow you, as part of my network, to go anywhere near the King of Refere, you must first secure another alliance." Her eyes narrowed, but she waited for him to finish. "As part of his coup, Lord Alexander wants to turn you and your family to the streets. Secure his favor, and I will see to it that you are placed on duty in Refere, as queen, if you wish." His smile turned impish. "Having a queen in my employ would be rather useful."

"You cannot decide who Lordan will marry." That was too high a claim, even for a man like Grey.

Shadows gathered as his face turned down at her. "You would be surprised at what my network can do. Are you willing, my lady?" His brows waggled. "To accomplish this, you will have to hurt your brother and Aly. And, I suspect, your mother also."

Elise spun slowly until her eyes found her brother, hands behind his back, face staring up at the sky. Her stomach churned. Nearby, Aly lurked under a suspended flame. The peace of this moment was a strange veneer over the tumultuous reality they all faced. A usurper wished to push her brother off the throne and her family into the streets. Canyon beasts leaked into the world in alarming numbers. Kassia was in hiding, no doubt planning something to ruin them all.

The thought of hurting those she cared about tasted sour, but

Elise swallowed it and turned back to an expectant Grey. "Easy," she said, chin lifted. "When do I start?"

Grey frowned. "This business, it ruins people."

In her head, Elise replayed Lordan's kiss, so soon before his betrayal. *I'm already ruined,* she mused. "I am not afraid of that."

"Oh, my lady, you should be." He tapped a fist against an open palm, clearly agitated—a rare state for a man like Grey. "I will likely regret this. But know that I'm doing it to show you that one day, when you have the chance to hurt Lordan, you will come to realize that it won't satisfy you. Instead, I hope you might choose to forgive him."

"Like you forgave your father?" Her caustic tone must have slapped him because he stopped walking.

In his eyes, there was appraisal, surprise, and, finally, clarity. He'd not known Elise until this moment. She'd been the prim princess, always using the right grammar and the best compliments. His gaze swept the party, then said, a hint of sadness in his tone, "I've thought of your first assignment."

6

RED

A bell rang above the courtyard, the summons to dinner. Conversations stopped, champagne flutes returned to passing trays, and people funneled toward the stairwell leading to the grand dining hall overlooking the Gulf of Eseda. Stars burst out across the moonless night sky, reflected in the calm harbor.

The peaceful scenery and the grandeur of the celebration mocked the feelings of betrayal thundering through Red's veins.

Since parting from Grey's company, he'd not been present in the chatter taking place around him. One word—*depose*—replayed in his mind, cutting deeper and deeper with each repetition. Aly had used that word. It was succinct and it smelled of treachery.

As the crowd carried him along toward the dining room, Aly found him. She noted his expression and, without a word, a coolness blew across his face and his skin chilled. The crowd pressed them into the stairwell, and her fingers traced against his for only a moment. At her touch, tension dispelled from his knotted muscles.

The corner of his mouth twitched upward. She could always

sense his distress. Perhaps it was her ability to see into his Truth-well, or perhaps it was simply her uncanny ability to read people's faces. Aly's masked face remained politely facing forward as they mounted the stone steps adjacent to the court-yard. Though people left deferential space around the sovereign of Tandera and his Royal Sorcerer, he walked close to Aly, the broad shoulders of her cloak brushing his.

Within the folds of her large cloak, he found her hand and grasped only her smallest finger, certain his action wouldn't be noticed by those behind them.

They needed to talk, to strategize, but they had a dinner to attend. *Depose.* He hated the word. He needed to act, to press toward home, not leaving it in the hands of a would-be usurper.

Sensing his frustration, Aly said to his mind, *There is little we can do right now.*

"We could plan," he grumbled.

"We will," she assured him.

At least there was a *we.* He had Aly, Tandera's most powerful sorcerer. No man could steal his throne as long as she stood by his side.

"Brother?" Elise called.

He snapped from his thoughts, unsure where his sister's voice had come from. He peered around. She was coming up behind them, people parting to allow her to pass. As he'd turned, his hand, the one linked with Aly's, had become visible between them.

Elise's eyes stared at their retreating fingers.

She still wore an expression of ill humor, perhaps at Lordan's half-hearted declaration of love. Red was in no mood to smile either. Some things weighed too heavily to fake contentment.

He nodded at her, mentally approving of her gloominess. At least it matched his own.

"Do not fret," he said, opening his arm to allow her to step up beside him. "We leave tomorrow."

Elise's eyes narrowed. "Yes, yes, what of it?" She waved a hand, drawing the eyes of those clustered on the steps. "I wish that we could stay. Do let us stay!"

A few Referen courtiers cheered happily, which caused the people already on the balcony above to turn to face them.

Red lifted his brows at her sudden change of mood, surprised she didn't want to leave Refere as soon as possible. "We must leave. You know we must." He couldn't say aloud that a usurper wanted his throne, and Elise would not expect him to wait around in Vona while Alexander took control of Mardon. What was this about?

At the top of the stairs, she snapped, "I am happy for you! The person you love cannot run away. Like it or not, she is bound to serve you. Must be a good arrangement, from where you sit."

Before Red could respond, Elise spun away and, with a hand pressed to her mouth as if shocked at what she'd said, darted down the balcony away from the dining hall. All the eyes in the crowded space turned back to Red and Aly as Elise fled. Even as the princess dashed through a door into the palace, the whispers around them rose: "The Tanderan king is in love with his sorcerer."

The guest wing of the palace contained several grand suites, and Red had insisted Aly share Elise's rooms during their stay in Refere, rather than a separate, smaller chamber reserved for the Royal Sorcerer. Now, as he walked toward Elise's room, trembling in a mix of rage and embarrassment, he hoped his sister would not be there. This had turned into a wreck of an evening.

"Aly!" he yelled, banging on the gilded door. One look after Elise's words, and Aly had vanished, retreating into her solitude and escaping from the stares of Lordan's guests.

Red's personal body guard, Veeter Yin, stood against the wall several strides away. Since Bulvarna, Red had been mostly unsuccessful in having any moments alone, save the ones where he was with Aly, practicing their magic. Only then, and once the doors were locked at night, would Yin willingly let the king out of his sight.

No answer.

Maybe Aly hadn't come here. But where else could he look for an invisible person?

"Yin!" Red called.

His Okwan guard walked up, his tight braid tugging at the corners of his aging face. "Sire?"

Red ran a hand over his chin. "How bad?"

"I assume you are referring to—"

"Yes, yes. Tell me how it sounded. You heard her."

Yin nodded. "It was clear, I think, to those who heard Lady Elise."

"Just say it, Yin. Don't sugar coat."

"Very well. From what your sister said, it would appear you are in love with your sorcerer and that she—" he paused as Red groaned and began knocking one fist against the wall, "—that she willingly submits to your…attentions."

With a grunt, Red clunked his forehead against the doorframe. "I had no idea she was capable of that kind of vitriol. And now the world thinks Aly is my…"

The door swung open, revealing an angry Aly. "Your *what*, exactly?"

Red turned to Yin. "Leave us." He waited until Yin was out of sight. "Aly," he pleaded, facing her. Unfortunately, nothing he thought of sounded appropriate in this moment. He shook his head.

Aly marched unceremoniously into the dining room of the suite, leaving the door open for Red to follow. The chandelier hung over the mahogany table, and someone had lit candles and placed fresh flowers along its reflective wood. A sweating bucket full of ice and a bottle of champagne sat on the buffet against the wall. A note perched beside the bottle.

Aly ignored the bottle and snatched up the note to wave it at Red. "Do you know what this says?" she asked, tone a notch higher than normal. "It is a note from Lordan to Elise." Aly glanced down at it. "For you, my love." She tossed the note onto the table. "That snake!"

Red kept his face flat, not wanting to say anything that might offend her further.

Aly huffed and waved her arms. "Why would he do this? Send her champagne and a pointless note that calls her 'my love'? Why would he do that after botching her ultimatum?" She yanked off her gloves and held them, apparently waiting for an answer.

"Ah, I don't know. Perhaps he thinks he upheld it." Aly was upset about *Lordan*? That wasn't what he was expecting.

This was the wrong thing to say. Nearly snarling, Aly slapped her gloves over the back of a chair. "I'm sure he does."

Almost afraid to speak, Red said, "He doesn't love Elise."

Aly blinked, then nodded. "She was so hopeful, Red."

"In Mardon, she told me she wanted to hit him," he countered, confused.

Pulling out the chair, Aly sat. After a small laugh, she said, "You clearly don't understand women."

In her evening gown, her hair arranged just so, his sorcerer was stunning. Red stared, knowing he should not, but also knowing that he should apologize to Aly for what Elise implied and also that whatever he said would not right the accusation thrown at him from his own sister. An accusation that, he was certain, would not only create backlash from many angles but could create doubt in Aly's mind about him.

He'd never admitted to himself that he loved Aly. It was, after all, completely not allowed. But Elise had spoken those words so easily, as if everyone knew them as the plain truth. Did Aly know this?

Now was not the time to ask.

"Red, please stop."

He pulled his attention away from her and stared instead at a flickering candle. Of course, she knew. She had to know.

That moment on the train burned into his memory like a brand. It filled his dreams and fueled his hopes. It had been barely more than nothing—no more than a touch of her hand and a spontaneous comment.

She's off limits, he reminded himself, not wanting to believe it.

Taking the chair across from her, he sat. "What she said, I...I am sorry she said it like that."

"Like what exactly? The part where she said you loved me, or the part where she said I am no more than your...*slave*." She dipped her head at the last word.

A flush colored Aly's cheeks. She turned away.

The word stung Red, but he could tell it bothered her even more; there was something about the defeat in her shoulders, the blush on her face, the inability to look directly at him. "You're not my...it's not like that." Heat, along with panic, crept up his neck to his ears. "You don't feel like that, do you?"

After an agonizing moment, Aly shook her head. "People will wonder now. What should we do?"

"What do you think we should do?"

"I don't know, Red. You are the king. I follow your ord"—she cut herself off, face purpling now as her unfinished word screamed in the silence.

They stared at one another, neither willing to speak.

Finally, Aly said, "Well, it's true." She stood and walked toward the large glass doors to the balcony. As she opened the door, she added, "It is simply how it is with sovereigns and sorcerers." Again, she left the door wide.

Red followed. He propped against the doorframe, watching Aly as she leaned against the balcony railing and looked up at the stars. The harbor was lined with anchored ships, and even though the sun had set, the docks rang with the sounds of commerce.

He needed to close the distance between them. Aly was drifting away, like a feather on the wind.

Once, he'd failed to trust her, and it had nearly gotten him killed. Now he needed to reassure her, regain her trust; he could not imagine facing tomorrow, let alone the dangers ahead as they continued their fight against the Canyon, without her trust.

"When I was in the Canyon," he began, stepping out onto the balcony, "you kept me from losing my mind. *Light overpowers the darkness*, remember? I sort of lost it there for a little while, but I didn't fall entirely. And that was because of you." He leaned over the railing, far enough away to say he understood her frustration.

She watched the harbor for several long seconds. "The *Verad* kept you from losing your mind, not me."

"But you reminded me of those words. Truth has power, but we so easily forget what is true. Without you, I'd be dead a dozen times over." He offered a small smile and she did not turn away.

She leaned on one elbow, ever so slightly tilting toward him. "Are you ready for what will happen?"

His chest tightened like a hand fisting inside him. "I will not let Alexander take my throne."

Aly looked down. "I meant about what Elise said. Rumors will spread like wildfire. Your character will be called into question." She met his gaze. "As king, you should be equipped to handle gossip. What people say about me isn't really that important." A small amount of pain edged her words.

He wanted to take her hand, but he gripped the balustrade instead. "Gossip, I can handle, but I don't want people thinking poorly of you."

"Why? It's not like it matters."

"It does matter." He stared at her. Why would she think it

didn't matter how people viewed her? "Elise was pretty angry. I think she will be calmer when we reach home. She needs time away from Lordan. It will be good for her to see Carolyn—and our mother. She'll be all right."

"Eventually." Aly stared out across the water.

"Should we destroy the note? I don't want her to hurt more than she has to."

Aly sighed. "No. That's not up to us. And you can't make her stop hurting, Red. You can't fix everything. Only time will do that."

"Possibly not, but I can ensure that she never has to see Lordan again."

"What are you going to do, confine her to your palace? She's her own person—and a princess. You can't control her life."

Red's tongue thickened like cold gravy. *Am I really that controlling?* His intentions were to protect, to *help*. He spun away, one hand rubbing his jaw.

"And anyway, we can't avoid Lordan forever," she continued. "We need him as our ally. Without his sorcerer's help, more people would have died at Kassia's hand." She avoided admitting that her father, via Kassia's control, would have been the one to inflict more damage. "We'll need him in the fight to close the Canyon."

He faced her again, his expression softening as he took in her wide eyes, her determination to see this wild plan to its end. "Their sorcerer may be incredible, but I'll put my money on Tandera's. If Lordan doesn't join us, we can still defeat the Canyon's evil. I know it." On a whim, he grabbed her hands.

Aly closed her eyes, her hands limp but not retreating. "Don't."

He shook his head. "Let me finish. Maybe we don't even need Lordan. Maybe all we need to close the Canyon is you."

Aly's cheeks darkened. Her fingers began to withdraw, but he held on. "Red, come on."

"You're stronger when I trust you."

She yanked her hands out of his. "Don't be ridiculous."

"But you keep saying that the Beacon and Beholder—that *we* —will save the world. What if we simply need to trust that more?"

Aly dropped her shoulders and lifted her chin in annoyance. "I never said *save*, I said *change*."

A loud, grating crash sounded from the docks, which sat clear across the harbor from the palace.

"Must have dropped a crate," Red suggested.

Aly's hand shot out toward the water, a look of fear on her pinched brow. Dust-like specks of light pooled around her hand before a lightning bolt fired from her fingertips across to the harbor. After another muted crash, she added, "It seems the Canyon is polluting the waters of the seas now too." She turned wide eyes on him. "That wasn't a crate. That was a monster."

A knock at Red's grand suite the next morning broke his concentration as he, Grey, and Aly poured over a map of Mardon. He could not escape this palace fast enough. Open windows admitted the sound of crunching gravel as carriages pulled up and trunks were loaded.

It wasn't only the Tanderans leaving the palace today. Since the news of the sea monster's attack spread through the city, every noble guest and royal visitor was packing up to leave the coastal city.

Red yawned. None of them had slept. "No more visitors. No more comments." He pressed his fingers into his forehead and leaned over the painted table, over his still-full breakfast plate. The crepes had grown cold. A delighted fly had found the open jam and was feasting on the king's forgotten meal.

Aly had killed the sea monster—her magic left it sprawled

on the wharf where it had surged up to devour a worker unloading a late-arriving shipment of rugs and coffee. Neither Red nor Aly had ventured to the docks, but they'd received the report, along with the other royal residents of the palace, of a tentacled creature as large as a whale. Some had called it a giant squid. Others had called it an octopus. There were rumors of fangs.

Red didn't know what to call it, but Aly's magic had sensed the darkness within the creature and confirmed that it felt and behaved like a Canyon beast.

The Black River pollutes the seas now too. No longer were the beasts of the Deep confined to the land. He recalled Lordan speaking of a ship sinking at sea. Perhaps another beast?

"Here," said Grey, pausing his discourse to hand Red his coronet so he would look the part of king when their visitor arrived. Grey, who seemed unusually eager to hand him his crown, was finally filling Red in on some of his secrets. Their conversation this morning was on the workings of the gangs of Mardon and, more importantly, which nobles secretly funded them and thus gained a profit from their dealings. Grey knew more about these gangs than Red had imagined was possible to know, unless one had first-hand knowledge. But he wasn't here to question Grey or his methods. An informant gathered intelligence in whatever ways necessary.

Always know more than your opponent, Gevar had told his son, and Red needed as much knowledge of his country and the powerful wealthy as possible. Alexander, for instance, owned a mill in Mardon under a pseudonym—a mill where a gang was known to convene at night.

Heavy footsteps preceded Seb's voice arguing with Veeter Yin. "I promise he'll want to see this."

"Sire, I told him you desired no visitors," Yin said flatly.

Seb pushed into the room, ignoring the protocol of polite society and plopping unceremoniously on Red's couch.

"See what?" asked Red, grateful for a break from the intensity of the night-long conversation.

"This." Seb pointed at his face and flashed a wide smile.

"I'm glad we had a glass of humility this morning," quipped Red.

Seb leaned forward, scanning the breakfast array on Red's table. "Hey, they gave you more crepes, and I think your strawberries are bigger." He stood, nabbed one off the king's plate, and popped it in his mouth.

"Privileges of running a country."

Seb walked over to the large windows and made a face at pair of passing Referen women. "That's right. You want entertainment —I'll give you entertainment." He spun around. "Have you had many gawkers this morning?"

"A few," Red admitted, rubbing his tired eyes. At least their planning had kept his mind mostly off of the awful rumors started by his sister—rumors that had swept the palace like a virus and caused a few passing courtiers to hurl hateful remarks through his open windows. He wished his suite weren't adjacent to the vast lawn within the largest of the palace courtyards. "One woman earlier called me a disgusting wretch."

"Where can I find her? I'd like to give her a hug," Seb crooned.

"I can arrange your marriage, if you'd like. She was probably sixty."

Seb cringed. "What are you going to do about them, then?" He waved excitedly at a group of young women strolling by to glimpse Tandera's king and Royal Sorcerer.

"The rumors? They sort of pale in comparison to the larger issue here."

Seb's brows rose. "Which is?"

Red sank onto an overstuffed chair. "Alexander is attempting a coup."

Laughter burst from Seb's mouth. He recovered, noting the

expressions watching him, and said, "Oh." For once, the man was at a loss for words.

Aly stood and stretched. Red forced himself to look away and stared instead at the map on the table. "Grey, we can resume this conversation on the train ride home."

Grey stood, nodded, and left the room.

"What are you going to do about it?" asked Seb, his voice unnaturally grim. He took a seat at the table, ate another strawberry, and peered down at the map.

Red looked up at Aly. He could trust Seb, and he wanted to tell his friend and council member about what was happening, but he couldn't share what he and Grey had been discussing. He opted for the broader context. "We were sketching out options… if Alexander won't see reason."

Seb leaned forward. "You think he will step aside when you return? *Pfft.* Even *I* know a man isn't stupid enough to announce a coup, then simply walk away when the former king shows up."

Red frowned. "One can always hope."

"You're *too* hopeful, brother. Kings should be pessimists, if anything. Always planning for the worst possible scenario, then rejoicing if events don't end badly." He pinned a finger on the map, right over the palace. "Being an optimist leads you nowhere. Plan for the tossing *world* to catch on fire, then maybe you'll be able to handle it if it does."

From her stance near the corner, Aly tilted her head back and forth in an appraising way. "That's actually pretty good advice," she admitted.

Seb saluted her, then winked. She rolled her eyes.

Red slid the map out from under Seb's finger. "Alexander plans to move into the palace before we return. He's starting rumors that I've been corrupted by the Canyon, that I'm rash and villainous and evil."

Reaching out, Seb slapped a firm hand on Red's shoulder and said, "You are rash, but I'd say *evil* is taking it a bit far." He dropped his hand and stood, pacing the room with a contempla-tive scowl. "So, all you need to do is prove yourself the most qualified sovereign."

Red chuckled in annoyance. "It's *my* crown."

Aly stepped forward. "He's right."

"Exactly," Seb said. To Aly, he muttered, "See, we're going to be friends." Then, to Red, he said, "Tandera must want *you* instead of Alexander."

Red looked between them, surprised to see them in agree-ment. Eventually, his eyes softened. "What am I to do? How am I to earn my own crown back?"

"That's exactly it," Aly said, taking his arm. He startled when she touched him voluntarily. "You must *earn* it. No, listen," she insisted, cutting off his rebuttal. "In the eyes of the people, you need to prove you're the best option to rule this country."

"Inheritance isn't based on popularity." *Though I used to think it shouldn't be based on blood, either.*

"No," Seb admitted. "But the army's allegiance is. The allies you can garner are. The people's adoration is. Alexander calls you rash; we can change that. And as far as you being corrupted, we can prove him wrong there too. Hear me out," he said, lifting a hand. "Prove to the people of Tandera that you are wise. Prove to the people of Tandera that you can rule better than Alexander can. And—" he glanced at Aly then back at Red, "—I suggest you do it without magic. Win this crown back completely on your own."

Aly nodded at Seb, as if he'd spoken what was on her mind.

Red remained silent a moment. *Without magic, I'm no more than a man in a piece of jewelry.* What did the crown really mean, without the magic of the sorcerer to render it powerful?

His father's words echoed in his head: *The crown symbolizes authority; the scepter symbolizes power. Together, they comprise the sovereignty of our nation. Separate the two, and you have neither the ability to enforce your hand nor the respect necessary to warrant enforcement.*

The crown was about respect, about authority, about leadership. He'd have to garner the respect and loyalty of his people if he hoped to retain authority over them. Maybe Seb was right: magic might not be the best method for securing devotion.

"All right," he said finally. "But how?"

7

ALY

The train rattled down the track, the tall pines of eastern Refere shrank into the distance as Tandera's border approached, unmarked and unnoticed by the passengers as they rumbled homeward.

The Borrain Mountains loomed ahead as the train curved around a small valley. Little had been said since they'd boarded the train hours ago. Elise had slipped into her private compartment, and Red into his. Seb, Grey, and the others traveling with them had not once bothered the king. Aly, unsure where her place was—visible or invisible, to sit with Red or to give him space—took up a comfortable chair in the dining car and poured over a copy of the *Canticles of Magic, Volume III*. She'd not spent as much time with the third volume, as it was the smallest and therefore contained the least amount of information.

As the train chugged past the distant façade of the imposing Mount Crent, Aly read through a poem, written three centuries after the creation of the Canyon.

> Light passes
> and night the steady rhythm does employ,

of faces hid and suns to drink,
the chosen child, the world to brink,
and none without can e'er enjoy.

The book in Aly's lap jostled with the movement of the train, propelled by the railway's own Protector. With her finger, she traced the words *chosen child* and a purple smear appeared around the words. She flipped to another poem, penned by another Master, written a half-century earlier. It had the same phrase, *chosen child*, but it was plural, *children*. She'd thought originally that the poems spoke of all sorcerers as chosen, as they alone had been gifted by Theod with the power to Pull energy from the truth woven in the fabric of the Maker's world. But what if this poem was speaking of only one person—a Beholder?

She wanted to find out what her purpose was. *If Theod has placed this burden on my shoulders, shouldn't he also give me a few clues as to what to do?*

The next stanza held little clarity.

Press, O world,
Into the dawn alight with songs of joy,
When night lies down and breathes its last,
The faces shine that once were cast
And none within can e'er destroy.

Aly peered out the window, her gaze absently passing over the landscape. A poem had led them to the Canyon, to Red's cure. It was odd that she was searching again for answers in poetry. The *Verad* spoke of a dawn that would bring about an end to darkness, but there was something in the *Canticles* that made it personal, like the sorcerers who penned these poems ached in their very bones for this long-awaited dawn, and with their ink-dipped quills attempted to beckon it to them faster.

Her mind wandered again to Red's Truthwell, to the brightness fluctuating within like a thousand trapped fireflies. Her magic uncaged them, yet they never diminished, never truly flew away. They obeyed her. No wonder Theod had limited Truth-pulling to so few people.

Her father's masked face popped into her mind, and instantly her stomach tightened and turned a sickening flip. Theod had gifted the world with magic, but inevitably, that gift had been distorted, even defaced.

All good things cast shadows when held up to the light, and magic was no different. To some of the people in the town where Aly had grown up, no magic could be trusted. To the Zealots, the reverse was true: no magic could be considered wrong, no matter its outcome or its motive.

Aly rubbed her eyes and touched Red's Truthwell with her mind. He was pacing in his cabin.

It felt like ages since they'd left Mardon for Bulvarna, though it had only been a few weeks. So much had happened. So much had changed.

Aly sensed Red's arrival before Yin opened the cabin door and preceded him into the dining car.

Red paused when he saw her. The smile that lit his face evaporated all gloomy thoughts from her mind. She returned his smile with one full of hope.

Then his expression collapsed so suddenly that Aly hopped out of her chair.

"What's wrong?" she asked, steadying herself against the rocking of the train.

He dismissed Yin, never taking his eyes off of her. As he walked toward her, she couldn't move. There was a world within his eyes she'd never seen or known existed. It was full of terror and pain; she wanted to hide from it.

"Red?" she pressed.

He walked right up to her and reached toward her cheek, then withdrew his hand, leaving only the ghost of his warmth on her skin.

"Tell me about your vows," he said, voice deep and choppy, like he was fighting to speak what was on his mind.

She blinked several times, puzzled at his words. "My vows to serve the crown are Binding, you know that."

As the words left her mouth, it hit her.

The crown.

She pressed a hand to her mouth. Alexander was vying for the crown—the crown she was sworn to serve.

He grabbed her shoulders. "Tell me you can break that vow if necessary."

Shaking her head, her braid trembled at her back. "If I break that vow, I die."

His shoulders slumped, and a heavy breath hissed out of his mouth.

The notion that Alexander would succeed with his coup was too ridiculous to accept. She'd never allowed herself to picture a reality where Beacon and Beholder were separated. It made no sense. Why would Theod allow that?

He wouldn't.

Aly straightened, confidence clambering back up after a quick fall. "He won't win," she whispered.

"Tell me plainly, Aly, what happens if he does?"

"If Alexander wins the crown, I'll be Bound to him."

Mardon's ancient walls rolled past the coach windows as Aly's magic propelled them home. Dread and relief mingled in Aly's core. She was coming home, finally, after being away so long. When they'd left, Red had been cursed and her father had been the force behind her nightmares.

Those threats were gone. Kassia was still at large, but she'd remained completely hidden from view for weeks now. The scouts sent to the Candul region had discovered at least two witnesses confirming she'd been there, but could not determine her exact whereabouts. She was an expert at disappearing, almost as good as Aly.

Now, rolling toward the palace, Red and Aly were returning to troubled waters.

Grey's intelligence had arrived in bits and pieces, none of which were good or uplifting, but Aly had maintained hope that Alexander's attempted coup would be a farce, a worthless endeavor.

Because if it wasn't, and if Alexander really did usurp the throne, Alexander would break her Binding to Red. How she'd missed that, she had no idea. Purposeful ignorance, perhaps. He was a Beacon, she the Beholder. A bond like that was not only rare, it was crafted by Theod to change the world —wasn't it?

Along the streets, only a handful of curious peasants and stiff-necked merchants peered at the passing carriages. Aly spotted few noblemen among the Mardonians assembled to witness their king's return.

This isn't good. She glanced at Red, whose face was twisted away to look out his window. She couldn't read his expression, but his shoulders were a bit scrunched.

Red had worn the crown for barely three months, and already it was changing his posture, his resting facial expression. For a small bit of metal, it weighed as much as the world.

Aly turned her gaze back out to the city. She plastered a smile on her face, hoping the sight of her half-mask might enliven some of the crowd. These people hadn't seen her yet. They hadn't seen what the Referen citizens already had: Aly beside Red, not merely protecting him but...*beside* him.

She'd hoped it would bolster him in their minds, but the rumors started by Elise had traveled faster than the king.

The faces Aly observed on the street looked skeptical. Slitted eyes and taut mouths accompanied finger pointing and uplifted, judgmental chins.

These people have heard the rumors, and they believe them. Aly wondered which rumors, exactly, were circulating in Mardon. As with any bit of truth-lie mixture, the lies grew like yeast in dough, transforming the original lie to something more. *What are people saying about me? About Red?*

Alexander was attempting to smear Red's name, to make people believe he was not only unfit but *unworthy* of the throne, and that Alexander was the upstanding alternative. Alexander's maternal line had distant blood tied directly to the king's ancestors, so his claim to the throne was based on blood *and* character. The savior. The rightful leader.

Aly pushed out her awareness, searching for threats, for lyths in particular. The Canyon, unguarded as it had been for weeks now, was pouring its beasts into the world. They didn't need Grey's network of spies to know that much. Aly didn't sense any beasts of the Deep nearby, but she did discover a large gathering of people at the palace. A cluster of Truthwells, all lined up perfectly. Too perfectly.

"The army," she gasped quietly enough that Red wouldn't hear. The king was rolling toward a firestorm. Alexander couldn't possibly think of attacking Red with the military.

Aly's shoulders hunched as she watched the city roll by. To serve in the light, no longer protected by her invisibility, meant to invite both the eye of admiration and the eye of criticism. As king, Red knew he must to endure this. As Royal Sorcerer, Aly had never imagined she would as well.

This was what it felt like to truly live—to be seen by others and live among them was to take the good with the bad. A glance at Red reminded her he was worth it.

Mardon was the largest city in Tandera, teeming with people. Yet, for their king, no one came with banners, no one came with bells. Only a few curious faces peeked out along the sidewalks between the buildings and from the upstairs windows at the royal procession.

She remembered traveling home with Gevar on many occasions. Banners, confetti, rose petals, trumpets. None of that was present for Red's return.

What has Alexander done to this city?

Aly waved at a wide-eyed young girl walking with two older women. The girl smiled but, at a gesture from one of the women, shrank back. Aly's smile faltered. She'd wanted to be seen all her life, but at times like this she wished she could slip under her shroud and disappear.

It took all Aly's self-restraint not to look away when someone made eye contact from the sidewalk. She was used to people looking through her, around her. When their eyes caught hers and moved with her, it produced a strange sensation in Aly's muscles, triggering her desire to flee.

She glanced again at Red. He caught her movement and turned his brown eyes toward her, offering a small smile. In that smile, she could see the disappointment weighing on the corners of his mouth. He was worried.

But she held his gaze. *His* gaze was one she'd grown rather fond of, despite the fact that his very presence disturbed her otherwise unwavering concentration on her magic. This man, who'd morphed in her mind from a boyish prat to a man ready to risk his life for her safety, for his people's safety, made her feel the world was welcoming as his eyes found hers.

Even now, when he's facing this terrible welcome, he's trying to comfort me with that smile. She reached across and found his hand, squeezed. He pressed his thumb against hers and squeezed back.

"We're home," he said.

The palace loomed ahead. She thought it took longer to ride through Mardon, but she'd never ridden in the carriage with the king before either. She'd always been on top, and those rides were much more uncomfortable, therefore seeming much longer.

She was grateful for the change, for the comfort of a plush seat, but with it came different difficulties and discomforts she had never imagined.

Who was *she* beside this man? Just a shadow shield, as she always had been, nothing more. A Protector. An employee of the crown.

And yet there was more.

Her hand held in his proved it.

In the Canyon, there had been more. That moment in Kassia's garden after they had defeated her father, there had been more. Those precious few days on the train, when there was nothing but Red and her and the mystery of what was between them, there had been more. Yet with the news of this coup, and the strangeness of the rumors surrounding her relationship with the king, a distance had grown between them, a small chasm she feared would widen as soon as the carriage doors opened and they stepped into this new Mardon twisted by Alexander's lies.

As they drew nearer, her vision sharpened, and the shapes of soldiers emerged.

Red's hand slithered away. She quickly withdrew as heat burned in her cheeks and her chest. These soldiers didn't look like a welcome party. They stood across the gates, barring them.

"What's he up to?" Red said under his breath as the carriage slowed to a stop. He grabbed the door handle.

"I wouldn't," Aly said, using a bit of magic to push back against him, so he wouldn't open the door before he was ready to step into the crowd, before he knew what his actions would portray.

His eyes were fierce as he turned back to her. "If I do not step out of this carriage, it will make me look afraid. I will not stoop so low. Let me out, Aly."

She pressed her eyes shut. "I know. Only think about what Alexander is trying to do. Think about what he said about you."

Red's breath was loud as a pinned bull's. "Like I could forget."

Aly cringed as she released her magic, wishing she hadn't said or done anything. He was the king, not a little boy. She shouldn't try to school him on politics, like she knew anything about that realm. Maybe he wouldn't let his rashness spill out in words he would regret, but if he did, that was his choice to make. Aly climbed out of the carriage behind him, into the hot sun.

Before Red could take two steps out of the carriage, a bald man emerged from behind the soldiers, smiling.

Lord Benedict Alexander's large mustache sat atop a wide grin. "My dear boy, you have returned to us," he said, arms open wide.

"Do not speak thus to me," Red said, voice nearly shaking with rage.

Aly wished she could calm him. In his Well she sensed a swirling darkness touching the edges of his brilliant light. He was fighting lies within his mind, but even those whisps of shadow failed to dim his surging luminance. Alexander, however, boasted a Truthwell rife with shadows. Within his Well, a vine of darkness coiled and slithered among the otherwise bright light. The man was either living a lie or had been persuaded to believe one darker and deeper than most petty lies, whose shadows never took such pronounced shapes.

She nearly reached out a hand to stop Red from stepping toward Alexander, but she knew one Truthwell couldn't pollute another just by proximity.

Fear and anger were drawing out the shadows in Red, coaxing them forward without any curse at all.

"It offends you that I welcome home our young prince?" Alexander asked, arms wide.

"I am your king," Red retorted.

"Ah, but the coronation has not happened yet. Your Accession was a temporary crowning. A trial period, as it were."

Red's limbs twitched at his side, the energy inside him pulsating, humming. "You will remove your men and let me into my house."

"I will do no such thing, my dear boy." Alexander clasped his hands behind his back. "You see, the military answers to me now." His words carried across the pavement, bouncing against the stone walls of the buildings nearby, as if this new truth were flooding the streets like a summer downpour. "It was a simple matter of explaining to them that their leader—in this case an eighteen-year-old boy with no experience leading an army—had been corrupted by a rather unwise trip into the very dwelling place of evil. You admit you have been to the depths of the Canyon, and you think we do not see the truth of what you have become. You cannot deny the corruption in you."

"I am not corrupted," Red snarled, unable to keep his voice level and calm.

Alexander nodded. "That is what a corrupted man would say. When you rose out of the Canyon, your rash decision resulted in the death of our closest and strongest ally, as well as the death of the Royal Sorcerer of a country we would have preferred not to have offended. We have lost an ally and gained an enemy. That is no action of a king."

"Lordan is with us." Red's voice trembled with what was surely rage. Aly cooled his body, but she wasn't certain it would be enough to calm him.

"Lucien's son, Lordan, is as reliable as a wet napkin," laughed Alexander. "We cannot trust him."

Red stiffened. It was one thing to call into question the loyalty of an ally in secret, but to do so in public would reach Lordan quickly, given there were likely Referen spies in the crowd now gathered around to watch this exchange. It was bold for Alexander to make alliance-breaking statements, as if the crown were already settled on his head and he drove the nation as he willed.

"As I was saying," Alexander continued, "these men answer to me now, and we have decided it is best if you reside elsewhere until the lawful change of power has occurred, after the official coronation at summer's end."

A few people in the crowd passed hushed whispers. Aly resisted the urge to bite her lip. She wasn't used to having to hide her expressions. She knew, based on the way Red's energy moved in angry fits and careless sloshes, that he wanted to destroy this man. She blinked and stepped backward, automatically recoiling from the rising anger inside of Red.

I can remove them all, if you wish, she whispered into his mind. She couldn't bear the disgrace of this affront to Red, and she didn't want him to draw a blade and attempt to take on Alexander by himself, not with the army standing like so many branded cattle behind the usurper.

Red's jawline twitched as he ground his teeth. There were at least a hundred people watching, not counting the soldiers. Whatever happened here would be announced all over the continent.

She never before wanted to see inside of Red's mind, but right now, she wished he could speak silently to her the way she could to him. *What does he want me to do?* They'd agreed she wouldn't use her magic to win him the crown. But they couldn't let Alexander succeed.

Red cleared his throat. "We will not force our entrance here. No one need die today for this man's ignorant actions."

Aly exhaled a long, slow breath.

"Ignorant?" barked Alexander. "I am wise to save the country from your corrupted hands!"

A chorus of *hear, hear!* raced through the crowd.

He'd already won their allegiance. *But how?*

Red stepped back toward his carriage, turning his attention to the crowd. "Perhaps you forget that Theod chooses who wears the crown."

A few people nodded and chanted their assent.

Alexander sneered. "Indeed, he does, my boy. Indeed, he does. At summer's end, we will see who Theod has chosen."

"So be it," said Red. He spun on his heel and slipped back into the carriage, shadows whirling in the energy of his sun-bright Truthwell.

Inside the carriage, he hammered his fist on the cushioned side panel. "If I cannot stay at my house, where am I to sleep?"

Aly could think of only one place. "Grey Manor."

The ivy-covered walls of Grey Manor grew larger as the royal carriage rolled toward Aly's former home. She had only lived on the estate for three months, but it had proved a pivotal time in her life. Her residency here had been the bridge between her old self and the person she was now.

She'd grown up a girl afraid of her magic, afraid of what it meant that she could change her body temperature or heal a person from afar with no more than a thought. She had been uncertain and uneducated in the ways of magic, until Grey had found her, and he had brought her here, whisking her into the world of ballgowns and ballrooms, kings and sorcerers. This place had been the place of her becoming, and also had been a place that had broken her.

She cracked each one of her knuckles, then her wrists, then rolled her neck.

"Is everything okay?" Red asked, his voice stiff, the first words he'd spoken since they'd left the palace.

"I'm fine."

Her mind flashed to the first time she'd arrived at this house in a carriage. Her mother had sat opposite her. It had been the last time she'd seen her mother. Aly fought down an unexpected tightness in her throat.

Lord Weston Grey, who'd only recently arrived at his estate as well, emerged from around the house on horseback.

Is that Miss Turner? Aly chuckled at the sight of the bay mare. She was getting old, but Grey still sat atop her like she was a prized racehorse.

"Something funny?" Red's brows twitched. He looked uncomfortable.

"I rode that horse to spy on Grey once," Aly answered.

"Spying on a spy? How'd that go for you?"

Aly's eyes narrowed. Red was touchy. She couldn't exactly blame him, but she wondered if part of that tension was from the man now dismounting his horse. Red didn't know much about her time with Grey. She wasn't sure she wanted Red to know everything. "Grey likes his secrets, let's just say that." *We all do.*

Red grunted. "That's why he's good at what he does."

Grey's current footman, a man unknown to Aly, opened their carriage door. "Welcome to Grey Manor, Your Majesty."

Though Grey had traveled the same distance as Red and Aly, his crisp black suit looked barely rumpled as he strode toward them. His hair, on the other hand, was wind-tossed, and his hand raking through it did little to help.

Red waited as Aly descended into the sunshine. Aly met Grey's eyes and grinned. Smiling at him came easily; it felt familiar.

He tucked his riding whip against his side and bowed low as Red emerged from the carriage. "Your Majesty, you are welcome here as long as you please." The skin around his eyes twitched, his jaw worked as he swallowed.

Is he nervous? Aly wondered. Lord Weston Grey didn't get nervous. He fought the beasts of the Deep like they were stray tomcats.

His gaze danced toward Aly. She wondered if, despite his legendary bravado, Grey was apprehensive about her returning to his house. She kept her chin lifted and willfully did not look back at him until his attention returned to Red.

Yates approached Aly with a smile. The night butler had now become the day butler, it appeared. "Would you like your old room?" he asked. Aly stared at him blankly. He spoke as if she were some young woman returning home after experiencing the cultures of the world. He cleared his throat. "Very well. Your things will be brought up."

Grey reached out a hand and placed it on Red's shoulder to lead him inside. Aly assumed she was the only one who noticed the tightness in Grey's motions, the way it taxed him to act so cordial. *What's bothering you?* she thought as she stared at the back of Grey's head.

"Come, Your Majesty, I will show you my latest additions to my trophy room. I've a large moose that I think will impress even your skilled hand."

Red nodded, then paused on the top step before entering the house, his face half obscured with shadow. "No. We need to talk strategy. We need to figure out how I'm going to reclaim the palace."

Aly sighed to herself. Grey turned, his expression almost pained, as if he were truly offended the king didn't want to see his hunting trophies. Red was not one to relax while a task needed completing. He needed a plan. He needed hope.

What will be your mad hope this time? Aly wondered. *This time, it cannot be me.*

Thinking of how rash he could be when desperate, Aly nudged his Truthwell and lowered his body temperature. He was all steam and hissing tension, a train attempting to slow down from full speed. Watching his face relax, Aly suppressed a smile.

"Yes, of course. I'll call for tea," Grey added, shuffling them all indoors.

Once inside, Aly's eyes turned automatically toward the room to the left, but its doors were closed. Then her gaze flickered to the painting in the foyer. She grinned at the familiar art. "Hello," she whispered to the painting, which portrayed death as a woman about to strike an oblivious man on the helm of a ship. She'd never fully appreciated the painting during her stay at Grey Manor. Now, she rather liked it.

Grey sidled up to her, arms clasped behind his back. "You used to hate this painting."

"It's grown on me."

He chuckled. "Art has a way of telling us things about ourselves we didn't yet know." When he met her gaze, there was a mischief in it, both a mixture of the impish Grey she'd known and a glimpse of the stoic Grey he'd become from his time at the Canyon. One thing was certain: secrets hid in his dark eyes.

Red, shoulders stiff and hands fidgety, lumbered up beside Aly on her other side. He didn't even look at the painting, but instead looked between Aly and Grey. "What of Carolyn? My mother? Have you heard Alexander's plans for them? I insisted Elise wait to enter Mardon until we'd assessed the situation at the palace. Should I send orders to bring her here?" he asked Grey.

"She is, of course, most welcome. However, I believe Alexander may not turn her away. For now, the queen and Lady Carolyn are allowed to remain at the palace. I believe Alexander will see the value in allowing Elise to return to her mother and sister." Grey scratched his cheek, where a new beard was shading his features. "Alexander understands that the best way to defeat an enemy is to remove those who support him. Elise is more valuable to him *away* from you."

Aly watched Grey's eyes, but the man was harder to read than a poem in ancient Edrean. He knew more about the situation than he was sharing. He would have his reasons, and though she'd learned the hard way not to trust his reasons, she had to believe they were for the good of Tandera.

Most courtiers knew Lord Alexander did not approve of Gevar's marriage to Isabelle. He'd accepted it because Gevar was king. Now Isabelle and her daughters were living under the same roof as a man who considered them of no more rank than Isabelle's carpenter father.

Red snorted. "If he even thinks about casting them out onto the streets!"

"He won't do that," Aly said. Her body swayed closer to his, and she wouldn't have noticed but for Grey's presence on her other side. "He's vying for a crown. He knows the people adore your mother. To cast her out would be to make enemies of the common folk."

"She's right," Grey added. "But we can't count on him extending his grace toward them forever. If he...succeeds in his coup, Your Majesty, I believe he will demand they leave the palace."

Red lifted his gaze to the painting. For a moment, he stared in silence. "If I can't keep my crown, my family will be homeless."

"We will arrange for them to visit you tomorrow," Grey announced, changing the subject. "I know you're eager to see them."

"Very good," Red said with a nod. "Do you still have that painting of my mother here?"

Grey chuckled. "It isn't a painting of the queen, but yes, I have it. It's my favorite Yvesy. I keep it in here." He turned and opened the doors to the drawing room off the foyer. As the two men stepped out of the foyer, Aly stood a moment alone in the vaulted space.

She was struck by the memory of when she'd first entered this house. The smells sank into her senses, and she was sixteen again and Weston Grey was standing in front of her, staring at a large painting, asking her about art. With effort, she avoided glancing at the place where a bench had been. She'd noticed immediately upon entering the house that the bench was gone, replaced with a large buffet dotted with candlesticks. Maybe Grey didn't like remembering that night either, the night he'd brought her news of her mother's death.

She glanced to her left into the sitting room. The painting *Clarentine* hung exactly where she remembered it. Relief washed over her. For some reason, if that painting had been moved or sold, Aly would have missed it.

The likeness to the queen really was striking, and the characteristic Yvesy strokes and colors brought a smile to Aly's face. They also brought back a quick sting as she recalled another Yvesy: the one hanging in her rooms at the palace. They were the only flowers a man had ever gifted her.

A gift from Grey.

Grey's back was to her as he gestured at *Clarentine*. He might be a warrior with little heart, but he loved art. Aly *humphed*. Grey had always been a conundrum to her. Her time at the palace had only cemented her confidence in choosing to step away from him. He was a spy. Indifferent. A skilled killer. His own family avoided him. He could lie better than anyone she knew—his job as the king's informant demanded it.

Her attention shifted to Red. Warmth blossomed in her chest and hands. He was rash and ridiculous at times, but Red cared so much. Too much, perhaps. His emotions drove him in all directions, despite his efforts to anchor himself down with action. She smiled. He was still young. He hadn't experienced the battles and death that Grey had. He hadn't even carried the sovereign duties of a nation for long.

His touch was tender. The way he looked at her made her not care if the rest of the world could see her. Grey's touch had been tender too, but in a cautious way, a fumbling way. Now that she could compare the two, Grey's hands had been deceptive. He'd held her when he'd known he'd have to give her up. He'd done it knowing his actions would hurt her.

Red, that night she'd healed his headaches for the first time, had fallen against her with such rapt attention as if nothing, not even the Canyon, could stop him.

As if feeling her gaze, Grey and Red turned around at the same time. She thought she saw Grey's throat bob as he looked away. This was going to be awkward, all three of them staying under the same roof.

8

RED

The following day, Red's family arrived at Grey Manor ahead of a scheduled luncheon on the grounds. Elise stepped out of the carriage before her mother, a look of disdain on her porcelain face.

The former queen and the princesses arrived as the sun was reaching its highest point and temperatures soared. It was the first time Red had seen his mother and youngest sister since leaving for Bulvarna. Gnats pestered Red's eyes as his sisters and mother appeared in all their finery. Red and Grey bowed to the women. An unmasked Aly curtsied.

"Oh, my son!" Isabelle rushed forward, clasping her son's head and drawing him into an embrace.

After a moment, Red started to fidget. "Mother."

She released him. "You almost *died*. I am allowed to hug my son." She patted his chest. "Are you taller? It has not been that long, has it?"

Red shook his head and turned to his sisters. He offered Elise a curt bow and then opened his arms to accept Carolyn's violent embrace. He groaned as she squeezed.

"Hi!" Carolyn said, turning her attention to Aly. She curtsied. "I have always wanted to meet you," she said.

Aly's eyes widened. "And I you."

"But surely you have seen us the whole time. You knew us."

"In a way," Aly said.

Carolyn clapped her hands. "I am so excited to meet this mysterious sorcerer." She straightened, casting one last hesitant grin at her brother that confirmed she'd heard Elise's rumor as well. "I have never visited Grey Manor," she added, turning toward the grand house. "It is huge."

Their mother nodded. "Finest house in the county."

"I thought Wyndall's was," Carolyn added, ignoring Grey's cough.

"Carolyn, my dear," Elise said, ever concerned about manners.

"We are most pleased to see you, Lord Grey," Isabelle said, nodding her head at their host.

"It is my honor," Grey replied with a formal bow. "Luncheon is on the patio. Shall we?" He offered his arm to the former queen and led them through the house to the back terrace.

An ornate display of flowers anchored the tablescape and added a fresh scent to the setting. Grey's Comforters would have their work cut out for them to keep them the summer heat at bay.

Red moved to the head chair opposite Lord Grey and, as he took his seat, he reached out and pushed Carolyn's head forward playfully.

"Don't touch my hair. How many times do I have to tell you?" Her hands patted her head to see if any of her golden red curls had fallen.

"Oh, leave it alone, I'm your brother. I'm allowed to mess with you."

As soon as they were all seated, a heavy silence fell over the gathering as they avoided discussing the reason why they were meeting at Grey's house rather than the palace. The topic would be broached soon, and Red was not looking forward to it. Wine was poured and sips were taken.

"Tell me, how is life at the palace?" Red finally asked.

"Wonderful," Carolyn said, picking up a fork and examining the pattern at the end of it. "These are lovely," she said and placed it back on the table.

Red tapped his fingers on the tablecloth, annoyed with Carolyn's answer.

"Alexander has been most kind to us," Isabelle said, a consoling tone to her voice.

"Well, that's fantastic," Red snarled.

"Son, I meant that as a comfort."

"He has not treated us harshly at all," Carolyn agreed.

"But what he has done to you is unspeakable," his mother added, "And I am certain that he will not see this plan through."

"But it *is* a possibility," Carolyn said, perking up.

Everyone shifted. Red cleared his throat. "And what exactly do you mean, Carolyn? Do you believe I am not the rightful king?"

She shook her head. "That is not what I meant. I, of course, believe you are the king, but Alexander has convinced a lot of people to believe otherwise." She became aware of the darts in her brother's eyes and the warning simmering in her mother's gaze. She slowed her words. "What I mean is that Alexander might win. It is a possibility we must not ignore. That is all."

"Oh, that is all, is it?" Red scoffed. "I was ordained by Ondorian. I said the vows. I wear the crown."

"Yes, you wear *a* crown," Carolyn said. "But did you know he does, too?"

Isabelle closed her eyes, and Red leaned forward. "What?"

"Yes," Carolyn continued. "When he's about town and when he's in the palace, he wears a crown. The big, red one."

Red swirled his wine glass, watching the liquid reach for the

CROWN OF DUST

edges like blood about to spill. "He wears my crown." Aly's
breeze was doing little to stave off the sweat on Red's forehead.

"Oh, brother," Elise exclaimed, jumping into the conversation,
"you seem so possessive of it, yet you only had it for such a short
time."

Aly gaped, but she quickly recovered by taking her glass to
her lips.

"And *he* has no claim on it whatsoever!" snapped Red.

"He has served the kingdom longer than you have been
alive," Elise said, charging on.

"Are you on his side?"

"Please," Isabelle raised her hands toward her children. "We
are here to see our beloved Frederick. I am so thankful that you
are alive after what happened in Bulvarna. I am grateful that you
are home."

Red leaned back. "I am not exactly home."

"But you are here and you are alive."

He nodded at his mother and attempted a small smile.

"So," Carolyn blurted, drawing all eyes. Isabelle raised her
hand to caution Carolyn. "Oh, Mother doesn't wish me to speak
of it."

"Speak of what?" asked Red.

Isabelle sighed. Carolyn beamed at her brother. "Edward."

"Edward?" repeated Red, brows lifting.

Carolyn's smile was so bright it was contagious. "Edward
Alexander. Lord Alexander's nephew."

Elise nodded, satisfaction on her freckled face. "He has been
courting Carolyn ever since your council returned from Bulvarna." She leaned on the words, like a knife slicing through her
brother's confidence.

"Mother doesn't wish me to speak of him," Carolyn said with a
glance at Isabelle. "But I can't help what his uncle has done." Her
smile faltered for the briefest moment. "He's an excellent dancer,"
she added, spreading her hands over the tablecloth. "I always

needed a man who could dance." Beaming, she added, "He loves my inventions. Says they're brilliant. Oh, he's studying to be a doctor."

"How noble of him," Red said, resting his head in his hand. Now his youngest sister was being courted by someone from the enemy camp.

"He's at the university."

"Can we not talk about him?" barked Red.

"Oh, it bothers you, does it?" Elise snarled. "Alexander is not holding our relationship to you against us. You shouldn't do the same to your sister."

"Contractions," hissed their mother.

"We will see," Red said. "The man is nothing but a snake. If he is treating you well, it is because he has a reason."

Elise lifted her chin. "Or perhaps he is simply a gentleman."

"Who steals people's thrones," Red muttered.

At that moment, the first course was brought out and laid in front of them.

The meal passed largely with small talk punctuated with awkward silences, quick glances, and clinking cutlery. Red was grateful when it ended and, though sad to see the tension in his mother's eyes, glad when his family departed.

Elise had transformed from his confidant into something altogether foreign, something sinister. Needing to escape from company and desiring to mull over how to win his country—and his sisters—back, Red dismissed himself for a walk around the grounds.

"But it's blazing hot," Aly protested, her hair drifting in a magical breeze.

"I'll survive," he said with a smile at her objection. She tossed out a spell as he walked away, and the snow-bright flecks of magic cooled his skin where they landed.

He glanced over his shoulder at Aly, noting the way her brows tilted up in concern. He wanted to wipe the worry off her face, to assure her their Binding would not break at summer's end. *But is her desire to remain Bound to me due to my light as a Beacon or is it more than that?*

For him, it was more than that.

The only way to ensure he could remain by her side was to win the crown—the crown that was rightfully his.

Dead summer grass crunched under Red's feet as he paced through the back field at Grey Manor. The large house squatted in the distance, its pale walls matching its name.

How am I supposed to win this nation back?

A king was born, not chosen based on merit. He knew his father had been a good king, a wise leader, but he didn't know how it could be measured and replicated.

As he walked, he forced himself to consider Carolyn's words, that Alexander might win.

Aly's magic, when she had first Bound to him, had intoxicated him. He'd not understood how much he would come to need her by his side.

"But it's not about the magic," he said aloud, to no one. He wanted Aly by his side, but not because she was powerful or even beautiful; he needed her steady counsel, her temperance against his incendiary nature, her commitment to what was right. She, like an anchor to a drifting ship, kept him moored, and he couldn't allow anyone to cut the chain that prevented him from wandering into troubled seas.

But remaining Bound to Aly couldn't be his only reason to want the crown.

Why do I want to rule? It seemed as if the answer to this question was paramount to his success, and he wasn't sure he truly knew the answer.

Tandera was a powerful, rich country, and she deserved a strong leader. Red would show the world that he could lead his country as well as his father had. He would prove that Gevar's marriage to Isabelle had been right and that their children were the rightful heirs of the throne.

"Now, how do I prove I'm the rightful king?" he mused aloud.

He heard footsteps. Lord Grey marched toward him with a determined expression.

Red whipped around, embarrassed that he had been caught speaking aloud to himself.

"My lord," said Grey, offering a curt bow. "A man just arrived from the palace. You've been invited to speak with Alexander in the morning."

"Invited to my own home. How kind of him." Red frowned.

"If you desire, I will accompany you."

Red studied him. This man was good at secrets. He was, after all, the king's liaison to the illegal shipping industry and underground crime rings in his city. Kings were to know everything that transpired in their country, good or bad. The only way to know was to have a man on the inside. But was such a man trustworthy?

Grey fixed his eyes on the king, his posture open, as if to conceal nothing. Then again, he had been trained to look innocent.

"Very well. Yes. I would like that."

"He wishes to intimidate you, sire." Grey said, chin lifted. "You are not to let him."

"Of course not," Red retorted. His palms were sweating and the summer sun was heating up his already inflamed emotions. "Perhaps Ondorian should join us, too. Might as well draw the full council together."

"He is taking some much-deserved rest, I'm afraid. Traveling until fall."

"He chose an odd time to be away," muttered Red.

Grey chuckled. "The high priest is an odd one, but he's a good one."

"The best," Red agreed with a small smile. They were sharing something, a common knowledge, and Red desired this more than he had anticipated. His shoulders loosened a little.

Grey looked around. "This is where Aly…" He stopped.

"Where Aly what?"

A stiffness came over Grey, their moment of comradery truncated. "This is where we practiced stopping bullets. She knocked me down a few times. Many times, actually." He ran a hand over the back of his neck, wiping away sweat.

Is he trying to open up? To be friendly? Red wondered. *Or is he trying to tell me to stay away from Aly?* Aly was the one who could read people. Red had never mastered the art. As crown prince, he had looked very few people in the eye or studied their faces as she had.

"You trained her," Red stated.

Grey nodded and said, "She's told you of us."

Us.

Red needed to read Grey, and he needed to infer the right information about him. If Grey was a friend or an enemy, Red had to know. All of their future endeavors would hinge on whether or not Grey was truly on their side. Though Red disliked giving that much power or credit to one man, he somehow knew Grey was an important player in the game ahead.

"She doesn't speak of her life before the palace," Red admitted.

Grey stared at his king, his stoic expression unreadable. "You should ask her about it sometime." He smiled, and it seemed genuine. "And sire, you must prove to Alexander that you are not giving up without a fight. Alexander needs to see strength. Your people need to see it, too, my lord. Tomorrow will be a good opportunity to demonstrate just how wrong Alexander is about you."

∾

The smell of the palace brought forth both a wave of nostalgia and a flash of hot anger. This was his *home. What am I coming here as a guest?*

His heartrate soared as he combatted the feeling of injustice surging through him. Somewhere in the palace, his sisters and mother reposed. He wondered if Carolyn was cavorting with Edward Alexander, drawing herself deeper into the enemy's hands. And Elise's coldness since leaving Refere was a mystery to Red.

When the councilors filed into the council room, the cool air of the tall chamber greeted them along with the crisp bow of Lord Alexander, moustache peeling away from his mocking smile, as if to widen his grin.

Sebastian Thorin sat at the council table—no, *lounged*. He had one arm draped over the back of his chair like he'd ordered a round of drinks for the room. Red wished for once that his friend could sense the gravity of the situation, but he was glad Alexander hadn't dismissed Seb from the council—yet. Alexander sat at the head of the table, in the king's chair.

Outrage rioted in Red's blood, but he had to convince these men that he was not rash, not corrupted. He took a long, quiet breath. "Is your sorcerer here?" Red asked Alexander as he watched the usurper occupy his seat. He assumed the answer was yes, but he wanted Alexander to admit it. The man would have someone acting as Royal Sorcerer. Why couldn't this person, whoever it was, serve Alexander if he won the crown? Why would Aly have to serve Alexander?

Alexander said nothing, but offered a sly smile, being difficult.

Riode Liere, the Referen consul, remained erect at the table.

"Liere, good to see you again."

Liere had arrived in Vona before Red and Aly, and he had been present for the return of his late king's body and Lordan's coronation. He, too, had hurried back to Mardon.

Liere nodded but didn't speak. Heat flared in Red's cheeks. Not addressing a king when he spoke was madness, an offense no friend would commit. So, Liere was with Alexander. Rage threatened to forge Red's next words, but he remembered Aly's words. *Convince them you're the right man for the job.* "I believe Lordan will serve Refere well," he added with a polite smile.

Red needed to show that the other countries would support him over Alexander, and the only one that he currently knew supported him was Refere. He hadn't had a chance to speak to Virienne's king or Okwa's emperor, though the Okwan emperor would likely not side with either of them, choosing instead to remain aloof from the civil dispute. And Bulvarna was leaderless at the moment, though Mira apparently had taken up residence in Kassia's palace as queen regent, while their official monarch was still missing.

A large crown rested on Alexander's head. Red wore his coronet. Two crowns at one table. It couldn't last—and everyone in the room knew that.

"May the Maker guide us," Alexander and Red said simultaneously to open the meeting. Alexander's boldness clawed at Red's throat with annoyance. That was the king's opening line.

Peace, Aly spoke silently to him, anticipating his growing anger. *Win them with charm.*

"What have you got for us today, Alexander?" Red said, hoping to seem cavalier. He was going to try everything he possibly could to win these men back to his side. If they desired to see power, he would show them power; if confidence, he'd exude it; if level-headedness, he'd display it at every turn.

To do so, he'd need to kill the rage inside him with each breath he took.

Alexander cleared his throat, covering his mouth with one knuckle. "How eager our young Frederick is."

Red bristled but remained silent.

"Gentlemen," Alexander continued, "this young man, as you

know, descended into the Canyon itself. His actions were reckless and resulted not only in his own corruption but in the unnecessary death of Refere's former king and the sorcerer of a kingdom we all wished to remain *unprovoked*."

Red slammed a fist on the table, already forgetting his former resolve. "I was not the one responsible for Lucien's death, and you know that! Toss it all, man, you were *there*."

Alexander's mustache quirked in satisfaction. "According to witnesses, King Lucien died fighting with *you*."

Shock stole Red's words for several seconds. "He was fighting alongside me. Get your facts straight."

"Witnesses have claimed otherwise."

Red's knuckles turned white. *He's using lies to undermine me.* Alexander had thrown another high card; as it stood now, he was winning this hand, thanks in part to Red's childish outburst. Liere leaned against his elbow, cursing Red with narrow eyes. Though Red and Lordan had an agreement, Liere had either not heard of it or was beginning to question its validity. "Seb was there," Red finally said, looking to his friend to save this conversation.

Everyone in the room turned to Seb, whose gaze snapped up in surprise. "Red did not kill King Lucien," he said.

Red nodded at Seb.

"Of course, you would say that," Alexander quipped. "You have grown up with this boy. Why should we trust this man's word? His shenanigans are known far and wide throughout the city."

Red stiffened, wanting to speak, but a glance from both Aly and Grey silenced him. They knew something. Maybe they could read the tension in the room better than he could. He could only ride it like a wave, unable to see straight through it, but rising and falling with it.

Alexander leaned forward, wrists on the table. "We have to discuss what we will do with you, Frederick." He didn't include any terms of respect, only the king's first name, like he was no more than a boy. "I see your sorcerer is with us today. This is new. And she is sitting at the table like a man." A grin tilted the lord's mustache up at one end.

"Indeed," Red blurted, wanting to defend Aly. "She is my closest advisor."

Alexander snorted. The rustle that circled the room indicated that these men had heard the rumors of him and Aly and had questioned the gossip until this moment. Instead of appearing gallant, he'd sunk lower in their minds.

"She is not on this council. Thus, she is not fit to make decisions for this country," barked Alexander.

"She is fit to protect my life. Does that not qualify her to also advise me on occasion?"

Alexander's face darkened even as he smiled. "She, in case you were unaware, is *fit* to serve the King of Tandera. Truly, her life is tied to the man who wears the crown." His eyes flicked upward, indicating the crown on his bald head.

Heat blasted through Red's torso. *He wants Aly's magic.*

As if he could feel Aly's thoughts racing toward him, Red glanced at her before her words entered his mind. He'd realized it as soon as she had, and her words felt like his own thoughts spoken in her voice. *He means to make me his sorcerer.*

The glare he turned on Alexander could have lit damp logs. "You will not take my sorcerer from me."

"Oh, is that because you two are so well *connected?*" He allowed time for people to join him in laughing at Red, but none did. "The Binding comes with the crown."

At Alexander's words, the fortitude Red had constructed before arriving at the palace disintegrated into desperation.

Aly was loyal to him, but if Red lost his crown, he would lose Aly too.

Grey leaned forward. "Proceed with your agenda, Alexander."

"Very well." Alexander combed his mustache with absent fingers. "I wish for you to be fully removed from this city by the week's end. I desire you to leave voluntarily, but as it stands, if you are still here by the start of next week, the soldiers have been commanded to remove you by force."

"You scheming usurper. How dare—"

"You will address me as Your Maj—"

"I will address you as I desire." Red leaned over the table. "This is *my* house. *My* council. *My* country."

Alexander did not retort, but swept his eyes around the room, as if laying claim to the men, the position he had among them, and the room itself, effectively proving Red wrong on all accounts with nothing more than a glance.

"I will show this country who is the true king," Red snapped, ready to leave. "At coronation, it will be me, not you, wearing the crown."

Alexander chuckled. "You descended into the Canyon while claiming to hate it. You sought the Black River, the source of all evil, and you think you can regain the loyalty of your countrymen? The trust of the men in this room? You are an abomination to the truth and the name of Theod."

Red stood up, his chair scraping on the floor. "You know nothing of the truth. Only Aly—" he pointed straight at her, using her first name without hesitation, "—knows what happened down there. As a sorcerer, she cannot lie. If you want to know the truth, ask her."

The whole room stared at the point of his finger and then followed the line slowly to her masked face.

"Your sorcerer is not allowed to speak at this table, as has always been the case," Alexander said.

Aly, apparently adhering to tradition in Red's time of need, remained silent. If she but spoke now, she would dispel the fears of these men.

No, I told her not to interfere. She's only doing what we agreed. He needed to win this country back on his own. Even in this, Red could not rely on Aly to fix his situation. Fuming at the way the morning had unfolded, he wished he could end this right here and now and yank the crown off Alexander's head, but that was not how kingdoms were won. Not by force and not by blood. He wouldn't win that way.

Alexander sensed Red's capitulation and said, "By week's end."

"I will not flee my city."

"You will. For if you do not, I will punish whoever attempts to help you." As Red blinked in shock, Alexander added, "My military will enforce my desire, as well as my sorcerers." He emphasized the plural of the word.

"Kings only have *one*, as you seem to know so well."

"Ah, kings may only have one Protector, but that does not mean that they have only one sorcerer willing to enforce their work." He was throwing a threat out there that Red assumed was false.

No way did Alexander have an army of sorcerers behind him. Protectors did not fight individual battles. They served the nobles, loyal to their employer. The soldier-sorcerers among the army served Tandera by choice. Lordan, too, had alluded to an army of sorcerers at his disposal. What was Red missing? Did Tandera have an army of sorcerers, concealed in secret? Red turned his eyes to Grey. If there was a secret sorcerer army, Grey would likely know.

Red toyed with the handle of the ash blade at his waist. The rage and offense inside him pushed him back toward reck-lessness.

Grey had told him to show strength today. Red was losing too much ground.

His father's words, spoken in this room, entered his mind. *Strength is not only in arms or might to hold others down. Sometimes strength is holding up those who are too weak to hold themselves.*

"I will win this nation, Alexander." It was a pointless thing to say, but he couldn't cower out of the room.

"All right, then. That was special," said Alexander, amused. "In one week, you will be gone. After that, I do not wish to hear from you again."

9

ALY

The following night Aly slipped through the cobblestone streets of Mardon, well after the city had gone to sleep.

She tried, for the second night in a row, to find a place suitable for Red. He insisted he would not leave Mardon. Aly, scanning the city with her magical awareness, looked for unoccupied buildings or unlet rooms. She had agreed not to intervene directly in his efforts to secure the crown, but she could help in small ways. He needed to win back Tandera, and she needed to let him.

Privately celebrating his determination, Aly walked with an air of confidence, assured she would find a place for this city's sovereign to sleep. She was glad he was not willing to accept defeat. His strength may be deeper than even he knew.

Red and Aly needed a place to hide, a place easy enough to slip in and out of without disturbing anyone. Aly could shroud them, but they needed *space* to sleep, to eat, to bathe. She explored all the unrented rooms in town, trying to find one that would not be hard to live in without being noticed, since Alexander had placed threats on anyone who aided and abetted Red.

Aly's senses scanned for threats, blasting through the city like a sudden freeze, unhindered by walls or locks. The Truthwells of a hundred thousand people blinked in her mind's eye, as if the city itself were made of stars.

And still Red's burned brightest.

He remained at Grey Manor, but would only be safe there one more night, as Alexander had approached Grey about his loyalties. Grey had said what Alexander wanted to hear, and had later told Red that he would continue to aid him however he could, but it would need to be hidden from Alexander's prying eyes.

Grey should have little trouble hiding his actions and his loyalties from Alexander, but it didn't solve their problem of needing a place to sleep.

Warm night air hung lazily in the streets. During the day, the stifling heat of summer exacerbated the smells of the city, and only when the clock neared midnight did the stench ebb. The wealthy neighborhoods, which Aly left behind after not finding any vacant rooms, had the privilege of Comforters to keep the smells of latrines and animal droppings at a minimum. But as the streets narrowed and the residences squished closer together, the smells became harsh, biting Aly's nose even at this late hour.

"How do they stand it?" she asked no one, holding a finger under her nose.

With a flourish of her hand, she spat magic toward the walls, the streets, the very air around them. The spell was a strange one; she'd rarely used magic to alter scent, but the words were true, and the *Verad* never failed. With the ancient words to guide her, she shaped her desire for sweet air. Within seconds, the stench was gone.

She pursed her lips, satisfied.

Around the next corner, Aly's nose was again offended by a rancid smell. Then she spotted a water well adjacent to a nearby building.

"Oh," she exclaimed, stopping short. She raised a hand for

more magic. Aly gagged. "That can't possibly be the smell coming from where these people draw water!" She often spoke aloud while under her shroud; it helped her feel less alone.

"It is," came a stranger's voice, startling Aly so much she yelped. "Unfortunately," the voice continued, "many of the wells in this part of town have been polluted and are thus of no use, other than as community dumping grounds."

A cloaked figure stepped out from the shadows. Aly trembled. Only another sorcerer could hear through a shroud, and only if they meant to. The mask had feathers and might have been a raven, but it was too dark to tell.

The sorcerer paced across the small space, angling toward a road on Aly's right. Maybe she'd simply crossed paths with someone else out patrolling the night streets. The raven's beak nodded politely and moved past her as if to carry on.

Aly hesitated. She rarely spoke to other sorcerers. Part of her still yearned for their comradery. The figure was slipping away. "Where do they draw water?"

The sorcerer paused, turned, and studied her a moment from beneath the feathered black holes in the mask. "They pay a small fee to draw from other wells."

"That isn't fair."

"It is not, but no one from this neighborhood has attempted to clean out the well, either." He—for the voice was that of a man— shrugged beneath his wide-shouldered cloak.

Magic came with mystery. It had always been that way, but Aly wished she could see this man's face, the face of someone like her. With a small spell, she sensed the energy fueling his Master's ring.

"Couldn't you?" she whispered into the dark as the man walked away. Her words were muted by the terrible reality of these people's living conditions. Life in the cabin near Kitrel where she'd grown up had not been this bad. At least she'd lived with fresh air and fields of wildflowers.

Or perhaps our king could, replied the man's voice, directly into her head.

She startled so sharply she felt her pulse in her fingertips. She'd only ever received a handful of mental messages, sent from the Protectors of important men, meant for Gevar's immediate attention. It had been a while since anyone had spoken to her mind.

The man's shadowy figure faded into the dark. She stared down the narrow road he'd taken. He'd said Red could fix this, not her. He'd called Red *our king*.

Red had allies in this city.

Aly's lips curled up. If there was one lone sorcerer loyal to Red, there would be more. Maybe the family this man served was loyal to Red as well.

Many Mardonians already sided with Alexander, welcoming the usurper with open arms, as if completely forgetting that the crown rightfully belonged to Red. No one had known of Red's death curse, had no idea why Red and Aly had chosen to descend into the Canyon.

Truth would save them, if only the truth could reach into the darkness created by Alexander's lies.

She wanted to clean the well, but she agreed that Red should be the one to order this task, as this man suggested. That way, he'd garner the respect of this neighborhood.

But what could it hurt to give them clean water now? A simple spell, pointed directly down the well, purged the water of all filth. Surely there were other wells Red could clean out.

As she turned down a narrow street lined with tall tenant buildings, Aly's mind slipped again to Alexander's words at the council meeting. The thought of having to serve Alexander sickened her, but the vows of a Royal Sorcerer bid her protect the sovereign until death claimed her.

She clutched at her twisting stomach, knotting her fingers in the fabric of her cloak.

The thought of losing Red's Truthwell brought with it an ache deep inside her, the ache of an artist told to abandon his brushes and paints. But it was more than losing his light—to lose his Well would be to lose *him*.

If she were no longer Bound to Red, she would have little opportunity to see him, especially if Alexander banished Red from Mardon. The thought of cutting him out of her life entirely brought with it a flare of rage she did not expect.

Alexander can't win. She knew she couldn't fight this battle for Red, but she would give all she could to help him succeed.

I need you, she said, pushing her words out into the void of night, not far enough that they would reach Red's mind, but the thrill of thinking he *might* hear her was enough to stir a restlessness within her that hurried her steps.

Shrouded, she slipped into a building, crept past the unoccupied front desk, and darted up the stairs, using her magical sense to locate the empty rooms.

As she climbed past apartments full of sleeping families, she mused on the dilemma she now faced. Six years ago, she'd chosen to serve the crown over her own heart. She'd thought it was her only option, the only path to her and Grey's survival.

The pain of that choice had dulled over time, and now that her heart beat faster around Red than around Grey, she couldn't imagine having made a different choice. Her Beacon, her king, her...whatever else he could be to her might be destroyed if Alexander succeeded.

Her shroud kept her feet from making noise, but the stairs still creaked with her every step. Two flights up, she cringed at a loud floorboard. She heard movement and saw a Truthwell moving behind the wall to her left.

A man poked his head out of his apartment door. "Oy, you squatters can find—" He paused, eyes narrowing in the dim hall light. "I know I heard you!" He glanced up and down the stairs. "When I catch you, I'll turn you in!"

Though her shroud hid her body and her breathing, Aly remained motionless for a moment after the man withdrew into his room, not wanting the floorboards to conspire against her.

With a deep breath she launched herself down the stairwell, conjuring a spell to help her coast to the next landing without stepping on a single stair.

If this neighborhood was rooting out squatters, Aly needed to head farther into the city.

As she turned down a crooked street, one crisscrossed with a ceiling of hanging sheets draped overhead like ghostly flags, Aly sensed the darting light of a small Truthwell. Animal, judging by its size.

The reeling sensation hit a moment later.

This was no escaped pet. Only the Truthwell of a Canyon beast could burn so dim. Any other animal, unaffected as they were by lies, contained no shadows at all within their Well. A Canyon beast, however, was the very product of twisted truth, and emanated only the faintest glow.

Aly's mind sharpened. The hairs on her arms lifted.

A spell cut through the night as she hissed the words toward the trotting and oblivious, beast. The size, the speed, and the fact that it was alone suggested it was a foxblood. They were bolder than the woodwolves, sneaking deeper into cities than the pack animals, but their bite was less dangerous. Still poisonous, but less likely to kill. Her spell must have startled the beast, for it skittered out of the way as the magic was about to hit. Instead, the spell crashed quietly into the cobblestones.

Aly leapt to a window ledge and clung to the thin iron railing holding one end of a laundry line. The beast slunk closer, alerted to her presence.

"You will wish you'd chosen a different target," she snarled down at the foxblood, whose eyes glinted up at her as it found its prey.

With a stab of her hand through the dark, she aimed a spell at the beast. *The whole earth bends to the Maker's hand,* she spat, her magic obeying the words and the thought that drove it toward the creature of the Deep.

As the magic washed over the beast, it tripped, twitched, and did not stand up.

Aly settled once more on the street and stared down at the dead foxblood. The Maker had designed the fox. The Canyon, somehow, had made this beast with its broader snout, longer fangs, and nearly lion-like mane. She noted a bit of blood on his chin.

Aly cringed. He'd already taken a victim. Perhaps whomever it was would be healed and would live.

Another series of spells lifted a few cobblestones, opened up a hole, and devoured the dead animal under a mound of earth.

Though she'd saved additional people from the foxblood's ceaseless hunger, one thing was certain: the beasts of the Deep had come back to Mardon.

10

RED

They walked arm-in-arm down the street, shrouded and protected by a spell Aly had recently perfected, the one she'd created after cleaning out the city wells—a spell that altered their scent should a woodwolf or foxblood come slinking by. He ignored the fact that they were invisible, pretending as if the whole world could see them, nonchalant, strolling down the city streets, without fear of beasts or coups or wicked queens.

"Where are we going?" he asked, ready for sleep after walking half the city, listening for the pulse of the people, where their loyalties lay and their reactions to Alexander's new governance. Their outing had returned little of value, other than the fact that most Mardonians didn't appear to care who governed them; they were more concerned with the appearance of two more foxbloods and the constant struggle to put food on the table, exacerbated by a crop of wheat ruined by the drought. Red was frustrated with his and Aly's efforts—and the soreness in his feet.

People care primarily about their lives. If your rule does not affect their lives, they will not care. If your rule does affect their lives, it better be for the good or they will hate you for it. Gevar's words pressed Red forward, toward a solution, toward a better Mardon, a better Tandera. He needed his countrymen to care that *he* was the one wearing the crown, but that was becoming much more difficult than he'd hoped.

Aly offered a weak smile as she held his arm. "I found an abandoned building last night. It's not too far from one of those wells I mentioned."

Red hated to think that some of the city's wells had been turned into dumping grounds. What an awful misuse of a needed resource.

Mardon's lanes were less busy at this hour, though many pedestrians bustled about, returning from taverns in the heart of the city. Aly led Red down narrower and narrower lanes, until they reached a small triangle-shaped common space between lopsided buildings. The small cobbled area had a bench and a well and, before they reached the well, an awful stench pierced Red's nose.

He slapped a hand over his mouth and nose as they approached. Aly lifted a brow and shrugged, as if to say, *Here you go.*

"The people here pay to use other wells?" he asked, reasserting what she'd told him. "If they hadn't poured refuse into this one, they could use it."

Aly crossed her arms. It wasn't necessary for her to say what was on her mind. Talking about pointless things that *should* have happened wouldn't fix this problem. He sighed and nodded, thinking through how he could fix this without magic.

Oh, but magic would be easier.

He backed away from the gut-curdling smell. "I think we can make an exception on this one. What do you think? Or would you prefer we locate some shovels and muck boots?"

At that moment, Aly froze. Her arms danced around her, then she spun. This was not a playful maneuver. She sensed danger.

He knew better than to interrupt.

She whirled back around, arms falling to her sides. "There are sorcerers out. I think they're looking for us. What we did today, speaking with so many people, it made its way back to Alexander. He knows we're still here."

"We only spoke to the commoners. I didn't think Alexander would have much concern for who walked among them."

Aly frowned. "It appears we've underestimated his reach and his desire to win this crown."

"Will they be able to find us?" Red forced himself not to glance around. Aly would keep him safe.

"They likely were instructed to memorize your Truthwell. I'm not sure how far their awareness can reach, but I don't think it's as far as mine." She grinned. "After all, they don't have you as their source."

That was a small comfort, but these sorcerers would eventually find them. Their time was running out.

Aly fanned her hand in front of her nose. "I can clean the well, but that won't *keep* it clean."

He blinked and looked again at the dark, reeking hole. He understood her meaning. They needed to solve the issue surrounding this nasty well. "True. At least we can give these residents a reprieve from the smell." He nodded at the black hole in the cobblestones.

With a shake of both hands, Aly blanketed the hole with a fine dust of pinkish light that sank down into the darkness. Within seconds, the awful odor dissipated.

"We should have sorcerers assigned to keep the city clean," he said, admiring her work. The worst job imaginable for most men was a flick of the wrist for Aly.

She peered at him with a smile curling half her mouth. "Now *that* sounds more like a solution, Your Majesty."

"Now that I think of it, why *don't* we have them?"

A small frown tugged at her lips. "Not all kings walk the city like this."

He grinned back at her, sensing a small victory more from the way she looked at him than the solution he may have found. "Now, where shall we pass this lovely evening?"

They walked to an abandoned building abutting the edge of a merchant neighborhood.

Red swallowed. He'd never slept anywhere but in a plush bed, with attendants no more than a bell away. Even on long hunts, the tents erected and the meals provided for the royal family were of the highest standards.

"What happened to the roof?" he asked, spotting places where it looked unfinished.

"Fire," Aly replied, striding to the front door, which was boarded up and secured with a large chain and lock. With a flourish of her fingers, the lock fell open and the chain lifted free of the handle.

Taking in the buildings nearest to them, Red realized they'd walked onto Graves Avenue, known to him only as the street that caught fire two years ago. The blaze had devoured nearly the entire block before the Comforters controlled it. The other buildings had been repaired, but on this one, black stains crawled out of the upper windows.

As they walked into the building, the acrid smell of burned wood was overpowering, even so long after the fire. Red glanced around at the bubbling, peeling wallpaper and crinkled his nose. The fire must not have reached this floor, as the lower floors were easier to soak with the water cannons. The summer rains had warped the floorboards near the windows and a mouse scampered from view as they stepped through the boarded-over front door.

It has come to this, he thought, scraping his foot through the dust and soot on the floor.

Aly lifted her arms and, with a gentle word, the dust dissipated and the floors looked polished, pristine. Next, she purged the stains off the walls. The plaster on the ceiling still contained a few holes in places, but with another word and a quick flip of her fingers, these too melded back to normal, seemingly untouched by disaster and neglect.

When she finished, he shook his head.

"What?" she asked, cracking her knuckles.

"You're amazing."

She smirked and walked forward into the room, putting her back to him. "Since we are to sleep in such confined conditions, I would appreciate it if you didn't...say things like that."

His cheeks blazed. How exactly *would* they sleep? The arrangement made his palms sweat. For them to stay together alone in an empty building would only grow more rumors about their relationship, if anyone found out.

As if playing a magical game, she began pulling objects to herself. First boards from the exposed ceiling beams, then planks from the stairwell by the door. With several spells, she stacked them edge to edge until there was a small partition in the floor, sectioning off one corner.

"Now, it feels a bit less like we're in the same room," she said, dropping her hands.

He laughed, grateful. "Indeed." Inside, however, he was very much aware that they *were* going to sleep in the same room. The small barrier between them was not enough to barricade his mind.

He sat down on one side of the wall and she on the other. He rested his back against it and began to remove his shoes. Her nearness was like an itch he couldn't reach. *If you cannot rule your own mind, why should you rule a country?* Even now, his father was instructing him, as his wisdom rolled through Red's thoughts, constant as the ocean waves. Red *humphed* and reined his thoughts in before they rode away like wild horses.

"Aly," he said after only a minute had passed. "How am I

supposed to sleep here?" His question hinted at both privilege and propriety.

Her movements made swishing sounds on the other side of the small wall. "You'll manage."

Though she couldn't see him, he nodded, running a hand along the now clean floorboards that were to be his bed. "Can't you summon a bed or something?"

At her cough, he realized he should have mentioned *two* beds, but she replied before he could add this. "Kings can sleep on floors like anyone else, if it's all there is. Goodnight, Red."

"Goodnight, Aly."

Red stretched out on the floor, his surcoat folded under his head as a pillow. His backbone and heels pressed against the stiff, unforgiving wood.

Staring at the ceiling, trying not to think of Aly's nearness, he poured over a dozen ideas, ways to regain the city's trust, the people's allegiance. He needed to win the hearts of his people, the way his father and mother had, without losing the loyalty of the nobility.

The nobles would follow the crown. Their loyalty wasn't much deeper than that. *No, it's the rest of the city that I need to win.* The people whose opinions could be swayed were the working-class folks, even the merchants. He needed to find a way to earn their trust. The nobles might not care who the masses loved, but Red felt to his bones that to lead his country well, he would need to gain the love of *all* his people, not only the wealthy.

It was a radical idea, perhaps, but once it lit up his mind, he had no desire to put it out. He fell asleep trying to think of ways he could become more familiar with the poorer citizens of Mardon.

~

Two days later, dressed in his finest suit that had been altered slightly by Aly to look sleeker with fewer gold embellishments, Red settled into the back row of Mardon's cathedral. Hushed comments and discreet gestures poured from the nobility seated at the front of the church. Aly's white cloak stood out, a beacon against the dark pews and the drab clothing of the commoners—a jewel among river rocks. The commoners' expressions ranged from delighted to terrified; most displaying an expression of mild shock.

The lady beside Aly scooted away so that no part of her dirty clothing might touch the sorcerer's attire. Aly smiled at the woman from beneath her half-mask. The woman smiled back, trembling as she covered her mouth. Red exchanged a nod with the woman and her husband.

Lord Benedict Alexander sat at the front, sporting the large crown reserved usually for ceremonial events. Even from the back row, the tall crown—with its red velvet cap beneath golden arches—stood out among the hats of the nobility. He turned as Red and Aly took their seats, but his reaction was well-controlled. Whispers rippled through the crowd, but no one bade them leave, as Red had expected. Alexander couldn't banish someone from a house of worship.

Before the crowd settled into silence, a small commotion at the front preceded Seb's appearance in the wide aisle. He smiled and hurried back to where Red and Aly sat, squeezing his way onto the bench beside Aly.

"Nice seats," he mock-whispered across Aly, his hissing words not quiet at all. His suit, unlike Red's, was flashy; silver threads burst like seafoam up the front of his white lapels, onto his collar. He winked at Aly, and turned his attention to the altar.

An unfamiliar priest occupied the pulpit, filling in while Ondorian was traveling, and he preached a sermon on venerating the Maker as the true sovereign of Tandera. Many people yawned, but Red tried to focus. Theod chose kings, after all, and

Red was hoping Theod's choice would rest on him at summer's end. Red's plan for regaining the crown revolved around extricating the truth of who he was from the lies Alexander had spread about him—surely this was Theod's plan as well.

Heads turned at intervals to catch a glimpse of Aly and him. Some faces sneered, and not only among the nobility. Laughter issued from a few of the less subtle noblewomen.

Red glanced at Aly, brows raised. Was there a stain on his suit he couldn't see?

After the service, one young man walked down the nave toward Red and Aly. Red recognized him as Lord Nock, a relative of Alexander's. "It looks as if you're taking up your seat in the back row quite comfortably," he said.

Alexander walked up behind the man.

Red bristled, trying to hide his movement with a shoulder roll. Alexander's ostentatious, borrowed crown loomed above them. It took all Red's control not to knock it to the cathedral floor with the back of his hand. Aly must have anticipated his flash of anger or sensed it in his Truthwell and, as she turned, she casually brushed his shoulder with the edge of her wide cloak, a small warning.

He knew what she was thinking, even before she spoke into his mind. *We're trying to convince these men you are not rash. Don't give them more evidence that you are.* He'd failed at the council meeting. He couldn't afford to fail again in a much more public setting.

Seb slapped Nock on the shoulder. "In the back, no one notices when we fall asleep. But don't worry, we all saw your head drooping after the first ten minutes."

Nock frowned.

"Do not become too comfortable back here, Frederick. You will, of course, be leaving town quite soon," Lord Alexander added with a small chuckle before the two of them walked away.

Aly, who wasn't very good at hiding her expressions, shifted her weight and chewed her bottom lip. Red watched them depart, his teeth grinding as he bit back the responses he wanted to hurl their way. Saying nothing might make him appear weak, but yelling insults wouldn't improve his reputation as hotheaded.

Perhaps the complaints against him did have a little truth in them. He grunted quietly enough that only Aly and Seb could hear.

The priest, swamped by parishioners after his sermon, navigated his way through the crowd, offering polite apologies to those wishing to speak with him. He stepped up to Red and offered a curt bow. This gesture of respect cooled Red's hot blood.

"I enjoyed your words this morning," Red said.

"How is the sound from the back, my lord?" he asked with a smile.

Red wasn't certain if the priest was mocking him or merely making conversation. Faces of commoners and merchants and a few remaining nobles watched him.

Whatever his intentions, the priest had just handed him an opportunity.

"As good as in the front," he said. "Excellent acoustics."

"I am pleased." The priest's eyes squinted with a hint of shared understanding. Maybe this man was on Red's side, though it was difficult to be sure if a priest took sides in matters of state.

Nearby, a few of the commoners cheered. The people pushed toward him, as if his comment made him more approachable. He loosened his posture, accommodating what he hoped they were thinking, but his resolve faltered as the nobles walked past with chins tilted high. Seb jerked his chin up at each one of them in turn, as if defending his friend and sovereign with looks alone.

Some of the commoners followed them through the large, sunlit square like a parade of excited puppies. Red tried to hide his discomfort at the smells around him, wondering how people could arrive at worship smelling so foul. Their clothing looked as if it hadn't been washed in a week. He always thought that people came to church clean and well dressed in their best. *Have I really never noticed the people in the back?* Admittedly, he'd usually been escorted in and out of the cathedral through a private door used by the royal family near the altar. He had never had to walk out with the crowds.

The sunshine felt pleasant against his back, but the day was heating up and the morning's chill was fading. He hoped his face, the tightness of his jaw and pinch of his brow, didn't reveal his discomfort. He had never really been this close to the commoners. The two times he'd walked through the city's poor districts with his father, they'd been surrounded by soldiers.

The commoners slowed and eventually hung back, whispering excitedly until Red and Aly were several paces ahead. Interrupting his thoughts, Aly's voice slipped into his mind. *They need a reason to follow.*

Grey and Aly had said he needed to win the hearts of his people. He spun around to face the crowd, heart pounding as he whipped together a plan. "I shall walk through the city," he announced.

Occasionally, his father had taken walks after worship, strolling through his city, talking to the people. He had mostly walked the streets of commerce, rarely straying into neighborhoods. It had been a way to be visible, and the king needed to be visible to his people. Red had not had the chance since Gevar's death to take up this tradition.

The crowd jostled but did not move forward.

"Anyone may join me and my sorcerer."

Excited laughter and smiles spread among the Mardonians. They surged forward. These people weren't too proud to be seen following their rightful king.

Seb chuckled. "Looks like you have enough company. I'm going to leave you to it." He clapped. "Food. Then a nap." As he walked away, he smiled and waved at every woman who looked his way, which seemed like all of them.

Aly gave Red an amused smile from beneath her half-mask before they turned back to the street ahead. Along the way, Red intended to listen to his people's complaints and brainstorm ways in which he could offer his help. It was his responsibility to meet these people's needs.

Red had heard reports of a bad crop of wheat in Tandera, and he wanted to see if these were true. He no longer had his typical resources available to him for information. All of his previous chancellors and advisors, save Lord Weston Grey and Seb, now reported to Lord Alexander. Both Grey and Seb were playing dual roles, attempting to remain in Alexander's good graces. Seb, Red trusted could do so without any disloyalty. With Grey, Red didn't have the same level of confidence.

As he began strolling through the city streets, Red turned left and then left again. He knew the way to the poorest district, but he'd only been to it twice and never to the one building he had an in mind. He wanted to see a mill he'd heard several people discuss, a mill owned by Benedict Alexander. It had a poor reputation among the people who worked there, which might serve Red well. As he walked, the crowd of people tapered off, the merchants peeling off to head towards their homes as the king strolled deeper into the city.

Then, as he and Aly strode past the homes of those who did not attend church, more gathered. Some ran out of their doors. Ladies poked their heads out of upper windows, pointing and shouting, "There goes the king!" Just as many, if not more, said, "It's her! It's the Sorcerer!"

They walked past a bakery, the delightful smell alleviating the oppressive odor of poverty. A large crowd followed him now, collected almost entirely from this part of town. The people's clothes matched the color of the streets, which matched the color of the walls—the monochromatic grayish brown of cobblestones and old plaster.

"Tell me," Red finally said to one man walking near his left shoulder. "What do you do for a living?" The man looked around and pressed a scarred hand against his chest. "Yes, you." Red smiled to encourage him.

"W—working, work at the mill."

"And do you find this work satisfying?" asked Red.

The man's brows rose. "Satisfying, my lord?" The man clearly wasn't sure how to address Red.

"You will address him as Your Majesty," Aly offered, saving Red from having to say anything.

The man crumpled over into an unpracticed bow. "Of course, Your Majesty. Sorry, I wasn't certain."

Red swallowed. This man wasn't sure if Red was still the sovereign. Red waved his hand to dismiss the offense. "Tell me about your work. Does it pay well?"

A few people scoffed or covered laughter. "Does the mill pay well? I can barely afford to feed my family, if that's what you mean. Your Majesty," he added with a quick nod.

The sun and the exercise produced a steady sweat now, plus Red had just stepped into hot water. "Well, that doesn't seem very good," Red admitted.

"Do you know anything about what happens in the city?" the man asked, incredulous.

Red had wanted this. He'd invited it. Still, this manner of address was new and unexpected. He excused the man's lack of propriety—he'd likely never spoken to a king before. "It is my city. I know enough."

"Do you?" Apparently, Red's casual manner had emboldened him.

Let them choose you, Aly had told him. He'd known she was right, but it didn't make him feel better while this stranger was berating him for his ignorance. "I'm here to learn," Red replied.

The man tilted his head, arms crossed. "Now that's interesting," he said. The man's posture relaxed. He turned to the crowd still walking behind them. "You hear that? The king is here to learn about us," he said, lifting his arms. A few people laughed.

Another man in a brown hat stepped forward. "He knows nothing of what it's like to live in this part of town." Disdain oozed from the man's words. "He's stuck in that palace."

Red cleared his throat. These people didn't know Red had been kicked out of his home.

Another young man jumped in. "He's *here*, ain't he? That's something. Man says he wants to learn. Let him! Tell him what it's really like in the Creaks."

Cheers rose from the crowd. Red, fueled by the enthusiasm of his people, blazed forward. "Yes, tell me. Er, what is your name?" he asked the man in the brown hat. "What's life like here? I want to know," he added firmly.

"Donner," he replied. "Samuel Donner, Your Majesty." The man offered a quick bow, briefly removing his hat. Then he sniffed, wiping the back of his hand across his nose.

The summer cold. Of course, these people would have it, or many of them. "You're sick, aren't you?" asked Red, infusing his voice with true concern. These men didn't have Comforters to ease the conditions. They didn't have Protectors to dismiss sickness.

The man studied Red, gauging whether or not the king actually cared about his health. "We leave the windows open, but it doesn't do much good. No matter how many windows we keep open, the sickness always comes."

Now that Red was looking for it, he noticed several people with running noses, pink cheeks, tired eyes. He was surrounded by a mob of sick Mardonians.

So many of them, and they carry on about their day as if they were well.

The summer cold, as most called it, was the cousin of winterspell, the more fatal counterpart. It swept the poor districts every year. Most could survive the summer cold, but it strained the population as people had to care for sick children or elderly parents.

"Henrik Baas, Your Majesty," said the younger man who'd defended Red a moment ago. He shook hands with the king. "Aye, the summer cold is brutal, but then the winter comes, and it's much worse." He hooked his thumbs in his belt loops.

The people nodded. Donner again took the floor. "Winterspell floods these places every year. The weak among us—children, the elderly—they die. In *droves*."

Stillness halted the crowd. Red peered among the faces of his fellow Mardonians, aware of the immense gap that stood between his own life and theirs. He saw on their faces the ache of loss, a pain he still felt every single day since his father passed.

He'd heard of winterspell. He knew it could be bad and that every year many died from it, but he'd never heard of these sweeping waves of it, coursing through the parts of town no one at court talked about.

"But none of your lot care what happens here," said Donner, scratching his chin. "Least of all the people in your palace."

"That isn't—" Red stopped himself. "I hope to change that."

Donner cocked an eyebrow. "Do you? What are you going to change it with, your own two hands? I hear you're not the king no more."

The pressure of Red's fine golden coronet, usually unnoticeable, pinched against his scalp like a great claw. Donner and the others waited for his response. Red's temples flamed, his mind raced. He had to answer this man.

"Donner, how do you help your family?"

The man sneered, head tilted sideways in scrutiny. "Go to work every day." A few laughs and some loud assents trickled from the crowd. "Put my time in at the mill. I'm paid—not much, but I'm paid. I go home. My wife buys food. We eat. Then back to work."

More cheers from the crowd.

Red nodded along with them. "He's right. What I plan to do to," he said, raising his voice so more could hear, "is work. I plan to work for Tandera. I am your king. I will *remain* your king." A few people clapped. Most looked confused.

"What's a man like you going to do to work? Your idea of work is signing papers with your fancy pen." Donner was a tough man, hardened by labor and likely a lifetime of barely scraping by.

Red straightened and faced him, unphased. "Your wages come from the owner of this mill; is that true?" He pointed down to the road to the very mill they'd been discussing, the mill he'd come here to visit. During his walk of the city, he'd ascertained that the mill was recently purchased by a wealthy merchant— perhaps because Alexander had needed to remove his hand from all his secret dealings in the city. Donner nodded. "Then I will speak to him."

Donner laughed. "Not likely, Your Majesty." Red wondered if he was using the term of respect in earnest or in jest. "He and Alexander, they're buddies. I hear Alexander wants you out of town. Says he'll punish anyone who helps you."

A weight sank in Red's gut. It seemed everyone in this town was siding with Alexander. How had the man secured so many men loyal to him? "Nevertheless, I will speak to him. I am still the King of Tandera." Some of the men and women offered impressed expressions, others more skeptical ones. Red wasn't sure how he'd secure an audience with the mill's owner, but now he'd made the promise and he had to follow through.

"And now, to the sickness," Red continued, turning to face those who stood behind him. "If the conditions are that bad, I will see what I can do to improve them." Again, several people applauded, others snickered. "You need more housing. I will find more." *And more Comforters,* he added to himself, wondering how he could find Comforters to work for the good of the common folk.

"How can you do that?" asked a woman holding a young boy on her hip. She immediately shrank back and muttered out an apology, as if appalled she spoke directly to the king. He nodded kindly to her and she flushed a deeper crimson.

"You're not going to build, that's for Deep sure," Donner spoke up from behind Red.

The man Haas stepped forward, holding one arm out to stay Donner's ire. "Your Majesty, we're low on wood here. We can't get hardly any at all."

Red forced his face to remain calm, but he was starting to feel overwhelmed by the unending bad news. He was so ignorant about his own city. Buildings were going up left and right, that much he knew. "No wood?" he asked, keeping the skepticism out of his tone.

Donner swatted Haas' hand away. "It's all being used for them fine houses out by the edge of town. And that fancy hotel down by the river. None left for such as us."

Could that really be true? No wood at all? Aly's half-masked face wasn't giving anything away. Contrary to her norm, she was keeping her expression completely unreadable. Not that she would have any answers for him here, he simply wanted to see a face that trusted him. "We will find more wood and we will build more homes before the winter." The promise was out, carried by the wind and his good intentions over the heads of the desperate crowd. He had just made a pledge he wasn't sure he could fulfill. He blazed on. "We will do this. I will see to it."

"Okay," said Donner with a shrug. "I'll believe it when I see it." Several loud assents rose from the crowd. Some people voiced their thanks to Red.

Despite the fear and disquiet throbbing inside Red, he did not feel anger at this man's lack of trust. This was not about Red or his kingship, not really. He could see that now. This was about the people of Mardon. They were suffering, and no one had done anything to alleviate their troubles.

Gevar had been a good king, securing stronger trade and better foreign relations, but had he done so at the omission of better *local* conditions?

Red would shoulder the peoples' distrust, even their anger, until he made things better. If he failed, perhaps he didn't deserve to be their king.

A little boy broke away from his mother and ran up to him. "King, king," he said, tugging on Red's jacket. Red recoiled instinctively from the little boy, more out of surprise than disgust. As soon as he'd flinched, he hated himself for it. The boy shrank back. The faces nearest him frowned. "Apologies, my young squire," Red said, squatting down. "You startled me, is all. What can I do for you?"

The boy blinked at him. "My daddy's a farmer. He said if you're here to help, then you will do something about the food."

"What about the food?" Red's voice wavered.

"There wasn't much rain," the boy said with a shrug, "but it still got the scab."

Red stood. "Where's your father?"

"He didn't..." The boy stopped. "Well, sir, he didn't want to speak to you, but I said I would."

"Where is your father?" Red asked again.

The little boy pointed behind him. A man with thumbs hooked on his overalls stared at the king, his face tilted back in contempt.

Careful, Aly's voice whispered silently to him. *Don't make any more promises you can't keep.*

Red nodded in a small way only Aly could see and stepped forward. "Tell me of this spoiled crop."

"Our wheat comes in every year," the man began, unhooking his thumbs from his suspenders. "We need it to live through the winter. Perhaps you at least know that. Only thing is, whole tossing lot of it got blight this year. Scab like you ain't never seen." Murmurs from the crowd. "And now we ain't going to have the crop I was promised by the seeds I planted. The crop *I* promised so many others." He inched forward, a grimace forming on his weathered face. "You want to help? Can you grow another crop before winter?" His laugh punctuated this ridiculous query.

The little boy stood beside his father, shoulders lifted in pride but unable to capture the same arrogance on the man's face. Red's stomach knotted. He, as well as all these people, knew another crop couldn't be grown in time.

Suddenly, Lordan's words about his newly developed wheat thundered through his mind: *It grows faster and lives through almost all conditions.*

"How much of the crop was lost?" asked Red.

"Hardly any fields were spared."

Red's mind clambered toward possibilities left and right. "And exactly how much was this, in weight?"

The man laughed and cocked his head to the other side. "We won't see no winter this year if we don't get it, *King*. Winterspell won't even be the reason we go. It'll be hunger. And it hits the young and old the worst. This boy here." He placed a hand on his son's head. "And the ones too small to be out here on the street right now. Those are the ones who will go," he said, as if pronouncing a death sentence. His son's wide eyes filled with terror.

Red rubbed his chin and glanced at Aly. The man hadn't answered his question, but he could ascertain the typical amounts harvested in the fields near Mardon. Likely Seb would know, or he could find out from his father. Otherwise, that information was stored in the king's ledgers in the palace, locked away with Alexander.

"Lordan can help us," he began, then realized no one knew

what he was talking about. "The King of Refere spoke of a new crop developed by the scientists at his university in tandem with the sorcerers there. It's a crop that is hardy enough to withstand cooler temperatures. It can be harvested later than standard wheat." The crowd shifted and shuffled. "I will have a shipment sent here."

Donner, as well as a handful of others, glanced at the farmer to see his reaction. The people of the Creaks might not like the mention of sorcery or science solving their problems, but if the alternative was to face starvation....

The farmer stared hard at Red, then after a moment finally leveled his chin and squared his gaze with his former king. "If you see to that, sir, I will not only personally bow my knee at your feet, I'll follow you into battle."

Red's heart leapt. The people erupted into applause. The farmer tousled his boy's hair and then scooped him up. At this man's word, the once hesitant people were with Red. It was that simple. One man's approval won the crowd. Donner, however, still sulked.

Aly turned and tugged her hood low over her head. As she walked away, her voice jabbed his victorious thoughts. *I warned you not to make promises.*

Now he had to set about fulfilling them before Alexander discovered him.

11

ELISE

The palace corridor smelled of Benedict Alexander's pipe smoke. He only used it when he was alone or in company he trusted, which these days was a compact group. Any usurper had to be careful who he allowed in his inner circle, especially before the official coronation, when he'd claim the crown for his own.

Elise smirked to herself, wondering what the old man would think if he knew Elise was eavesdropping on him. The problem with sneaking up on someone who employed a Protector was that the sorcerer could sense the approaching Truthwell long before any words could be overheard. Her presence couldn't be hidden, so she needed to be clever when it came to sneaking about.

Grey hadn't laid out specific instructions, but she'd taken it upon herself to become as useful as possible, obtaining whatever information she could, on whomever she could. That mostly included Lord Alexander, but was extended to anyone living in or visiting the palace.

If the pipe smoke was her guide, Alexander was hiding in the seldom-used parlor adjacent to the trophy room. Unpleasant as it was with old, creaky furniture and no art to lighten its dreary papered walls, this room was one of the places Alexander had commandeered for the meetings he assumed were private. Of course, Elise couldn't actually overhear their words, given that they were shrouded, but if she timed herself just so, she could catch to *whom* he was speaking before the shroud enveloped their conversation.

She clunked her heel on the wooden floor of the trophy room and walked heavily toward the unlit fireplace.

After a moment, a head peeked through a door that looked like part of the paneled wall. It was the door to the parlor.

"My lady, what are you doing up here?" Lord Alexander asked.

He was clever to reveal only himself and not his companions. He'd not been as clever the first time Elise had tried this trick.

"My sister was arguing about which of these animals had the largest antlers. I told her it was the elk, but she insisted it was the moose." Elise pointed at both animals. "I cannot quite measure them from here, but I think I am right. At least among the animals present."

Alexander snorted. "Perhaps that is only because that moose was young."

Elise smiled a winning smile. "Either way, I will tell Carolyn I am right." He turned to withdraw into the side room once more. This was her chance. "And I shall mention that she too may be right, if we can find a moose to replace these antlers."

The usurper paused, nodded. His arm on the door straightened as he did this, revealing two men in the room, one bearded and one wearing a white cloak. That was all she needed.

Tonight, at the dinner, I shall determine the identity of the bearded man.

She strolled away, pleased with herself, happy for the distraction from the painful thoughts of Lordan. She'd win Alexander's trust, and soon enough, she'd be allowed to know who was in that room. Grey would see her usefulness—she'd fool them all.

~

Alexander had hosted three balls already, and he planned to hold one every week until coronation. Much like Lordan, he'd woo the nobility with parties.

Elise wasn't complaining. It livened up the palace, which was always cleaning up from or preparing for another event. She had dresses made. She and her sisters could remain visible to the wealthy families, moving among them. It *helped* their case, but Alexander failed to see this. If he cast them out after parading them around at his fancy dinners, he'd be harangued as a hypocrite.

These parties also gave Elise ample opportunity to hone her skills as an informant. She began speaking less and listening more, perfecting the facial expression and head motions of one enthralled by conversation when in reality her mind was roaming, searching, prying for scraps of useful information.

She wished she could disappear, shroud herself like Aly or any other sorcerer. She was trying to figure out why Grey used non-magical spies in his network. There had to be a way she could be of use, learning this trade as well as any other spy. *Sorcerers can't lie*, she remembered. *At least not without great cost.*

But *she* could.

The dinner table was set up on the back terrace, a more intimate gathering than his previous one. Alexander was also playing favorites, inviting only a choice group to these smaller balls. It made them feel important and wanted, a ploy that almost never failed to win the invited people's affection.

Cool air wafted over the table, with candles flickering angrily in the artificial breeze created by the Comforters stationed along the back wall of the palace. Blue hydrangeas billowed out from centerpieces all down the long, white table runner. Elise drifted lazily down the table, scanning nametags and ignoring the chatter of an older noblewoman beside her.

She spotted her name and stood behind her chair. To the right, she read a name that made her frown: Sebastian Thorin.

"Hey, look who I get to pester all evening," his deep voice intoned as he took his place beside Elise.

She pinched her lips and inhaled. It was one thing to tune out the conversation of this noblewoman, who now waddled down to her seat, but it was another thing entirely to attempt not listening to Seb's annoyingly loud voice. "How delighted I am to see you."

He gripped the back of his chair and leaned over, trying to force eye contact with her. "Oh, you've learned sarcasm since I last spoke with you. How much more fun this is going to be!" He cackled and stood straight.

His absurdities would never end. "You could bother the person to your right."

Seb didn't even glance away. "You're my best friend's little sister." And that seemed to seal her fate to be forever his favorite target to annoy.

"My brother is nothing to me now." The staff stepped forward to pull back chairs. The women sat, followed by the men.

Seb resumed the conversation with a pronounced scoff. "Doesn't change the fact you're his sister." He had the audacity to elbow her. "Look at this!" He ogled the descending bowls of soup, decorated with spirals of white cream.

"Oh, soup! How exotic," Elise sneered.

Seb cast her a strange look, but she didn't reward him by turning his way. "You've changed."

"People will do that now and again."

He laughed softly. "You're not a kid."

"Well spotted."

His eyes remained on her a moment too long. "I guess I still thought you were like twelve or something."

Now she cut furious eyes at him. He grinned in victory, but a seriousness lurked beneath his flirtatious veneer, as if he'd really not noticed her age until now.

The meal passed with more frivolous chatter, and Elise was unable to listen in on anyone else's conversations. She caught words here and there, nothing more. She had, however, memorized the nametags she'd seen as she walked the table, so she could at least place every face with a name.

The bearded man who'd met with Alexander earlier was Samuel Donner. Not *Lord* Donner, so not a nobleman. Yet here he was, dining with the richest families in Mardon. He sat in the dead center of the long table, the least honorable place, considering the seats nearest Alexander and his wife at opposing ends of the table were the most desirable. Elise and her sister sat near the middle of the table, not a pointed showing of disrespect, but not a measure of favor either. They were, after all, unwed ladies of questionable heritage. Alexander made sure the two former princesses sat beside men of little honor. However, this afforded Elise the ability to hear Donner's accent, which was decidedly uneducated. Not only was he not a lord, he was poor.

How intriguing that Alexander was honoring a man like that with a seat at his table. There would be a reason, as Alexander didn't typically bring commoners into his inner circle. The man certainly didn't own anything of value Alexander wanted to buy or use to his advantage, and he wasn't influential enough to be of value in securing anything Alexander needed.

So what does this man have that Alexander needs?

Elise couldn't catch many of Donner's words over Seb's ceaseless drawl. She maintained a steady frown despite his jovial conversation.

Maybe Donner has information Alexander needs. Even a poor man can be rich in secrets. She peered down the table at Alexander. He looked like a chef surveying a spread of fine knives, as if everyone here were merely a tool to propel him toward his goal.

She was the tool he didn't realize would break right when he'd learned to trust it.

After dessert had been cleared away, Seb leaned over—as if he had to move closer to make his voice heard—and said, "Since you're not a kid, and you've had a pretty mean scowl on your face all evening, let's say you dance with me at least once tonight."

Elise nearly spat out her sip of water. "I will do nothing of the sort. Women who dance with you are…"

"Are what?"

"Idiots," she mumbled under her breath.

Seb cocked his head in mock offense. "Half the women at this table, then, are idiots."

Elise scanned the faces. "I can agree with that."

"You are ruthless," he said, tone glowing with approval.

Her ire wasn't working to repel him. She would have to try harder.

As the party moved toward the ballroom, Seb hung close. She wouldn't be able to collect much information with him trailing her like a puppy. "Why do you hate me?" he badgered, squeezing through the open doorway beside her.

She turned and walked along the wall, where several couples stood, gazing at the dancefloor. "You are despicable."

"Ouch. Why have I sunk so low in my friend's sister's opinion?"

She pitched her voice loud enough to be heard by those she passed. "I thought I made it clear I do not wish to speak of the former king."

Seb blinked at her statement, but he pressed on. "Despicable as in gross or despicable as in—"

"Deplorable. Morally unfit. An insult to this court," she finished for him.

His eyes grew wide. For a moment, no words exited his mouth. Elise sighed with relief—prematurely.

"Perfect. That means I don't have to worry about you falling in love with me." He flashed the grin that melted most women's reason.

"Is that what you think? That all women are just itching to speak to you, to dance with you? That every woman in this room is subject to your charms?" An angry flush threatened in her cheeks, but she had to remain unphased. A spy did not fall to the whims of emotion.

He leaned his head back and laughed, drawing a few eyes. "It has been my experience, yes."

She huffed, then scolded herself for allowing such a lapse in resolve. When she glanced up at Seb, he was shaking his head at her, his lips curled up in the kind of grin he typically reserved for Red. It was a smile of conspiracy, of friendship. Not the flirtatious smile he wore around women. "You may find it shocking, but not all women find you attractive."

"Do you?"

The question caught her off guard. Why did he care? Was it because he was under the prideful assumption he had power over *all* women, merely with his smile? Was it because, in this, he needed to feel victorious?

"No," she lied. His face was too pretty, as if cut from black marble by an idealist. His face was what defined the word handsome, and yet his entire demeanor, behavior, and existence poisoned his good looks with the stench of arrogance. He was dangerous, a menace to women.

He crossed his arms. "Excellent. That makes it even easier to be friends with you. Do you know how frustrating it is when women giggle at everything I say and fawn over me like I'm a prized stallion or something?"

Elise snorted in laughter. "More like prized bullfrog. All you do is puff yourself up."

Seb burst into laughter. Elise couldn't help but join in, entertained by her own insults. She'd never been one to say what was on her mind around anyone but her family. Until tonight.

When they'd collected themselves, a few faces stared aghast at their improper behavior. Elise realized the music had quieted and the couples on the dancefloor bowed to each other. They'd chosen a poor moment for such an outburst.

"Now, look, you're sweeping me in with your bad reputation. Leave me." Elise shooed him with one hand.

His shoulders still shook with residual laughter. He stepped away. "I'm afraid once you're soiled with my company, there's no recovering from *that*." An exaggerated cringe twisted his face. "Now, let me prey upon some poor soul who wants to fall in love."

Elise shook her head, struggling to erase the smile off her face. As Seb slipped into the crowd, she felt a weight returning to her cheeks, her lips, her eyes. *I have a job to do*, she remembered, and set off to find Samuel Donner and ascertain his role in this coup.

ALY

Using her mind, Aly peeked around the corner of the street up ahead. Truthwells bustled about at this hour, those of Mardonians all hoping to finish their errands and visits and dining before the unspoken curfew descended at nightfall—the hour when the beasts were more likely to roam.

Two days ago, a pair of woodwolves had attacked a family; their Comforter had not been able to stop the beasts before one poor soul had been taken from this world.

Frenzy and terror choked these people. Their Wells surged and frothed with the tangle of light and darkness that indicated their minds battled the kind of lies only fear could produce.

Aly's mind snagged on a spell—one so small it had to be either a shroud or a Master's ring. A quick exploration with her magic confirmed it was a shroud.

A sorcerer wanting to hide in daylight was either spying or looking for something. The only Master who was accustomed to hiding in broad daylight was the Royal Sorcerer.

"Wait," Aly hissed, her hand reaching out to stop Red from strolling onto the street.

Sparks of white-dust magic shot with rifle precision from

Aly's hands toward a shadowy alleyway across the road. In the light of her magic, the shape of a cloaked figure illuminated briefly then disappeared again as a shroud again hid the sorcerer's form.

"This way!" Aly shouted, shoving Red with a bit of magic to help him back the way they'd come.

They sprinted down the narrow lane, around a corner, and zig-zagged up toward another street. Aly slowed first. Red bent double and heaved a few breaths.

"It helps if you keep walking," Aly said, lifting her arms above her head. "Do like this."

Red shook his head, smiled, and copied her movement. "You know a lot about running," he teased.

"I hid for six years," she retorted, a blank expression on her face. "I know every possible way to disappear, including running away."

He closed his mouth and breathed heavily through his nose. "Are they following?"

Aly searched for the trace of magic that indicated another shroud. "Not yet. I think they didn't—no, wait, here they come."

Red shook his head, then leaned once again into a sprint. The heat of the summer evening tortured his heart and lungs, but he dared not slow down.

Aly could use her magic to fly them away, but then the sorcerers would be able to trace that magic to where they hid. She dropped all spells when they ran like this, even letting her Master's ring dissipate for the moment.

She hoped they could outrun the sorcerer's mental field of awareness, and Red's Truthwell would again be lost to their pursuers. It had worked twice before.

Around another corner, Aly slowed again. Over heavy breaths, she said, "Maybe that's far enough."

How far can you really look? She wondered at the ability of other Masters. She'd been told by both Grey and Gevar that she was stronger, more capable, than the other Masters. She was fairly certain her mind, fueled by Red's Well, could scan the entire continent, should she desire to. The concentration and power it would take to succeed in an endeavor that large, however, would render her completely unaware of her actual surroundings and thus would be stupid to ever attempt.

The sorcerer pursuing them must have turned down another street. Aly raked her hair out of her sweaty face.

In the moments they walked without a shroud, the other people on the streets could see them. To hide in plain sight, they had removed all identifying articles—coronet, cloak, mask—and hid them in an attic they'd stayed in one night.

A man brushed against Red's shoulder rather violently. "Sorry, mate," the man said, tipping his hat to Red.

Aly watched the man for a moment, making sure he wasn't a threat. When she turned back to Red, he stared at a note in his hand.

"Where'd that come from?" she asked.

"That man," Red said, fumbling to unfold the missive.

Curious, Aly stepped around him to peer down at the note, her senses keen for any approaching threats.

New Moon at sundown.

He held it up. "What?"

Aly snatched it and read it again. "Think it was meant for you, or was it a mistake? It was a full moon last night."

Red held out his hand and Aly placed the note in it. "The word *moon* is capitalized. Could that be a place?"

Aly slapped her hand to her forehead. "Of course! There's a tavern called New Moon. We passed it two nights ago. Or three nights ago—time is sort of hard to keep straight these days. It's in Cabrian Village."

Red glanced at the orange sky. "Sundown is pretty soon. If this was meant for us, think we should trust it?"

Aly lifted her palms up. Then an idea occurred to her. "Let me see it again." She held the paper up to the golden light of the dying day. A watermark appeared beneath the scribbled words. She squinted at it. Yes. "This is from Grey."

Red's brows rose. "And you know this, how?"

She showed him the watermark. "It looks like an infinity symbol, but it's actually a mask. See the pointy edges?"

Red shrugged.

"That's one of Grey's many symbols. Gevar acquired plenty of notes with that symbol on it." She grinned. "To Cabrian Village."

The New Moon tavern was a dingy place, despite its locale. Cabrian Village was a nicer merchant neighborhood, full of decent restaurants and a fairly well-attended theater. The greasy windows barely released the light inside, as if warning people not to enter.

The dining room was sparsely filled, which Aly found unusual at a time when many Mardonians enjoyed dinner, especially now that eating out after dark was less popular. Maybe everyone had already left and headed home to arrive before darkness took the streets.

"Okay, now what?" asked Red, as they shuffled toward an empty table.

A woman in an apron breezed among the tables. "This way," she said to Red and Aly without much of a glance.

Aly cast a quick trio of protective spells around them and marched behind Red. She searched out the rooms ahead, only to find the flickering Truthwells of people more comfortable with lies.

The woman led them to a door and waved a nonchalant hand at it before sauntering back toward the dining room.

The door was carved with a small sliver of moon.

Red tapped a knuckle on the door. "That's not a new moon," he grunted.

The door immediately swung open, revealing a smiling Grey. "You're right," he quipped with a wink. "It's a waxing crescent." He pulled Red and Aly into the room and shut the door.

Aly's face lit with a smile. Red, on the other hand, shuffled his feet and rubbed his palms down his torso. He returned Grey's small bow and continued fidgeting.

"Sit, please." Grey pointed to four velvet chairs arranged before a dark fireplace. Soot stained the wall and part of the ceiling. A pair of small lamps lit the room, but there were no windows.

Aly elected to stand, and Grey did not question it. "What is this, one of your lairs?"

Grey chuckled. "Sort of. I was hoping you wouldn't outrun my sorcerer earlier, but Aly, it seems you are good at keeping Red safe."

"That was *your* sorcerer?" she balked.

"I had to find you two. You are hard to find."

Red crossed his legs. "That's sort of the point."

Grey nodded at him. "Of course, Your Majesty, but I have news. I told my man you would drop all spells once you detected him, so that's why we chose to use the note."

Aly frowned. "So, he dropped his cloak and his magic as well?"

Grey nodded.

Uncomfortable that someone had slipped past her defenses, Aly crossed her arms and sulked in the corner beside a poorly painted portrait of a man. His face appeared to float away from his neck. Leave it to Grey to figure out her means of avoiding capture and slip right through them.

If Grey could figure it out, in time, Alexander's men might as well.

"What brings us here tonight?" asked Red, cutting to the point.

Aly's directness had rubbed off on him. She smirked.

Grey leaned back, ever the one at ease, and lit a pipe. "Your trainload of wheat has left Refere."

Red sat forward. "Indeed?"

Grey nodded. "I received a message this morning."

Red glanced back at Aly. "One week," he said.

She smiled. Red was following through on his promises—somehow, despite how radical his promises had been. He'd ordered the wheat from Lordan, reminding Lordan that he had promised aid to Tandera. In one week, when the train arrived, Red would be one step closer to providing food for some of Tandera's poorest citizens.

Grey slapped a knee. "And I might have found a Comforter or two to keep an eye on the fields of the poorer farmers when they plant. Best I can do right now, I'm afraid, since my hand in this whole ordeal must remain hidden."

"Very good," said Red. "Thank you."

"I am pleased to help the rightful sovereign," Grey said. "My allegiance with Alexander remains strong, and I plan to keep it that way. Always know more than your enemy." Grey tipped his brow at Red.

"My father always said that," Red replied.

"He was a wise king." Grey stood. "I must cut our time short. My whereabouts are watched. I hope you can find your way to the train station as the wheat arrives. In fact, I have a plan for a rather entertaining distraction to keep any interested parties away from the station when that train arrives."

Red stood and shook hands with Grey, like business partners. "Thank you."

Red was going to win this nation back. He would be a wise king, like his father. *And I will remain forever his armor, and nothing more,* Aly mused. The scepter was a tool, an instrument to wield, the way a shield stopped the arrows of the enemy.

She wanted more than that; however, to want something other than what Theod had crafted for her was to want something that could not be.

Her power would keep him safe, but it would not gain him his crown or govern his people for him.

Despite her insecurities at her place in this dance for the throne, Aly couldn't shake the proud smile off her face as they left the tavern by a back door. Knowing that the seeds were rattling their way toward them even now felt like a victory.

Now, they just have to make it to harvest.

Mardon's train station was quieter after all the passenger cars had emptied and all that remained were the cargo containers. Not as many suits and dresses flashed about on the platforms, but plenty of people milled around the cars as shipments were unloaded, and new ones were placed in the cars that would travel back to Refere.

Whatever distraction Grey had planned to keep Alexander's men from the platform must be working, because she hadn't detected any of them nearby.

Aly and Red stood shoulder to shoulder on the platform. The warm summer air carried the smell of burlap and sawdust wafting off the trains. The shipment Red had ordered from Lordan was on this train.

The promise he'd made his people was one step closer to coming true. She'd been wrong to question him.

"Sir," said a short, well-dressed man who approached Red with a tentative bow. "King Lordan has come through. Two cars, full of seeds!" The man pointed at the boxcars that had yet to reach the platform. Soon enough, the train would inch forward and the rest of the contents, including Refere's promised seed, would be emptied.

Lordan had answered his call quickly, sending bags and bags of the newly developed hardy wheat from Refere. How he had so much to spare was a question she and Red couldn't afford to answer—or how Lordan would decide to receive payment.

Whatever Lordan wanted in return, it would be well worth the cost. This wheat would be the answer to Mardon's food shortage. Aly pictured the farmer's young son. The little boy would not die of starvation, thanks to Red's actions. The people *had* to see this. How could they not want Red as their king? But it would take more than one thing to convince those who had already sided with Alexander. One farmer had swayed the crowd that day, but there were the merchants and the nobility still to win, as well as the working-class citizens.

Red was following through on his promises, though, and that was what mattered. His posture was triumphant as the empty wagons, ready to be loaded with bags of wheat, rolled up to the platform.

"Mardonians will not go hungry this year," he said, arms crossed over a proud chest.

Aly suppressed a smile. "Let's wait till the wheat is harvested and in people's storerooms before we celebrate."

He dropped his arms. "You think it will fail."

"No," she said, hating that she'd ruined the moment. "I know that sometimes...well, you heard the man—the last crop was ruined. I hope this wheat survives to harvest."

A slight pause preceded his words. "It's hardier."

"Of course." She nodded. "It'll be perfect."

"Can you make sure it stays warm enough? Gets enough rain?" Desperation tempered his words and his posture again slumped.

She sighed, sorry to have stolen the joy from this moment. "I can't ensure every field of this wheat grows to ripeness. I'd need to be in too many places at once, doing nothing other than directing the weather, and I'm supposed to protect *you*. The wealthiest farmers have sorcerers for that sort of thing. Plus, this wheat can grow in cold weather."

Red rubbed his forehead. "You're right, but I'm worried about those people, Aly. That boy. His father. All of them."

She bumped his shoulder with hers. "I know. That's why you're the best king this country could have."

He quirked a half-smile at her. "I've never felt hunger before. I can't even imagine what that would be like. Those people—you could see it in their faces that they've been hungry. I never want them to feel it again."

Aly glanced at her feet. Her mind shrank to a single moment in her past, and as her memories sharpened, her body began to curl in on itself. "Can you see it on my face?" she asked, voice barely a whisper.

In a flash, he was facing her, holding her shoulders and bending down to meet her gaze. "Look at me." She did. His eyes held both sadness and defiance and pity; amidst all that, there was acceptance. She could *feel* it in the way his gaze hammered into her, the way he'd noticed her posture shift and intercepted her before she could collapse back into her former self, the girl who'd been invisible for so long, in more ways than one.

He didn't answer her question, and for that she was grateful. He pulled her to him and wrapped his arms around her. To him, she wasn't invisible.

After a moment, she backed away. She wasn't crying or even sad, but she'd shared something of her past that she'd tried to bury, a memory of a winter full of a pain she never wanted to know again. Even alluding to her memories of hunger was awful. She'd never imagined she'd tell a soul about that winter, yet now Red knew.

He had a way of making her face her own truths, even the ones she wanted to forget.

Hunger wasn't just something that happened to other people. He needed to know that.

The fields were being prepared even now, so the wheat could be planted as quickly as possible. It was a gamble that these new seeds would take, and that the already depleted fields could support another crop. But it was that or let the poorest Mardonian families face starvation. Some farmers had chosen to plant potatoes to replace the lost wheat, sticking with something that they understood, something not touched by magic and science. If this plant was exactly what Lordan had said it was, it would be a victory for Tandera, for Red.

A wave of unease crashed over Aly as she considered what a great weight they were placing on Lordan's word. The man had edged around the truth before. If that happened here—she couldn't stomach the thought.

Red called the short man back over. "This train was guarded?" he asked as the final cars rolled up to the platform, moved forward by the simple spell of a Master Sorcerer employed by Excheter Rail.

The railyard worker nodded. "Every train is guarded, sire. Excheter Rail employs seventeen Protectors and thirty Comforters to ensure the safe delivery of our goods."

Aly covered a surprised cough with her fist. So many! There was an entire world of sorcerers she knew nothing about. A world in which she held the highest title, yet it was a world from which she was entirely excluded.

"This one had no trouble on its way from Refere," the man added and scurried off after a hasty bow.

Men slid the doors open and climbed in, shouldering bags of wheat and hauling them to the waiting wagons. The men coughed and hacked as they exited the boxcars. Soon, a strange odor wafted from the train. Red flagged one of the men and waved him over.

The trainyard attendant brought one of the bags and dropped

it at Red's feet with a heavy *flump*. Red paused a moment, staring at it. He squatted down, drew his ash blade from his hip, and slid the edge into the corner of the bag.

Immediately, two things happened. Seeds began to spill from the tiny slit and a wretched smell greeted Aly's nostrils.

White fuzz coated the seeds at their feet.

"They're rotten," spat the man standing before them.

In the man's words, Aly heard the growling stomachs of hungry children and the victorious laughter of Lord Benedict Alexander.

13

RED

He shouted in anger, jumping up, blade still in hand. A few eyes turned toward him. Red's promise to the farmers was as useless as the spoiled seeds before him.

This failure would be on him. Regardless of what Refere had sent, the seeds that Red had promised, the seeds he'd hoped would feed Tanderans, would not even have the chance to be planted.

Red jammed his blade back in its sheath, calming every urge to kick the bag and curse aloud. Beside him, Aly's hands cupped her mouth as she stared in dismay at the bag of seeds.

The man who'd dropped the bag had run back to the train, halting the workers with a whistle and a few loud shouts. One by one, the workers were cutting open the bags, checking the contents. The smell of rot overpowered the small platform.

"He promised," Aly whispered.

"It doesn't matter what Lordan did or did not do. I'm the one who promised my people these seeds."

With a few hand signals, the men unloading the train redirected their steps, hauling the bags off the platform and into the night. They were heading toward the large refuse pile directly outside of Mardon.

These seeds would be ash by morning.

All their hope, reduced to dust.

Aly placed a small bit of pressure on his upper arm, a gesture of both sadness and support.

"This train has been sabotaged," Red snarled. He stepped over the bag of spoiled seeds and found the railyard overseer, the short man they'd spoken with earlier.

"I assure you, sire, no one touched it."

"I will speak with Lordan about this," Red said, fuming.

"Could they have gotten wet in transport?" asked Aly.

The man seemed shocked the Royal Sorcerer was speaking to him. "No, ma'am. These train cars are secure. No rain in route. Our Comforters ride with the trains, especially ones carrying perishable goods, to ensure perfect conditions. The train was not the problem, sire," he said, giving Red a pointed look, as if Red somehow were the reason for the rotten seeds.

People will blame you for their problems, Gevar had once warned Red. Whatever went wrong in a country, it was the king's fault—always. He had to accept this.

But his posture slumped as he stared down at the floor beneath his feet. "We must think of something else," he said. "We need to find a way to feed our people."

"We will think of something," she said.

"I'll buy the wheat from Refere once it's harvested. Lordan will sell to us. He must."

Aly's small huff was barely audible, but Red caught it. She doubted Lordan, and he supposed it was for good reason. *But what other option do we have?* This was what alliances were born for. He would also contact the Viriennese king and the governor in Esvedara. Someone would have food to share with them.

He turned to leave the platform. "We need to send a message to Lordan, tonight. Can you contact his sorcerer?"

Aly's face paled, but she nodded. "Not here," she said, following him out into the night. As they exited the lit platform, Aly grabbed his arm. "Come with me."

She led him into a shadowy corner behind the train station. The sense of being led by her this way was strange, as if she weren't comfortable taking his hand. Only days ago, she'd held his hand like it was the most natural thing in the world.

It's just the stress of this discovery, he told himself. *There's nothing to it.*

In the darkness behind the station, the world quieted as Aly shrouded them from eyes and ears. Aly nodded, confirming they were hidden. There were still people about, but not as many outside the train yard.

Aly closed her eyes as she searched out the Truthwell of Refere's Royal Sorcerer. He didn't fully understand it, but she could memorize the pattern of a person's energy signature. It was one of the most lucrative skills of a Master sorcerer. Knowing exactly who someone was, behind a disguise or closed doors, even across cities, was knowledge no spy could provide. And Aly's magical sense could search farther than most, spanning the entire reaches of the continent.

There was something special about her magic. Theod had gifted her with power and talent far beyond an ordinary Master. Somehow, Grey had sensed this and chosen Aly to train to become the best sorcerer in the land. A part of Red still bristled at the unknown past between Aly and Grey. However, she was standing here next to him, not next to Grey—she'd chosen six years ago to walk away from him.

The night painted her freckled face with cool shadows. He enjoyed watching her while she wielded magic. It was a mystery, fascinating and intriguing. The way her face twitched in recognition as she found Refere's Royal Sorcerer infused Red with admiration.

If he and Aly were as powerful as the legends of the Beacon

and Beholder claimed, then escaping this predicament could be as simple as conjuring food out of the air, right? Magic should be able to solve their problems, but Seb had warned him that using magic to regain the throne would backfire, leaving Red without a crown. He'd agreed he had to win back Tandera on his own merit, but what harm would come from providing food for his people with a little bit of magic?

Not everything that matters takes magic. Ondorian had said this on many occasions. Some tasks had to be accomplished with flesh and bones. Feeding his people wasn't a problem to be solved with a single spell.

Aly began to tremble when lost in her magic. The curves of her lips loosened, but her eyes remained tightened as if she could see something he could not. He wondered what it was like to see Truthwells, to see their light burning in the world around him. He wondered, not for the first time, if it was merely his brightness that had warmed her affections for him.

She stood close, the way she had after the night they defeated her father. He cherished the feeling, but he still wasn't certain how to handle her nearness. In a sense, Aly was untouchable, and yet with that knowledge came a flicker of rebellion. He *wanted* to defy the way of kings and sorcerers and love her for as long as he lived. But even still, she would outlive him for a century. When he was gone, she would be the one to suffer.

He watched her until her arms began to relax and her fingers grew still. Before she opened her eyes, he placed one hand on her cheek. Her eyes popped open, bright and intense, as if lit from within. Her green eyes captivated him, but there was something in her expression that he couldn't place. A distance, perhaps a doubt.

"Did you send the message?" he asked. When she nodded, her face pressed into his hand. It was all he needed for encouragement. "Lordan will respond. I know he will." His hand fell away. "After all, he is still our ally, despite his weak promise to Elise."

"We need to rest for the night," she said. "I found a place earlier."

Red swallowed. He was homeless. The King of Tandera had been kicked to the streets. He extended his elbow to escort her, like a noble and his lady on the darkening streets.

No place for a king in his own city. He peered around at the empty street, his eyes taking in what should be his but what felt entirely unknown. His birth declared him sovereign over these streets and the people who occupied them, but he couldn't shake the feeling that he was the imposter. He had no claim to these streets, save the spot he'd sleep in, like a common beggar.

"What is it?" Aly asked.

"Nothing," he said. Red kept his face from faltering but the resulting stiffness refuted his word. "Where are we staying?"

Aly offered a sly grin. "It's nice. You'll like it. Better than where we've been lately."

"Oh, you mean there will be a five-course dinner and a hot bath?" He picked at the front of his shirt. "And someone to bring me a pressed shirt?"

Her face fell. "No, Red. Come on." She tightened her grip on his arm, and immediately the gritty feeling in his mouth and the stickiness of his skin melted away and his spirits lifted with the bats scattering over Mardon's rooftops.

Choosing to focus on Aly at his side rather than the shattered hopes of hungry farmers, he hummed quietly as they walked, invisible to the world. His cheerfulness eventually caught, like a small spark, and Aly flashed him the smile that made their situation not hurt so much.

Her. I get her. This was enough to make the homelessness, the exhaustion, the dirt worth it.

Once a king, now a vagabond. But life in the palace, with its silks and crystal and fine colognes, hadn't given him the feeling he now had as he stared over at Aly while they walked.

"You'd think you were just told you could move back into the palace," Aly said, her hand loosening.

He pulled her in tighter.

They walked down a thin street barely wide enough for a carriage. Drying linens created a canopy above them. Flowers hugged the window ledges and the music of a violin could be heard from an upper floor.

"Where are we?" Red asked. He paused to listen to the musician practice. He hadn't heard this kind of music in a long time. It reached deep into his bones and melted some of the tension buried inside him.

"Cabrian Village."

"Ah, you really are taking us to a nice place."

"No, it's right past this neighborhood."

Red's shoulders fell. "It would have been nice to stay in a comfortable place for once."

Aly looked away, pursing her lips.

"I'm sorry. I didn't mean that."

"You've only ever known comfort. Most of these people, even the ones who live in Cabrian Village, don't know comfort like you. If someone tried to scrape the crumbs from their table, they'd wonder what was going on."

Red *humphed*. "I never liked that either."

"Come on, it's this way."

They wandered a little farther. The streets of Cabrian Village abutted the Cresen River. Just across the water from the wealthy district of stone townhomes was Everett Street, which marked the start of the wooden and plaster buildings of the middle class.

A far cry from the Creaks, Everett and Johnston and Valmoro Streets still lacked the swept, pristine feel of the ritzier areas of town. The men's suits and ladies' dresses imitated those of the nobles, but there was something about the clothes here that marked them as less expensive. Red watched a pair of men walking. They had the same cut of suit as many of Red's. Their hats were of the appropriate height for the year, but the fabric and the way it fit indicated it was of poorer quality. He'd never known he could spot the quality of a suit this way, or that it was so easy to see.

He hated himself for even being able to note the disparity between himself and these men. *Not anymore*, he corrected himself. His own clothes reeked and had stains around the wrists. The two men he'd been scrutinizing turned a strange look upon him and Aly as they passed. They stared Red up and down and, without a doubt, cast him a look of disdain.

Red bristled. Then he remembered what he was to these men: *nobody*.

Their own king, stripped of his finery, was nothing but a street rat from the Creaks. His coronet was tucked away in the same hiding place where Aly kept her cloak and mask.

In the middle of the road, Red stopped. He watched the men as they walked away, returning their sneers with a look of complete astonishment.

"They hate me," he whispered to Aly. "Solely because I look like this." He lifted his arms.

Aly placed a hand on his upper arm. "Ignore them. Let's go."

"No." He pulled away from her. "Is that really how it is? Those with more look down on those with less?"

"Yes."

"Why?" Her brows lifted, and he shot her a puzzled look. "But I am not less."

She frowned. "Exactly. What makes a man less? Right now, you have nothing. Not a crown for your head, not even a pillow."

Red sighed. "I have you."

As she looked down, he spied the blush on her cheeks. "You know what I mean. What does it feel like to be looked down on simply because they assume you have nothing?"

In her tone, her eyes, her posture, there was a *knowing*. She'd been looked down upon. How very different their lives had been. He had been at the pinnacle of society; she, at the bottom. She'd begun this life afraid and alone, set apart from everyone. She'd risen, true, but she was still apart from everyone.

Save one person.

He stepped to her and grabbed her hand, pulling her closer. "It feels terrible." In his gaze, he tried to pour all his understanding, all his empathy. He might never know what it was to live as she had, but he was tasting a hint of it as his own city and country turned against him.

Arm entangled with his, Aly led him down Everett Street to a wood-and-plaster building.

"What's the story?" he asked.

"This one was owned by a rich man, as a second home for his…second life. The wife was a Master, and when she found out, she apparently came here and Truthstripped her husband and whomever he was with." Her shoulders rose and fell. "Since then, no one has wanted to go in there." She tugged his hand. "But it's just a building. Come on."

He walked up to the front door. It was ajar, but a sign on it read *no trespassing*. Someone had painted over the words with a suggestion of their own.

"No, this way." Aly led him to a gated alleyway. She lifted her hands and, with a whispered spell, removed the large iron lock.

They closed the gate behind them and stepped into a small, dark garden. Pots lined the walls. The plants had all died, their brown stems hanging limp. The only green was the moss that still grew over the stones on the ground.

"This is a sad place," Red said.

Aly nodded. "You'll like the inside."

Red tiptoed behind Aly through a narrow door that led into a side hall, as if a thief entering a house. The house smelled damp.

The small entryway opened up into a stairwell. The hall led

back to the adjacent kitchen house and forward into a paneled dining room. To their right was the foyer, where the cracked front door let in a line of thin light from the gas lamps outside. Muddy footprints lined the hall.

"Looks like we're not the first squatters to find this place." It still felt odd to call himself a squatter. Homeless. Destitute.

Most of the furniture had been removed, but a large cabinet still adorned one wall of the dining room. It was empty, cleared of its contents, but the piece itself was too big to move. The handles, however, had been confiscated by the truly desperate.

Other than the faint, sharp smell of mildew, the house felt clean, almost homey despite its emptiness.

"You're sure no one else will be here?"

Aly spun around in the hall. "I made sure the place was empty. Usually, it's first come, first served with squatters. I set up a spell to make it look occupied."

He shook his head. "I am officially a squatter." As he turned, his eyes landed on a tall piano in the sitting room opposite the dining area. Exhaling in pleasant surprise, he walked over to examine the piece. He ran his finger along the top, noting the dust. When he lifted the cover, he smiled. All the keys were still in place. "Thieves must not be that smart," he said. "These are ivory."

He pulled out the bench and sat. With an eager smile, he cracked his fingers and spread them out over the keys, as if petting a beloved dog. He settled his fingers over the center keys and, gently, tried the notes.

"It's *tuned*," he said.

Behind him, Aly's shadow approached. "I tuned it."

He swiveled and looked up at her. "How?"

"Magic." She tucked her hands in around her.

"Wow. I didn't know magic could do that."

"I thought you might like it." She bit her lower lip.

"Aly, you amaze me."

Turning back to the keys, he inhaled in expectation. Then, with gusto, he pressed his fingers into the first notes of a melody. Within seconds, he lost himself to the music. Swaying on the bench, he was back in the palace piano room, his grand Balunato before him. The music had never sounded as sweet to him as it did in this moment. He was *home*.

When the song drew to a close, he wasn't ready for it to end. He called on his knowledge from years and years of lessons and began the first notes of one of Nicere's finest and longest sonatas. The rich, deep melody cleansed him of the filth on his clothes but only increased the ache in his heart for his family and his home.

As he played, he felt another person join him on the bench.

He'd almost forgotten Aly was there. She sat backward on the bench, turning to stare down at his hands.

He watched her eyes until she looked up at him, his fingers never missing a note. At her eye contact, though, he stopped playing.

"What?" she whispered. There were tears in her eyes.

He lifted a hand and touched her cheek. "You're beautiful, you know that?" He leaned forward, his forehead tilting down. Her skin burned with so much warmth that he felt her before his face brushed hers.

They were alone. He wanted more than anything to keep things right between them, the way a proper relationship should be. But he'd left proper behind the first time he'd entered her chambers at night in the palace. Theirs was an odd courtship, where the rules were somewhat different. He'd spent the night in the same room as her for weeks now.

And yet, he hesitated as his lips moved toward hers. His nose bumped her cheek, then he pressed forward and kissed her.

14

ALY

Aly woke in the middle of the night, the memory of Red's kiss echoing in her mind.

She was uncertain what time it was until she settled her thoughts and reached out to the Truthwells around her. She could sense the stillness of the city's inhabitants. With a smile, she closed off awareness of all Wells save Red's. His lightning-bright energy was undulating peacefully. The deepness of Red's sleep indicated that he had been asleep for several hours. That meant dawn approached but sunrise was far enough off that the birds had not yet woken.

The memory of his kiss drowned out every other thought. She replayed it again and again, still startled by it, even now. Her body buzzed with energy. *Sleep,* she commanded herself, but it had been hard to fall asleep after feeling such a high. The kiss had been everything she'd wanted these past weeks. It had been *bliss.*

However...she knew they shouldn't.

For now, just let it be. She couldn't shove down the thudding in her heart or douse the inferno in her veins.

He'd been respectful, even in their solitude, even though not a soul could see them under her shroud. All it did was make her long for a life where they could be alone together without fear of discovery or rumors or separation.

But that was not to be.

I'm no queen, she told herself. Her magic and her Binding made sure she'd never sit as a co-sovereign of Tandera. Theod intended for magic and authority to remain *separate.* A scepter and a crown, never one and the same.

Into her mind, came a voice, deep and rumbling, shaking her from her thoughts of an impossible future.

Message from the King of Refere. The wheat berries were fine when we packaged them. Passed the inspection before departure. This is not our fault.

It was a short message, and it was one with little hope. Lordan's sorcerer hadn't seemed pleased, his tone on the edge of anger, as if her message had annoyed Lordan, and the King of Refere was flexing his muscles in response. She hadn't blamed Lordan, she'd simply stated that the seeds were ruined and that Lordan should know.

She sat up, knees at her chest, and pondered Lordan's message. If he'd told his sorcerer to lie, then he was asking his sorcerer to reduce his own power. No king would do that, not when the power of the Royal Sorcerer was what protected the king. *No, Lordan is too selfish for that.* Which meant he was telling the truth. The seeds were fine when Lordan sent them, which also meant he had upheld his end of the bargain. Maybe he could be trusted.

Someone or something ruined those seeds en route.

But who?

Almost in a panic, Aly hopped up to tell Red the message, but as she spied the king on the other side of her small partition, she paused. He was completely relaxed, his face toward her. The harshness he'd lately acquired in his expression was absent.

He needed to hear Lordan's message, but she allowed herself a moment to stare.

Red's breathing calmed her. His energy pulsed against her magical awareness in a rhythm she knew so well.

Aly sat back down, watching Red sleep and remembering what it had been like to watch him from the shadows, when he was nothing more than a handsome, arrogant face, forever untouchable. Meeting him in person had been under such horrible circumstances, and it had nearly ruined her opinion of him altogether. Until she'd seen his initiative, his reckless abandon for what he thought was right. He was rash, maybe, but he was also bold and brave and never idle. He got things wrong as often as he got them right, but he at least *acted*. He'd saved her life in the Canyon, even as she'd saved his. He'd fought with her against her father, a man against a sorcerer. Foolish, yes, but chivalrous.

She'd never considered that he would look at her the way he did, or that he'd care more about her than her magic—and that had changed everything.

What am I doing? she mused. *This will all have to end.*

Sovereigns and sorcerers were not meant to *be* together. They were merely meant to reign together, one from the light and the other from the shadows.

Aly pressed her fingers against Red's shoulder. She shook him a little, and he bolted upright, then immediately sank back to the floor with a groan.

"What is it?"

"Time to wake up," she said.

With another grunt, he clunked his head against the floor. She withdrew to her side of the wall with a huff. When she looked back, his arm was extended to where she had been. What would happen if she reached for him?

Instead of grabbing his hand, she scooted around the wall and sat beside him. He looked up at her with a small smile. She would tell him Lordan's news as soon as he stopped looking at her like this. No sense cutting it short.

"How did you sleep?" he asked, a warmth in his tired eyes.

She shrugged. "You?"

He sat up with a laugh. "I've never had a worse night."

"Privileged much?"

He knocked into her with his shoulder. "It's not my fault."

They sat like children on the floor, legs folded underneath themselves, the memory of last night's kiss filling the spaces around them.

"I received word back from Lordan," she said. Red perked up. "He said that the seeds were not contaminated at the railway's inspection, prior to departure."

Red raked through his hair violently with both hands, then let his head hang. She found his morning hair entirely distracting. "I expected as much," he finally said, catching her in the act of staring. "You like my hair?"

She wanted to reach forward and slide her hands into it, the way she had that night when she'd healed his headaches. The memory of her hands slipping through his curls was something she would never forget. She wondered if she would ever experience it again. A tight smile was her only answer.

Red stood, stretched, and turned toward the windows, where the first gray hint of dawn was rising. His shirt was untucked, his feet bare. He was marvelously handsome.

She laughed despite herself and their current predicament. His sleepy smile churned her stomach into knots. For a moment there was a sense of peace.

"Who sabotaged us?" Red wondered, reaching down to swipe his surcoat off the floor and shake it out.

She leaned forward, placing her elbows on crossed knees. "I don't know. A skilled sorcerer could have done it without the train guard knowing."

"If that's possible, then what good is a train guard?"

"A Master could fly, wouldn't even have to land on the train. It would be simple enough to send moisture into the bags."

"Even if the bags were sealed?"

She narrowed her eyes at his stupid question. "I suppose someone on the train could have done it. They admitted they employ a Comforter."

"All right," Red said, arms crossed. "The only person wicked enough to spoil this wheat on purpose would be Alexander. If he thought it had any chance of helping me regain the throne, he'd do everything he could to spoil it, and my chances. It was him."

Aly stood. "Even if it was, there will be no proof. The seeds are not a viable option now. We must think of the people."

Red nodded. "Of course. But—"

"What we must consider is who would have told Alexander of your plans. If we can't prove Alexander's hand in it, perhaps we can at least discover who among our allies is sharing information with him."

"A hundred people must have known."

"Surely not that many. We took aims to keep the information contained."

"But the employees of the train company knew, and the people on the street that day, and who knows who they told."

Aly pondered this. "We didn't specifically say the wheat was ordered by you to feed our people. The train company simply loaded the train with the goods and brought them from Refere. They were the transportation, nothing more."

With a sigh, Red sat on the windowsill. "Someone must have known."

"Grey could find out," Aly suggested.

Red's eyes narrowed before he turned his attention to the corner of the room. Grey was an odd topic with Red. Aly felt the air turn electric, as if charged by a coming storm. To ease his tension, Aly walked across the room and sat beside Red on the small sill, her shoulder pressed against his.

"Ask Grey," she said. "He will help."

Red huffed and stood. "We must find food for our people. We are too low on time to order more seeds, which would likely be sabotaged anyway."

"Is there another way to ship food here in time?"

"By sea."

"We could try that. Provide our own sorcerer to keep watch over the ship, given the recent...developments at sea." Aly blinked away her memory of the tentacled beast her magic had killed in Vona.

"You have a group of friends I don't know about?" asked Red, turning circles in the dim light.

Aly lowered her head. *No. No friends, Red.* She didn't say this aloud, but that reality stung her. She'd wanted friends as long as she could remember. Elise had seemed like a fast friend until the debacle in Refere.

"Seb knows people in shipping. So does Grey."

Again, Red laughed in annoyance. "Grey again? Yes, he can save us."

If she ever told Red about her dance with Grey, it would only anger him more, and they needed Grey. They had so few allies. Grey was powerful and his pockets were deep. If they pushed him away, they would have few others to turn to. "Why don't we go there now?" she ventured. "We can ask him."

Red eyed her, as if to assess her intentions. "I thought sorcerers were watching his estate?"

"They are, but he's not there." Red lifted his brows. She swallowed back the shame rising at her next words and how they would make Red feel. "He's not far from here. I believe his mother's house is in this part of town."

"I see," he muttered, eyes pooling with shadows as he turned away. "We'll put his family at risk to visit them there."

Aly pursed her lips. "Perhaps, but I think I can keep them off our trail. Plus, Grey's good at lying. He'll come up with something to escape trouble, if any arises."

"Fine. Let's ask Lord Weston Grey if he can save our people."

They walked into the street as dawn's light pinked the horizon. Rain was coming. She could sense the dull glow of energy hovering in the eastern sky.

"He's a few streets that way," Aly said, pointing.

Hands tucked in his pockets, Red marched down the sidewalk. The city was waking, the factory workers headed off to a day's labor, the kitchens firing up to feed families. "Do you keep tabs on his whereabouts all the time?"

The harshness in his voice stung Aly. "No."

"How do you do that?" He shrugged. "Find people like that?"

"I use you."

He barked out an amused laugh. "That sounds awful."

She elbowed him. "You know what I mean. Your Well." Their closeness tingled her skin. The summer day was muggy, causing a sweat even at this early hour. She dismissed her sweat with no more than a thought.

"Okay then," he whispered, his voice low. "Glad I'm so useful to you," he teased. He stepped nearer, but hesitated to close the distance, waiting for her word.

Her body turned rigid. This was what she wanted, what she *yearned* for. She leaned forward, her eyes on his. *Toss me, I can't do this!* She fidgeted and stumbled away.

His sigh of disappointment stabbed her like his ash blade. "What is it? Ever since Elise's comment, you've been different. We talked about that. She was wrong."

"We also both know you'll grow old at least a century before I do. And Theod forbids sovereigns and sorcerers from ruling...

together." Her voice shrank to barely a whisper at the last word. "I'm simply here to keep you alive as long as I can."

His laugh soured. "Oh, is that it? What happened to wanting to be looked at?" He reached for her elbow. "What happened, Aly?"

She crumpled into herself, diminishing as she attempted to disappear from her troubles. *You only first looked at me because of my magic.* She wanted to say it, to hear it disproved, but she couldn't. Instead, she bit her lips and said nothing.

Red's arms circled around her, drawing her in. He hadn't known her long, but he could tell when she wanted to shrink away from reality. His answer was always to pull her close, as if to remind her that he was a part of her reality, a part he would not let her hide from.

"Better?" he mumbled against her hair.

She nodded, enjoying the heady scent of his unwashed clothes. It was the smell of *him*, amplified and intoxicating.

He released her and ducked down to make eye contact. He didn't stand straight until she smiled at him. "Now, where is Grey?"

Aly pushed her magical awareness outward and honed in on Grey's, turning until she faced it.

"He's this way."

Aly had never met Grey's mother or sisters, but she'd seen them at palace events. Where Weston Grey was amiable yet subtle at parties, Grey's sisters were boisterous gossips, his mother a queen of condescension. Judging by the facial expressions of the people Aly had seen in conversation with Grey's sisters and even occasionally his mother, their presence was barely tolerated.

Grey's Truthwell led them toward one of the oldest neighborhoods in the city. The homes were large, made of stone, and had been owned by the same families for centuries. Grey's family was an odd case, considering the heir resided outside the city in the ancient estate, and the women lived in town.

As they entered the street, Aly froze. Red stopped and stepped backward, tensing to run at her command.

She raked the street, the homes, the carriages, for where the threat lurked. There were many Protectors on this street, as to be expected. She couldn't be certain any of them were out looking for Red and Aly.

But she couldn't be careless either.

She discovered that of the twelve homes on the street, nine flew the banners that indicated the family was in residence. Five homes were filled with Truthwells, and each of those five had a Protector or two within, including the house where Grey's Well lingered.

There was only one empty home with a Protector in it—the tiny spell for the Master's ring her only indication of the sorcerer's status.

That would be the one to watch out for.

Aly nudged Red forward with a hand. "I think it's okay," she muttered. "But there's a Protector in that house, and no one else." She kept her magic trained on that Well, ready to sense any spells cast.

"I believe this is their house," Red said as they approached a tall, imposing home with tall windows and stout columns.

The diminutive man at the door was visibly shocked to see the king and Royal Sorcerer standing there, asking for entrance.

"We wish to speak with Lord Weston Grey," Red announced.

"Of course, Your Majesty. Right this way."

The man led them through a narrow entryway into a vast sitting room where tall windows let in the bright summer morning. Clouds were rolling in from the east, passing fast shadows across the room.

"Lord Grey will be with you shortly."

Aly looked around the lavish room. The décor was decidedly

more modern than that of Grey Manor, everything basted in a garish green and gold leaf pattern. Paintings of women in fine clothing adorned the walls. As she turned, her eyes landed on a family portrait: a man and a woman with three children surrounded by the drapery that was common in paintings of the upper class. The man stood in a crisp suit with billowing ascot and a top hat popular in years gone by. There were two young girls and a boy. The boy stood by his father wearing a shining blue suit with cropped pants and a fluffy ascot.

Aly stared at the painting of Grey as a child. Their upbringings were very different, and yet here was a man who'd had a cruel father, just like her.

Gevar had been the father Aly had always wanted. She'd only known him six short years, but he still held a place in her heart that no one else ever would.

Grey was the one who had led her to the palace, to the man she had called Papa, and the king who now stood beside her. Movement behind her startled her out of her thoughts.

She spun to see Lord Weston Grey wearing a pale summer suit.

"Your Majesty. Very nice to see you. What can I do for you?" He bowed. "My mother and sisters are dying to come in here, but I insisted they wait until our business is concluded." He moved into the room. "I assure you, they will not bother us until we send word."

Grey sat on a sofa, offering the one opposite him to Red and Aly. She sat first, as was customary, but she jolted a little when Red sat down so close, his leg merely a hand's width away. A tray of coffee was brought in. Red took a cup and, to Aly's surprise, began sipping. He didn't normally drink caffeine, but he hadn't complained of headaches lately either.

Grey picked up a cookie off the coffee tray and nibbled the corner.

The awkward tension in the room prickled Aly's skin. She

couldn't dispel it with magic, so she leaped into conversation. "How is work at the, uh, New Moon?"

Red sputtered against his coffee. Grey, always composed, merely flashed his eyes at her above his cookie. She glanced at the men. "What?" She'd never learned the finer arts of polite conversation.

Grey placed the half-eaten treat on the couch beside him. His expression subtly shifted to amused. "I'm working for the palace, as expected," he said.

"I know it's all a game of tricks and false loyalties, but how can you possibly work for *him*, under any pretense?" Aly asked.

"I never said I was working for him."

She wished she could scoot a few inches away from Red, but this would only make it more obvious that she was uncomfortable. Grey needed to see her sitting next to Red, and she needed to be okay with it. "What exactly is it that you're doing for Alexander?" she asked in a shadowy tone.

Grey nodded at Red. "It might be best if we don't speak of this here. Let's just say, I am gaining ground in ways he is not aware."

Red held his coffee cup in front of his mouth, hiding whatever truths she might have been able to read on his face. "He's right, Aly," Red said with a nod back at Grey. "We need to discuss what we came here for." He set his cup down. "You know of our predicament."

Grey didn't even need to nod. Of course, he had heard of the seed shipment. Spies were tasked with *knowing* information no one else knew. Aly rolled her eyes. She should have expected Grey would already know about the wheat.

"You believe someone sabotaged the wheat?" Grey asked, driving straight to the point.

Does he know who did it? "It had to be Alexander," Aly said.

Red, whose eyes had drifted out the window, snapped back to

the conversation. "We can't prove it," he said, "but who else had a reason? It was meant to feed the people of Mardon."

Grey recrossed his legs. "Yes, but there's much more at stake here than the mouths of the poor."

Unfortunately, that's how politics worked. Aly knew, from her station in the shadows behind a sovereign, that the lives of the people at the bottom rarely factored into decisions made. Red's decision to buy the wheat from Refere, and his disappointment when it failed had proven different—he really did want to feed those people. Her cheeks warmed at the thought.

Red grunted. "How could he do that, knowing so many people will go hungry this winter?"

"Like you pointed out, we don't know the culprit. If you pin it on who you *think* did it, you will never find the truth."

Truth. Grey was a spy. His truths were everyone else's secrets. She'd once thought secrets were tantamount to lies, but Ondorian had steered her straight. Hiding a truth didn't make it any less true.

"Regardless of *who* ruined that wheat, we have nothing to feed these people," she said.

"What do you require of me?" asked Grey, again steering straight to the point.

"We need food," answered Red. "We need to have it shipped here. We can't trust the trains. You have a ship."

Ever the statesman, Grey smiled and nodded. "Indeed, I do." The curl at the edges of his mouth told Aly he was hearing the words Red had implied in his statement: *We can trust your ship— we can trust you.*

"The wheat must arrive. You have a sorcerer."

Here, Aly cringed. Red's unspoken words were not subtle enough. He was king, and he should be able to ask directly for Grey to send his sorcerer to protect the shipment, but something about his lack of tact grated on Aly. This sorcerer they spoke of was a person too, with contracts to uphold, which to a sorcerer were as binding as the truth.

Grey steepled his fingers on his leg and fixed his easy smile on Red. "This is true. However, my ship is far from here, and my Protector is always with me."

"You can afford another one," Red stated matter-of-factly. "One we can trust."

Aly bit her lips and waited for Grey's response.

"I could," he said. "But finding one that would we can trust might be difficult in such a short amount of time. When will the wheat be ready? Will we again be purchasing from Refere?"

The money won't even be his if Red loses the crown. How would they pay Lordan back if he lost?

Red shifted his legs, his movements betraying his discomfort, unlike Grey, who was perfectly at ease. "We must speak with Lordan. We can purchase some of the first harvest and ship it here. We could have it here in about two months, before the cold sets in," he said, thinking aloud. "Can you ship it here in two months?"

Grey spent a long minute staring at his hands. "Yes. I believe my ship could be ready. However, that will be after the coronation."

Silence settled over them. If Red lost, Grey couldn't use his own ship to do Red's bidding. Grey was loyal to them now, but what would happen if Red became nothing more than an exile? One thing was certain, if Red lost the crown, Grey couldn't openly help them; he'd lose all credibility with Alexander, and Aly wasn't sure Grey would risk that.

"You could use someone else's ship," she offered, though it was more a challenge than a suggestion.

Grey steepled his fingers. "Indeed. I have many ships in my network that are not tied directly to me. They are, however, tied to some rather powerful individuals who would not enjoy discovering they had taken a side in this tug-of-war for the crown."

Red frowned, as if offended by the way Grey implied this battle for the nation was a trivial game.

"Can we find a sorcerer in time?" asked Aly. "There are some who are loyal to you," she said to Red, recalling that sorcerer she passed the night she'd come across the festering well-turned-city-dump.

Grey laughed, and the sound rattled Aly's nerves rather than mollified them. "I will do my best to find you a sorcerer we can trust; you have my word," he offered. "I will collect the crew myself, and I will ensure that they are ready to sail when the wheat has been purchased and delivered." In his words was the unspoken truth that the wheat wouldn't be harvested until after coronation.

He stood. Red and Aly followed. The men shook hands.

"However," Grey added, "you are aware of the increase of trouble on the seas?"

Red's arm paused as it fell back to his waist. "Trouble?"

"Due to present circumstances, I have not been able to inform you of everything as I normally would." Grey offered a small bow. "My apologies, Your Majesty."

Aly braced for the Grey's news.

"To be brief," Grey said with a sigh, "the sailors described it like a dragon in the water."

Aly's skin tingled with dread. Memories of the dark shape in Vona's waters haunted her. It had not been an anomaly, then.

"Dragons aren't real," said Red.

"At one point, foxbloods weren't either," Grey countered.

If the entire ocean became corrupted, how could they possibly stop the evil of the Deep? If it was polluting the oceans of the world, no one would be safe. There was no way they could fight that.

Red leaned back and pressed the palms of his hands to his tired eyes.

"What are these beasts doing?" Aly finally asked.

"Attacking ships."

She groaned. "All ships?"

Grey chuckled, but it was a note devoid of humor. "In truth, mostly Tanderan ships. We can't figure out if it's simply because the beasts live closer to our ports than anyone else's, or if there's more at play." Grey tousled his hair, something he did to distract others from the present conversation.

She wondered if he was trying to distract her or Red and why. Everything he did had a purpose, premeditated and perfectly executed. He did not flounder.

"One of my partners lost a good deal of money when one of his ships was attacked. The shipping industry is feeling the effects. People are too scared to ship through our waters. If this continues, there's nothing I can do. Crews will refuse to sail."

Red tugged at his waistcoat. He shifted his weight back and forth like an impatient child.

She placed a hand on his upper arm and could feel Grey's eyes on her fingers. "It'll be all right," she said.

"If the seas cannot be contained, these beasts quieted, we will see great distress in Tandera. In fact, the entire continent will feel it." Grey's words pressed on them, cutting off hope.

She frowned at him.

"How could Alexander be behind these sea monsters?" Red asked.

"I'm not sure he is," Grey answered. "This seems far beyond his reach. He cannot control the waters of the seas."

Red gazed at the shifting shadows beside the window. "I wouldn't put anything past that man."

"We will proceed, Your Majesty. I will secure a crew and a sorcerer and a ship. I will do everything in my power to help you in this matter." He slapped a hand on Red's shoulder, a bold move, but one that showed he wasn't afraid to be friendly with his sovereign. Red's expression tightened, then he nodded. "We will speak again when the ship is ready. Until then, we should limit our communication. Now, my family will combust if I do not introduce you two." He smiled his winning smile.

Red quirked his brow. "Do they not care about Alexander's threats?"

Grey chuckled. "They are more concerned with having something gossip-worthy to discuss at their next dinner party. They'll suffer whatever Alexander throws their way, when he finds out you visited." He winked. "I'll tell him you came to visit me, but that I refused to help you. He'll pretend to believe me because he'll have no evidence to the contrary."

Just then, Aly's mind detected movement at the house where the sole Protector lurked. "Grey, who lives in the house two doors down?"

Grey paused. "It is Lord Nock's home, but he is not there. He spends most of his time at the palace these days."

"His Protector is home."

Grey stiffened. "Ah, I see. And you're worried he's detected you two? Perhaps I'll have Antony run some interference?"

"Antony?" asked Aly.

"My Protector." He flashed a smile and left the room.

15

RED

Red downed the rest of his now-cold coffee as Grey left to retrieve his mother and sisters. Red couldn't shake the feeling that Grey was toying with them; a spy who worked both sides of the game was not one he could fully trust, despite the fact that Grey had been nothing but kind to them.

Aly wiggled both brows at his empty coffee cup, like she could read his discomfort.

"Thirsty," he said, shrugging.

"If by thirsty you mean nervous," she retorted.

He gave a weak laugh. "Why would I be nervous?"

"Grey makes you act weird." He snorted at her words. She raised a hand, as if to touch his shoulder, but let it fall back to her side. "It's good he will help us."

Red nodded. "Yes."

Footsteps sounded in the hall, and Red straightened, tugging his waistcoat down. "We're not even properly clean."

"Don't worry about that," Aly whispered. "You're still a king."

Around the corner came Grey, followed by three women. The oldest was nothing short of elegance, her gray hair swept on top of her head in a massive pile. Jewels sparkled from every possible place, but they were not overly large like Queen Kassia's. They were all emeralds. The two younger women could hardly contain their giggles beneath flickering smiles. Both women had blond hair and paler complexions than their brother. They wore enough rouge to act as circus clowns. *No, they're blushing,* Red realized.

The women curtsied in unison. Red bowed politely.

"Your Majesty, you've met my mother, Lady Grey. And my sisters, Juliette and Madeline."

The younger women giggled in earnest now. Red tried not to sigh. They were both older than him by several years, as both were older than Grey, but he'd had women twice his age throw eyes at him at palace events. Power had a way of changing the rules of attraction. The oldest of Grey's sisters was already married, but she spent as much time with her unwed sister and widowed mother as possible, according to court gossip. Red never really cared for gossip, but Seb loved it, and Red had found that being crown prince—and now king—meant everyone's lives were, to some extent, his business.

"Pleased to see you," he said, his voice a little flat. He'd met them all at court, but not in such an intimate gathering.

As the women were executing curtsies, Aly touched the back of his shoe with her toe; a tiny gesture, and one hopefully no one else noticed, but Red didn't miss it. *Make them like you, remember?* She said to his mind.

He cleared his throat and flicked through discussion topics like playing cards. Everything he thought of—court, the latest ball, even the theater—highlighted the fact that he was no longer living in the palace, directing high society like a conductor. Since it was customary for the others in the room to wait for the king to drive the conversation, and he had remained silent long enough that he was edging toward rude, he finally burst out with, "Your home is lovely."

C. F. E. BLACK

Beside him, Aly tried to hide her visible deflation by fiddling with her skirt.

Lady Grey cooed with delight but did not offer any substance to the conversation.

Aly chimed in, rather boldly, "Lord Grey misses out on all the fun, doesn't he?"

The sisters exchanged a look and covered more giggles. Juliette said, "He's too boring for court."

Lady Grey eyed Aly with a slim mouth. The rules of decorum said that no one drove the conversation but the king. Aly of course knew this, which meant she had a reason for stepping out of bounds to steer the conversation. Red decided to go with the chosen topic.

"I do not blame him. Court can be tiresome," Red said.

Lady Grey sniffed. "Are you pleased to be away from it?"

Aly's mouth fell open, gaping so wide that Red could see it out of the corner of his eye. Perhaps she hadn't intended this turn of their discussion.

Red leveled a hard gaze at Lady Grey. Two could play the game of subtle jabs. He opened his mouth with a retort, but Aly's words rang in his mind. For once, he stilled his angry remark and said instead, "In truth, the break has been refreshing, but we plan to return as soon as possible, Lady Grey."

He'd said *we*. It had rolled off his tongue as naturally as water rolled downhill.

The Grey women tensed at the word, all three of them pinging their gaze between their king and his sorcerer. The rumors of their relationship, fueled by his own sister's words, had clearly tainted their opinion of Red and Aly.

Despite his efforts to be peaceable, he'd stepped in the very hole he should have seen coming and avoided.

An awkward silence filled the room. Aly couldn't bail him out of this one. Fortunately, Grey did.

"Mother, why don't we let the king and his sorcerer return to their business? We've taken up enough of their time."

The three women curtsied. Lady Grey's eyes were unforgiving when she looked up again. "What business is that, exactly?" Lady Grey asked, brazen as a bull.

Red was finished being polite. "Reclaiming my crown from that usurper."

Grey's sisters gasped. Lady Grey tilted her head, examining Red. "Very good. I was wondering if you had any spine in you."

Now it was Red's turn to balk. He recovered quickly, but her words shook him to the core.

"Mother, that was uncalled for," Grey muttered, trying to usher her toward the door.

"No, I want this young man to hear what I have to say. I support Lord Alexander because of what he has told me about you, Your Majesty. I would like to see it disproved." Grey nearly shoved his mother away, but she added, "You may be rash, like they all say, but in my opinion, rash is fine as long as it is also courageous. Unhand me, son." She stepped out of Grey's restraining reach. "If you believe Alexander to be a usurper, I expect you to at the very least *fight* for what you believe in. A king who is engaged in—" she eyed Aly, "—secret relations, that I do not mind, but who wants a king without convictions?"

Blindsided by her remarks, Red watched in stupor as she curtsied again and walked out of the room, followed by her daughters. With a rare apologetic look on his face, Grey shook his head, then bowed and silently left the room.

Red couldn't face Aly.

He couldn't face himself.

A minute later, he still stared at the door where Lady Grey had disappeared.

"Red," Aly whispered from behind him.

For another minute, he said nothing. *Any spine in you.* Her words carved him like a butcher's blade.

"Can we please not speak of this?" he asked, too embarrassed to turn to her. He strode toward the door, ready to be free of this place.

She followed, but he'd wager she was not content to remain silent about this.

Sure enough, as soon as they stepped out into the overcast morning, she said, "I think it was *good*, what she said."

He stopped so suddenly Aly knocked into him. She left one hand on his arm and stepped around him. Down the road, they could see a tree had fallen, blocking the way of two carriages, where a figure in a white cloak was now attempting to clear the way. She absently wondered if this was Grey's Protector's doing.

"She *wanted* to provoke you. You rose to the occasion."

"You make me sound childish." He rolled his shoulder.

She removed her hand. "That's not what I meant," Aly replied, lowering her voice. "You showed her you're not to be trifled with." She leaned forward. "That's the kind of king Lady Grey wants."

He shook his head, unable to accept that their conversation had gone well. "What she said about you…" He finally met her gaze. "I don't want people thinking that about you."

"Who cares what people think about me? It's *you* they need to like. It's your head on which the crown will fall at summer's end, not mine," Aly snapped, a note of exasperation in her tone.

Red blinked in confusion at the edge in her voice, but before he could think of what to say, she whirled around and stared down the road at the tree now being lifted out of the way with magic.

She added, "It's your leadership they want to see. What I do doesn't matter."

His freckled cheeks blazed with embarrassment. He'd been a fool not to see it before. Aly thought her actions didn't matter. He'd asked her not to win the crown back for him with magic, but that didn't mean he felt her presence was irrelevant or unnecessary. She was the power behind his authority, the steady hand that led him forward, the sensible one when his hot head lost sight of reason. It was her influence as much as anything that would help him win the crown at summer's end.

If the world had been a perfect place, he would have leaned down and kissed her, but at that moment, a carriage burst toward them from where it had been delayed due to the fallen tree. Rain began to patter their heads.

"Time to run," Aly said.

Red woke at dawn to the smell of smoke. Not the pleasing scent of a fire that warmed hands or cooked a pot of stew, but the acrid twang of a fire that destroyed.

He sat up from the hard floor with a jolt. Aly was already squatting by the window, her head craning to the left. They had spent the night in an attic of a wealthy man's house, a man they'd discerned was at a ball and wouldn't return until after midnight. They'd planned to sneak out early in the morning under her shroud.

The attic had been stifling hot but, thanks to Aly's magic, not uncomfortable as they slept, separated this time by two forgotten, old doors that acted as a neat little wall. He hadn't kissed her again, given their confined quarters, unsure if he could handle the way it tortured his mind. One day, perhaps when he was certain of his future, he would take steps to ensure that sharing quarters with Aly was proper and acceptable, in every sense.

That thought ignited his pale skin with another furious, telling blush, and he tried to tear his mind away from those wishful musings as he crawled to the window and kneeled next to Aly. There wasn't enough room to stand other than in the very center. The slim dormers afforded barely enough room for them both to peer out at the city. Aly squeezed over to allow him room, but he still had to press his shoulder against hers. He tried not to let his mind focus on this as he searched out the source of the smoke.

"There," she declared, pointing at the plume drifting over Mardon.

"What district is that?" he asked.

"I think it's the Creaks."

Red's pulse quickened. *Another one?* The Creaks had been battling fires all summer, despite the fact that fewer people lit fires during the warm months. He scooted backward, his body scraping against Aly's. She also squirmed out of the small space and scrambled to put on her shoes.

As he was tying his own shoes, he did a surreptitious sniff of his armpit and recoiled in disgust. He had never before smelled this bad. Self-conscious of how close he'd just been to Aly, he wondered if she had been repelled by his scent.

He recalled his visit to the Creaks two weeks ago, when he had first spoken with the farmers. He had smelled their poverty, and he had hated it. As a member of the royal family, he'd never understood what it was like to be unclean. Now, his skin had a greasy film to it. Aly's magic was adept at removing dirt but not as good as a proper bath. While he longed for a good scrub and clean clothes, they could no longer return to any of Grey's properties, as Alexander had heard of their visit to Lady Grey's and, true to Grey's prediction, had doled out a petty punishment under the assumption that the women were not at fault. However, in response to hearing of Red's continued stay in Mardon, and maybe in embarrassment at his exposed failure to chase off Red, Alexander had amplified his original threat of jail time to a threat of public flogging should anyone be caught aiding the former king.

So, for cleaning, their options were limited, unless they could find a tavern that would still let them rooms given the new threats from the palace. The wash houses of Mardon were filthy, smelly places Red was loath to visit. His opinion of them, however, was starting to soften.

Across the small space, Aly examined the ends of her unclean hair. It was strange spending so much time with her in close quarters. There was nothing romantic about it. Though at a different time in a different life, staying in places like this with Aly would have meant another thing entirely.

He couldn't think of that now; it didn't matter. All that mattered was securing the crown and the country and his future back from Alexander.

They were soon on their way through the busy streets of Mardon. It was market day. They avoided the main square with its carts and kiosks and livestock auction.

Even in this part of town, people spoke of the fire. Bits and pieces of the news fluttered to their ears. *Another fire in the Creaks. Tenant house. Six dead.*

"Six," Red whispered from the secrecy of their shroud.

Aly frowned. "Those people...they already have nothing," she said.

They turned down a street with smaller, less elaborate homes. As they neared the Creaks, the streets began to pile up with manure, the smell noxious in the summer heat. "Are there really are not enough people to keep these streets clean?" asked Red as he stepped over a particularly large pile left behind by what must have been a draft horse.

Red soon spotted the fire engine, pulled by two enormous horses. The large tank sat outside the smoldering building, the blackened windows indicative of the terror that had taken place. They stared up at the building, along with the crowd that had gathered.

Aly closed her eyes, and without any command from him, lifted her hands toward the rising smoke. She uttered a few words of the *Verad*, shaping her magic, as always, by the truths set down by Theod centuries ago. He watched for signs of her magic. Squinting, he noticed droplets of mist rushing toward the building. Within minutes, the fire had ceased.

When she was finished, she opened her eyes. The firemen whooped, calling out that the flames had finally stopped.

People huddled in the streets, and men ran with sloshing buckets toward the smoldering building. Mothers held crying children.

"Where will these people go?" he asked Aly as they stood under her shroud. No one knew she'd stopped the fire.

"There aren't very many tenant houses left with vacancies. Mardon is bursting at the seams. There's nowhere for them to go unless they leave the city."

"Why don't they leave then?"

She shrugged. "People are afraid to leave. This is their home. This is where their livelihood is."

"People dislike change," he said, including himself in this. An idea struck him. "Lower the shroud."

She balked, but instantly the sounds of the scene crashed in on them. People shot surprised glances at them.

"Oy! Tha's the king!"

Red steeled himself as all manner of comments hurled his way. When the people saw his face hadn't changed, they quieted. "Who will rebuild this home?" he asked. "And where will the people live until then?"

Faces turned to one another, no one bold enough to answer.

One woman stepped forward, a child on her hip. She was smeared with soot from falling ash. "There ain't no wood. My husband works at the lumber yard, and he says there ain't no wood in Mardon left. No one goin' to rebuild. We goin' to have find somewhere else."

A few people yelled their disgruntled agreement. *No wood?* This was the second time he'd heard that, though he found it hard to believe.

"I will see to it that wood is provided for this building," Red announced. With a swift bow, he turned away from the angry crowd. No one here seemed pleased with his word.

As they wandered back through the streets, uncertain how he'd fulfill this latest promise, he looked over at Aly, eager to think of something other than the city crumbling around him. "Tell me about Kitrel," he said.

She sighed. "You don't want to hear about it."

"Yes, I do. I don't know anything about you. Well, not about your past." He knew the way she muttered in her sleep—a fact that made his ears hot—and the way she could sense a person's emotional state merely from the twitch of an eye. He admired her stamina for living under her shroud, invisible to all save the king, as long as she had. Now that he'd spent so much time walking the city under her shroud, he felt the dismal weight of not being seen. That no one looked at them as they passed had been refreshing at first, but it had already started to drag on his self-worth. How she remained so strong despite being nonexistent, and therefore not missed, by nearly everyone in the world, he could only wonder.

She pursed her lips. "Very well. I'll summarize." She hurried her pace as she spoke. "My mother, Renna, fled here with me when I was born. She wanted to be far away from the Canyon and far away from those who wielded magic. I think she assumed that I was magical, but she didn't know for sure until I was five years old."

"Five? Is that when you first showed your magic?"

Aly made a strange grunt in her throat. "It's...difficult when you're younger. You can see the Truthwells, but you don't know everyone else can't. I think I mentioned them to Renna, but she wasn't quite sure what I meant. I wanted to know what the light and shadows were, and why she wasn't as bright as some others."

"Your mother's Well wasn't bright?"

"Oh, she was a wonderful person—" her voice hitched, "—

but she believed many lies about magic. She had to deal with some horrible things in life." Her voice dropped, and her shoulders settled.

Red nodded at this, walking with his hands clasped behind his back. "Keep going, if you don't mind."

She inhaled and continued, "My mother knew Dimitri would find me one day. She had been smart to protect me, but at the same time I hated it. I never really understood, and I held it against her. I shouldn't have. I should never have—"

Red wrapped an arm around her shoulder and pulled her sideways. Though strong, Aly's worst enemy, at times, was herself. She exhaled and didn't pull away for a few steps.

This was why she resisted talking about her childhood. He shouldn't have pushed her. His ideas of country life were possibly misguided and idealistic. She'd been poor, sheltered, and hidden away from the world, feared by her own mother. He tilted his head and pressed his lips against her hair. How had she become this powerful woman? This king's armor?

She stumbled; only his arm around her kept her from falling. Her eyes were round when she peered up at him.

"We need to see about the lumber," he said. "But first, I need a bath. And don't say Grey's," he added with a playful shove.

She pushed him back. "Alexander has threatened everyone." She pulled one corner of her mouth into a grin. "But there's one person who won't care about that."

He smiled. "Seb."

"But he's still at the palace, isn't he?"

Red shook his head. "He often spends weekends at his father's second home on the river."

Aly's face fell. "He might be punished by Alexander for helping us."

Grinding his jaw, Red stopped a moment. If he continued toward Seb's family's home, he was endangering them all. *Not if I win the crown*, he thought, turning toward the river.

16

ELISE

The grand homes of Preston Street stood before Elise. A noblewoman named Rebecca Van Hule waved goodbye to the former princesses from her doorway as a dozen other women emptied into the sunlit street to a line of waiting carriages. The party in honor of the noblewoman's daughter's recent engagement to a Viriennese earl had left Elise with sore cheeks from too much forced smiling and a stomach full of petite fours.

"Her desserts were exceptional, don't you think?" Carolyn exclaimed, hooking her arm through her sister's. She waved at their carriage driver and pulled Elise down the sidewalk. "Let's take a walk before we return to the castle."

The street burst with pink roses and orange zinnias, and a steady breeze nudged the leaves and the banners flying atop many of the gates. Carolyn broke away and twirled down the lane, arms wide. She always had a flare for the dramatic, but now that she'd met Edward, she was plain ridiculous.

"It's hot," Elsie complained.

Carriages trundled over the cobblestones as guests left the party, their occupants lazing out of open windows in hope of a breeze. Elise's gloves itched with sweat, but a lady didn't take them off while on the streets. She was glad they were still invited to society functions. Until the crown was settled on Alexander's head at coronation, the nobles of Mardon weren't ready to offend anyone who might still be a member of the royal family.

Carolyn grabbed her skirts and skipped, her golden hair flashing noticeably redder in the sun. "Seb is at home. Look." She pointed at a banner flapping in the breeze.

"Or his father is home."

"The Chancellor is in Esvedara or wherever." Carolyn waved a hand. "I heard Seb mention it last week." Now that Carolyn was preoccupied with Edward, her time constructing contraptions of destruction with Seb had waned. The trebuchet they'd built had been wheeled away somewhere.

The Chancellor of Trade often traveled for long periods, but his wayward son used the large riverfront home on weekends as a place for...whatever repulsive activities he participated in when unsupervised.

Elise rolled her eyes. "I hope none of the women from the party see him in an upstairs window. Any one of them would be sucked in by his mysterious ways and come back a ruined woman."

Carolyn covered a shocked laugh. "You talk like he's a harpy."

"That's a perfect description. The male harpy."

They shared a laugh. Then Carolyn added, "Let's say hello. I've never seen his father's home."

"Carolyn," Elise warned, "women who enter there toss their reputation to the dirt."

"Don't be ridiculous. He isn't as bad as you say. He hasn't even *kissed* that many women."

"And you know this how?"

Carolyn tossed her hair. "I asked him once. Women say bad things about him only after he moves on from them." Elise *humphed.* "He's Red's best friend. He's not a bad person. Plus, I saw you laughing with him the other night at the ball."

Elise mumbled under her breath, hurrying to catch up with Carolyn, who was skipping ahead.

One of Chancellor Thorin's massive oak front doors was already open. Cool air whooshed out of the house onto Elise's face. "Odd," she noted.

"Seb!" Carolyn called through the small opening.

They could hear voices. One of them was definitely Seb, cackling with laughter.

"Come on." Carolyn pushed her way inside, despite Elise's protests.

No butler appeared. Carolyn had a look of pure glee on her face, as if they were breaking into the national museum or the vault that held the crown jewels.

The voices originated from upstairs. Carolyn began ascending when suddenly the voices stopped. Elise hissed at her sister that they should leave.

"Carolyn?"

Seb stood at the top of the stairs, shirtless. Both women gasped.

"I knew it," muttered Elise, disgusted, as she bolted for the door.

"Wait!" Seb bounced down the stairs, a huge smile on his face. "What a coincidence," he said, lifting a hand. "Your brother just arrived."

Elise stopped, one hand on the door. Behind her, Carolyn yelped in delight.

"Red! What's he doing here?" asked Carolyn.

"He, uh, needed some clothes." Chuckling, Seb rubbed the back of his neck in a way that made his chest and abdomen entirely too visible. Elise looked away. "Come on up." Seb slapped his hand on the banister. "So sorry, ladies, I don't usually receive guests this way."

Elise frowned. "Why are you not dressed?" She followed her sister and Seb up the dark wooden stairs. Her eyes traveled along the portraits lining the way.

"Turns out our great king, who is now homeless, needs a style update. Before I head back to the palace, I wash everything, so all my clothes are down with Miss Graves right now. I gave him the one I had on." He turned around and whispered as if his words contained state secrets, "That way, no one will have to see him and turn my family in to Alexander."

"Convenient," Elise grumbled to herself as they arrived at an upstairs room.

The windows let in bright sunlight, casting Red in a golden glow. He wore a baggy white shirt and was busy fastening the buttons at his wrists.

"Sisters!" he exclaimed, rushing toward them. He embraced Carolyn and the two rocked back and forth a moment.

Elise cleared her throat. "Alexander will hear about this," she said. She had to play her role. *Red's not the right man for the throne,* she told herself, trying out the lie she'd been parading about in the palace. Somehow, while among Alexander's men, when her mind was set on becoming a world-class informant, the lie tasted less wretched, but while facing her brother, the lie not only soured in her mind, it crumbled like old wax. But if she played this part well enough, Grey would allow her to collect information on Lordan.

Seb laughed, "Not if you don't tell him." He plopped down on a settee, kicked his legs up. He was indecent and clearly did not care. In fact, Elise could have sworn he was enjoying displaying his physique to the women in the room.

"Where's Aly?" asked Elise, glancing around. Double doors opened onto a small balcony, allowing the breeze into the room. The house was cooled by magic, but the fresh air was welcome.

"She'll be up soon," Seb answered cryptically. "The two of them smelled worse than horse manure on a hot day."

Elise made a disgusted face, which only seemed to delight Seb even more.

The door opened and Aly slipped in, a surprised smile on her face. "Hello, Elise. Carolyn." She offered an abrupt curtsey and moved along the wall toward a window, always hanging on the fringes of a group, like a decorative tassel. Her hair was voluminous and curlier than Elise remembered it. Red's hair was still wet.

Where had they been bathing? Elise hadn't even thought about her brother's living conditions these past weeks. He was simply not around, that was all. She had been too busy collecting whatever scraps of information she could on the nobles, trying to discern where their loyalties lay, or any other tidbits that might prove useful.

Her heart sank. Red was truly homeless. He and Aly had come here when they had nowhere else to go.

"Why do you need clothes?" asked Carolyn, taking a seat on a couch.

Red coughed. Or possibly it was a laugh. He looked thinner. "I'm going to try to get a job at the lumber yard."

"No way!" Carolyn leaned forward.

Elise sat beside her sister, annoyed that the arrangement put Seb right in front of them.

"Or rather, I want to look like a man in search of work. I need to speak with the lumberjacks about the wood shortage. I figure they will speak directly and truthfully with a...with someone more like themselves." He glanced at Aly.

Seb hopped up. "And I said he could ruin whatever clothes he needed." He walked over to Aly and accepted something from her. Within seconds, a shirt tumbled down over his head.

Finally, Elise thought. She suddenly feared he might offer Red his pants.

"Thanks," Seb said, picking at the fabric until it hung to his liking. "No one saw you nab it from the laundry?" He waved off her response. "It was a joke. Hey, did you find what you needed?"

Aly nodded. "Thank you."

Elise noticed now that Aly wore a commoner's dress. A dull blue with no lace or pattern or extra petticoats. It was becoming on her small frame, but nothing about it spoke of life in the palace. She must have borrowed that too.

Carolyn rubbed her hands together. "You want those men to think of you as one of them?" She covered a chuckle. "You can't. You talk differently, you walk differently. You probably even sneeze differently."

"She has a point," Seb said with a wink at Carolyn. "Dressing like a lumberjack doesn't make you one." He clapped his hands. "Let's practice!"

They spent the next agonizing half hour attempting to teach Red to slump, shuffle his feet, and draw out his vowels. Elise busied herself with a copy of famous poems lying on the table by the couch.

After hearing Red's awful pronunciation of *wood* one more time, Elise snapped the book closed. "Carolyn, our driver is likely getting worried that we have been sullied." *Which my intelligence has been by this buffoonery.*

"All right, all right. But when will we see you again?" Carolyn asked Red.

He glanced at Seb and Aly. "I'm glad I saw you today, but I can't risk being seen about town. Alexander has promised harm to those who help me."

"We could meet here again," she offered.

"I've put Seb's family in enough risk coming here today," Red countered. "I won't do so again."

"Coronation is still a few weeks away, brother. If you go that long without another proper bath, *no one* will want you as their king. Not even me."

Red smiled, but it didn't reach his eyes. He was worried. On his face swam the possibility that he would fail.

If he did fail, Elise had to win Alexander's favor or else she'd lose her status and with it any possibility of being stationed in Vona's court; spy or not, no commoner would be allowed anywhere near the King of Refere. Her desire for revenge would die with her noble status if she were cast to the streets.

There was one step she could take to secure her favor with Lord Alexander. The notion struck her so hard she wavered, bending to place the book on the table as a way to cover her unease. When she straightened, she'd made up her mind.

Another spy in the Referen court could prove most useful for Tandera, so what she was attempting would eventually *serve* her brother. Nevertheless, she couldn't look at her brother as she spoke, so her eyes fell on Seb. This would hurt him too—perhaps him most of all.

"You're right, brother. Anyone who helps you will be punished." Her tone darkened, and Seb's eyes widened. "It really was a risk to come here today."

Red stepped toward her. "Elise?"

She gathered the courage to face her brother. To be a proper spy, one must deceive even those held most dear. He had to believe this ruse as well. So much the better, but inside, her stomach knotted. "Oh, surely you aren't worried I will betray the man who forced me away from Lordan?"

"Forced you away? Elise, he let you down, and you know it." Red gaped at her.

Aly's hands moved to cover her mouth. A last look at Seb prickled Elise's skin. He sank onto the settee, face in his hands.

I'm sorry, she thought, looking at Seb. *For a moment there, I thought we might be friends.*

She turned, marched out of the room, and began rehearsing in her head the words that would bring ruin on Sebastian Thorin's family.

17

RED

R ed had no waistcoat to tug, no jacket sleeves to fix. He fiddled with the loose hem of Seb's shirt, tucking it again for good measure. Then, with a grunt, he pulled some fabric out, reminding himself he needed to look comfortable in these clothes. He mussed his hair with both hands, his curls fresh and bouncy after his bath.

Maybe I shouldn't have bathed. Did he smell too much like a king? No, the bath had been necessary.

The clothes Seb had provided were mismatched so they neither looked like a noble's attire nor like typical commoner's garb. Seb had helped him rip a hole in the knee of his pants, and then Aly had patched it back together with a thread and a quick spell. She walked somewhere nearby, hidden under her shroud.

Elise's last words stuck to his mind like cold porridge. There was something odd at play. She had been angry when they'd left Refere, but he'd assumed it to be a passing storm. He *knew* Elise, and she was not one to betray family and friends. To turn Seb in for helping him was ominous.

"Can I help you?" asked a man with a day-old beard and a large belly. He hitched up his pants and walked across the dusty yard. Stacks of beams and planks of varying sizes lined two walls. A saw worked in a corner, the *switch-switch* sound indicating no magic was employed here.

Red furrowed his brow at the stacks of wood—a resource that didn't exist, according to the people he'd spoken to after the fire. "Looking for work," he answered, trying to stretch out the length of his vowels and clip the edge of his words, the way the poorer Mardonians did.

"Not much work here." The man grunted, as if this were common knowledge. "You new here?"

Already, Red had failed at being the poor Mardonian in need of work. A poor man would know the lumberyard was not hiring. "Yes," he said with a nod and what amounted to a grossly exaggerated sniff. He tried to squint his face and set his lips looser than his typically expression. He felt so incredibly stupid doing this. Everyone walking through the yard had stopped and now stared at him with hard jaws and narrow eyes, as if the very thought of another person wanting work might jeopardize their own jobs.

Forget this, Red thought, sweating under the pressure of their scrutiny.

He straightened his posture, not caring if it made him look like a king. The men here had decent posture and none of them hung about with their mouths open. "Aye, I'm new here."

The man scratched his neck. "Well, wherever you're from, sorry, but ain't no jobs here. We can't get enough lumber here to make nothing."

Red eyed the stacks of lumber. "Not enough?"

"Now don't get smart, lad." Red was amused the man called him *lad*. "That won't barely fix the wood that's been taken from us."

"Taken?"

"The fire! You really are new if you haven't heard of the fires this summer. The wood here wouldn't build a quarter of what's been lost."

"Really?" Red stared at the giant piles all around. He had no concept of how much lumber it took to build a tenant house. A home. A stable.

"Why did you come here, son?"

With a swallow, Red managed to keep the amusement off his face and hardened his expression to match the man's. "I need work." He shrugged. "After those fires, I figured you could use some help around here."

The man eyed him, tilting his head back and forth and re-hitching his pants. "Can you sling a hammer, lad?" The man stared at Red's thin arms.

"Aye," Red lied. He'd never done it, but how hard could it be?

"Yeah, bet you can," the man said with a laugh. "Right then. We can probably find something for you to do. Only problem is, we may not be able to find someone to pay you."

Red stopped as the man turned.

"Ah, yeah." The man wiped some sweat off of his face with the back of his hand. "Been a little tight around here."

"Who's paying for all this?" Red lifted a hand at the wood.

"Ah, that over there, that's for nobleman Fenmore's house. And that over there, well, it was claimed special by Lord Alexander."

"Alexander," Red snarled. His blood heated, but he reminded himself why he was here. This man believed Red was new in town. "Isn't he king?" The words hurt as they climbed out of his throat, but he wanted to see the man's reaction.

The man scratched his chin. "Eh, not king, just a man in a palace with a bunch of money. Sits on a throne, wears a crown, but no king."

Red's mouth curled into a smile. "What about the young king, the one who was there before? I heard something about it."

The large man shook his head, removing his hat to resettle it. "King Frederick, he up and disappeared, didn't he? Tossing coward." Red's entire body stiffened. "Nothing like his father. Say, you look a bit like him. Red hair," the man said, pointing.

Red ground his teeth, fists at his sides. He was increasingly unable to control his body language. His shoulders shifted back and his knees drew together.

The man squinted at him. "You looking like you're ready for a fight, boy. Remember you came here wanting help from me? You best watch yourself." The man breathed deeply, appeared to recover himself, and said, "Now, what's it gonna be? Do you like to work? Might be for free for a while, but stick around and you'll eventually get paid."

"Nobody works for free," Red said, trying to keep his voice from shaking with frustration.

"You sure ain't been here long, have you? You work for the promise of pay. The noblemen who run this city will pay you in time. Most of them are good on their word, at least on the whole. That Alexander will be good on his word to pay, deep as his pockets run. Granted, he's got his fingers in the country's treasury now." The man chuckled. "Guess he won't never run out of money now, eh? Good thing, since he's paying for all of his friends' houses and not the tenant houses that have burned to the ground. Shows you where his priorities lie."

The man had begun to ramble. His eyes drifted around the lumberyard. Gevar had told Red that when men ramble, they were often covering something up or trying to share a truth they weren't comfortable with. If Red was inferring this man's comments correctly, he was trying to say he wasn't in support of the man now claiming authority over him, the man with the ability to pay him or not pay him. It was a bold admission.

Red's mouth quirked up. He made a choice and ran with it. Rash? Maybe. He had to hope his quick decisions weren't all bad. Letting his voice slide back to his crisp, well-educated natural rhythm, he said, "What if we could rebuild everything that burned, and more?"

The man blinked. "We? Who are you to be talking like you own the city?" He looked up and down Red's stiff, kingly posture. The man's eyes widened. "Know how I said you looked a little bit like—" The man took off his hat, slid it down one side of his face and gripped it in his hands in front of his waist. "M-maybe I was a little quick to speak there, sir," he said, his brows lifting like two black caterpillars.

Red stared with satisfaction at the man. Should he reveal himself or let the man question? He had five weeks left before coronation. The city needed him. The country needed him. To secure the crown, he needed to act. That meant making decisions, some of them in a split-second. Taking the crown back from Alexander wouldn't come without risk, without betting all he had on his own success. He inhaled, a fleeting thought of what Aly would say passed through his mind. "I would like to rebuild the tenant houses." The man's eyes grew to a disturbing size. "Where can we buy the wood? I will pay for it," he said, with all the kingly authority he'd learned from watching his father. *That is, if I win the crown.* If he lost, here was yet another debt he would not be able to pay.

The man dropped his hat. With a glance at it, he chose to ignore it and instead saluted Red with the wrong hand. "Sorry, sir, but there ain't no wood. We can't work fast enough to cut the trees down and bring them here."

"What do you mean?"

"We only...we just can't get no wood. The ships, they're sinking 'fore they can get here."

Red worked his mouth. "I am aware of the problems at sea. However, we should not have to ship wood. There are forests all around us."

Shaking his head, the man said, "The workers won't go to the forest, what with the beasts and the bands of rogues. *Sire,*" he added apologetically. The man's voice had begun to shake. How quickly he had changed when he'd learned Red's true identity. This man was still loyal to the throne—or at least intimidated by it.

Red tried to relax his shoulders a little bit, to show the man that he could speak to him without fear. He mulled over the man's words. *Beasts.* The cases of foxblood and woodwolf sightings—and killings—were increasing. The man mentioned the rogues, or, as most people called them, the Zealots.

"What is the closest forest without a band of Zealots?" he asked.

While Red was thinking, the man had scooped up his hat and was attempting to brush off the dry dirt. "Every forest 'tween here and Refere has 'em." Red found that hard to believe, but this man clearly believed it. "Always a band of those rogues, sire. And the more trees, the more beasts can hide. Nobody wants to go in them woods."

Red hadn't thought of this. He'd not realized the ramifications of pushing aside Kassia. She'd been a threat and a menace, but without her, things were decidedly worse. The Canyon had to be contained, and Tandera's forces were only weakening as its military languished under a poor leader who cared more about the opulence of his private parties than the security of his own borders. "You are saying people are too afraid to cut down trees?" He rubbed his neck, no longer worried about his own decorum. "Our city does not have enough wood here to house its people, right, sir?"

The man trembled at the king's respectful address. "Your Highness, er, what am I supposed to call you, boy?" Appalled at his own slip, he glanced down at the crushed hat in his hands. "I apologize, Majesty; I called you boy. Again."

Red couldn't help but laugh and relax a little. "It's okay. Call me whatever you please." Another bold choice, but he knew now that people called Alexander *majesty* as often as they did Red. He wanted this man to choose him as his king, not to feel forced to do so.

The man balked. "Really? I never heard no royal saying that."

"Do I look royal to you?"

Gaging Red's light tone, he smiled. "You look a heck of a lot better than I thought you did a minute ago, coming in here asking for work with that puppy look on your face and no clue what was what. Sorry, sir." Red lifted a hand to indicate he wasn't offended. "But you didn't come in here asking for no work. What did you come in here for?"

"To see how bad the situation was. I've seen the fires. I heard of the lumber shortage. I want to help," he said, lifting his chin. "I want to rebuild what Mardon has lost, starting with the buildings in the Creaks."

"You came *here* to learn about the shortage, sir?"

"I'm having to do things...a little bit more hands-on these days," Red said.

"I get you. I, er, Your Grace."

Red laughed again. He paused. "Call me Red, if you want to. That's what my friends and family call me."

The man crumpled the unfortunate hat once more. "Shoot, that's what the folks on the streets call you too, but I always thought it was 'cause of your hair." He smiled. "Red, is it?" His mouth twitched as he called the king by his first name. His entire stature shifted until the man appeared several inches taller, several inches thinner. "Well, Red, there was a lumberyard up in the Crescent Forest. Good trees, hardwood. But the workers all up and left after a band of those rogues attacked. They shut down that lumberyard and won't nobody go back."

"Are you saying we should reopen it?" Red asked.

"I'm saying there's some good wood up there, sir."

"What would it take to get that lumberyard up and running again?"

The man nodded, considering. "Why, it'd take some brave souls."

"Brave souls? What else? Money to entice them up there?"

"Don't nobody want to go work around those rogues. Money might do it, but it'd have to be a tossin' lot."

Red needed to find a way to rebuild Mardon, even if it meant chopping down trees himself. He wouldn't let the poorest of his people suffer the winter without homes. "If we can ensure safety and good wages, could we entice workers there?"

"I believe so, Your Majesty." He spoke louder now, as if to announce to the people that the king was in their presence. Some people took off their hats when they heard him.

"Very well. Tell me your name." He extended a hand to shake.

The man stared at it dumbly. "Johnson. Sir." He slapped his hand in Red's and shook, hard. "Amos Johnson."

"Amos, good to meet you. Thank you for the advice. I am going to see what I can do about that lumberyard in the Crescent Forest. If you can find me some willing workers, I will take them up there myself, and we will cut down the wood we need. We will make this happen. Before winter arrives, we will rebuild the Creaks."

"Sir, yes, sir!" He saluted Red again.

Red offered him a half bow and walked out of the lumber-yard, wondering about how in the world they would cut and transport enough wood from the Crescent Forest to Mardon in time to prove to his country that he was the right man to wear the crown.

They had five weeks.

∼

"The Crescent Forest is dangerous," Aly said again, staring at him from across a small table in a dim tavern south of the Creaks,

a tavern frequented by poor travelers and those with questionable reputations.

"What can you tell me about the sorcerers up there?" asked
Red. He slumped against the back of a wooden chair and nibbled
on a crust of bread, his attention on Aly's wet hair. Taking the
opportunity, she'd bathed again, for the second time today. He
didn't blame her. After the heat of this afternoon, he needed
another bath too. She looked even smaller with damp hair, and
she mesmerized him with the way she toyed with the tangles,
easing her fingers through them with small, mechanical tugs.

With a word, she expelled the remaining water from her hair,
leaving it voluminous and completely dry. He blinked in
surprise. A small smile crept over his face.

"What?"

A few crumbs fell from his lips. "You look beautiful."

"We were talking about the forest," she said, turning her face
away as she tried to hide a growing blush. "The Zealots know how
to Truthpull, but they don't really understand what they're doing.
They've never been taught the *Verad*." She shook her head and
crossed her arms. "If they knew the *Verad*, they would understand
that magic is meant to be *controlled*. It's not meant to be wild."

"Uncontrolled thought magic…sounds disastrous."

Aly nodded. "You have no idea." She stared at his bread
crumbs, then without an audible word, they disappeared in tiny
poufs. "I think that's why, originally, they started living in seclu-
sion. They were too dangerous. They would set things—and
people—on fire, open up holes in the floor, destroy people they
disliked by burying them under mounds of earth. Weird things
would happen around them." She shivered in disgust. "So they
just withdrew, thinking magic was meant to be that way, that it
was some sort of gift that set them apart."

Red rubbed his face, trying to remove the mental image of
being buried alive. "They missed the point of magic, then."

Aly eyed him. "Yes. They don't use it to serve others. They use magic to serve themselves."

"Not every sorcerer wields magic in humble service to others," Red muttered, thinking of Dimitri and whoever was helping Alexander. There were certainly sorcerers who did not adhere to the *Verad*—the Canyon was evidence. "Okay, so they live apart from society. If they don't want anyone near them, why didn't they leave the men at the lumberyard alone?"

"You really don't know much about them, do you?"

"Never really had any tutors who thought *studying the ways of lunatics* was all that helpful in the education of a future king." He leaned forward, elbows on the table.

The server brought out a round of foaming ale to a loud table that sat under the massive wooden chandelier. One man drank his entire tankard in one go.

These people weren't concerned about who would wear the crown at summer's end. They cared about the money in their pocket, the faces of their friends smiling back at them, and their families back at home. Red missed the easy life he'd led as a prince, when the world was carried around on a silver platter for him. Now, he had to bear it all on his own.

Aly waved at him, drawing his attention away from the boisterous table. Her lips pressed back an annoyed grin. "I'm no royal tutor, but if it were *my* job to choose the subjects of a future monarch, I'd most certainly include the study of all possible threats to my kingdom." Her words sank in, leaving Red with a growing sense of dread in his stomach. "There are plenty of books about them in the library."

"Not likely to get our hands on those any time soon," he grumbled, leaning back again in frustration.

"Right. Sorry. I'm sure there're books about them at the University Library, as well. I never had to visit there. I always studied at the palace. There was enough material there to keep me occupied." Her eyes glazed with a far-off look. "So many more books I haven't had the chance to read yet."

"You have a list," he said matter-of-factly. She was the curious type, never satisfied, a bit like Carolyn in that regard. *Carolyn.* He wished he could see his sisters again, to cypher out what Elise was up to. He hoped Seb wasn't receiving Alexander's punishment even now.

"It's extremely long," she said. "Pretty much every book in the library. I want to know all of it."

"Well, at least you'll live long enough to read them all."

Stillness fell over them both. Aly stared blankly at her hands clasped on the table. Red looked out the small window in the thick, stone wall.

Aly moved on first. "I assume the Zealots don't want the lumberyard there because they think of it as taking away part of their home."

Laughter and a drinking song burst forth from nearby.

Red shifted in his seat. "But they can't live in the entire forest. It's huge."

"They may not see it that way. Remember, they think of themselves as *holy*, in a way. They think of their magic as inherently good simply because it exists. They think that if something is accomplished with magic, it was Theod's will. It's very interesting."

Red picked at some remaining dirt under one of his fingernails. "Do you think we can do it?"

"I think we should try," Aly replied.

"Are you only saying that because we agreed you shouldn't interfere in all this?"

She leaned across the dented table. "I think it's a brilliant idea."

He offered her a thankful half-smile. "We should talk to the sorcerers there. See if we can't form an agreement to allow the lumberyard to reopen without threat from them."

Aly tilted her head as if about to disagree. Instead, she said, "It'll be dangerous."

"You can protect us."

"Yes, but if the whole forest full of Zealots finds out we're logging again, I can't protect us against a hundred wild sorcerers."

"You say it like they're animals."

Aly snorted. "Have you read the accounts of their magic?"

"No."

"I can tell you what I know. Though they live as recluses, they have a bit of an alliance among themselves. Not a community, per se, but an organization of individuals, spread out over this massive forest."

Red ran a hand through his clean hair. "But you're a sorcerer. You could talk to them. They'd respect you."

Now Aly laughed aloud. "I'm the kind they hate. Once they learn that I used to be poor and live as a recluse, sort of like them, and that I came here and I chose *this* life instead, they'll really hate me."

For several seconds, Red looked at her with lifted brows. "Did you ever consider joining them?"

She looked up at him, repulsion in her eyes. "No. They are the antithesis of what I believe a sorcerer should be."

"Very well. Just thought I'd check."

"Red, you know I'm with you, right?" she asked, reaching for his hand. With a twist of his palm, he linked fingers with her. She gripped tightly. "With you," she repeated.

"You're with the crown, Aly." *And if I'm not wearing it in five weeks, you won't be with me anymore.*

His words stung her. "I'm right here." She gave him a closed-lip smile, as if trying to prove her words were true and his were ill founded. If they weren't—if Alexander won the crown and she Bound herself to him—then all of this would become a lie.

And that lie would destroy him.

18

ALY

Midsummer heat engulfed the carriage as Aly's magic propelled them toward the looming trees of the Crescent Forest. The mosquitoes flocked like birds here. Aly had never seen anything like it. Her magic could push the bugs away with a breeze or evaporate their tiny frames, but these pests were relentless. Before she and Red even reached the tree line, she tired of the concentration necessary to propel the caravan, cool the inside of the carriages, and dispel the blood-sucking creatures. She chose to push the bugs back rather than keep them cool. Sweat wasn't as awful as a face full of mosquito bites.

The two dozen men they'd brought with them were nearly all cut from the same mold: young, able, and out of work. Seb was no exception, though he'd never actually had a job.

After Elise had turned him in, his father quickly distanced himself, claiming it was only his son who'd engaged in conspiracy, and that the family shouldn't be disgraced by the actions of a misguided youth. Seb was promptly kicked out of the palace, forbidden from returning to his father's properties, and given a stern warning that should he show himself in Mardon's streets again, he would face a public flogging.

He'd signed up the instant Red had mentioned the lumberyard at the Crescent Forest.

With any luck, Red, Seb, and their men would have the operation up and running soon. The coronation loomed on the calendar, and with each passing day, Aly's mind twisted into a tighter and tighter knot of worry.

The trees rose high and dark and thick, stretching over the land like a heavy quilt. The forest was rimmed with a fringe of flat tree stumps that added an eerie quality to the already menacing ambiance. In the air, the creak of tall trees and the scent of green leaves greeted the newcomers.

Seb had stolen three of his family's carriages, and the other two had been procured by the men. The remaining men who weren't in the carriages rode on horseback, which meant they had to travel at the gait that a horse could comfortably manage, despite Aly's ability to push the carriages much faster. It had been six days since they left Mardon, and the saddle-sore men began to cheer as they neared the lumber camp.

"There's someone here," Aly whispered to Red, her hand darting to his forearm.

Her mind searched out the mostly vacant space where the remains of the lumber camp could be seen from the road. The lone Truthwell burned with fierce light, the thin shadows within darting quickly as if trying to escape. She'd seen this pattern before many times—in Veeter Yin. She let out a long exhale.

"It's okay," she mouthed to Red, thankful Seb hadn't heard her earlier statement over the sound of the carriage bumping over rough terrain. "It's Yin."

Red's brows furrowed, but he looked eagerly out the carriage window. Even before they reached the camp, Yin rode out on a pale horse to meet them.

He pulled his mount up beside the still-moving carriage and offered a small bow from atop his saddle.

"Yin! What are you doing here?" asked Red.

"Your Majesty, it is good to see you. I refused to serve the usurper, and it has taken me this long to discover your whereabouts. You are good at hiding, sire." He looked past Red and nodded solemnly at Aly.

"How did you arrive before us?"

"It is easy for me to cut across country, and I ride faster than your carriages roll."

Red laughed. "Of course. I am happy to see you."

"I am happy to serve the rightful king, Your Majesty." With that, he allowed his horse to slow so the carriage could enter through the broken gate into the grassy yard of the former lumber camp.

Once they entered through the wooden gate, the men's cheers ceased.

Red frowned as he looked around. Aly, careful to extend her magical awareness as far out as she could, searched for threats with both her eyes and mind. The buildings were in pitiful condition. Doors left open. Windows broken. A fire had eaten away most of a roof on one building and scarred the ground, leaving only small, bright green weeds.

"Well, here we are," Red said with a sigh. He darted out into the hot sun.

Aly watched him as he greeted the men descending from carriages and hopping off saddles. His birthday was coming up; he would be nineteen. Still so young to be a king. She wondered if they would celebrate it in the lumberyard, or if they would be back in Mardon by then.

Alexander had heard of their outlandish goals to reestablish the lumberyard here. He'd made it clear, via an announcement to the entire city, that although he was willing to accept whatever resources the men could provide, the former king better not attempt to return to the city without any lumber.

To win the crown, Red had to succeed. This was his last chance.

And that meant Aly had to protect them, no matter what. They *had* to return with wood, and when they did, Red would be the savior of Mardon, the humble king willing to do anything to help his people, even the most destitute.

Aly snickered at the groaning and grunting of two dozen men as they stretched after a long journey. Red joined in, reaching for his toes, which surprised several of the older men and made a few of the younger ones laugh.

Aly walked forward in her white sorcerer's cloak and half phoenix mask. With Red fueling her magic, she closed her eyes and pressed her awareness farther into the forest. The Wells of the trees were beautiful: old, sparkling with the light of ancient truths. She smiled, despite the whine of a mosquito in her ear. To perform this bit of magic took all her concentration away from her other spells.

These men relied on her for protection. They knew they were walking into something dangerous. Stories from the disaster that had driven men from this place haunted their minds. Aly, however, was the only one capable of truly understanding the horrors of what could go wrong here. Magic—untamed—was hideous. To Truthpull without aim, without the *Verad* to guide the sorcerer, was to invite disaster.

She brushed past the Truthwells of the ancient trees, the new growth, the birds, the air itself, and finally encountered a Well that made her pause. A bursting, thriving, rushing Well—a river. Once her mind grasped what it was sensing, she pushed onward, outward. The forest was vast, and her mind began to grow hazy with the discovery of so many Wells.

Their light called to her, especially the river, with its ever-surging source of energy. She ignored it all, searching for something else.

Then she found it.

The bright, burning Well of a human.

Her eyes popped open. The men were picking their way around the camp, examining their new abode. Red stood watching her.

"Anything?"

She swallowed, closed her eyes again, and nuzzled her mind into the comfort of his Truthwell. When she again felt her feet on the ground and that her body was stable, she looked at Red. "Yes. There's a river that way. And over there, about a league," she pointed east, "is a sorcerer."

In the direction of her arm, a scar of stumps stretched off into the trees where small saplings reached for the sun. The forest was taking over again, reclaiming its right to this space. A large tree grew through the roof of one of the abandoned bunk houses—a feat considering the place was only abandoned five years ago, not long after she'd taken over as Royal Sorcerer from Augustus Penwater.

This Lumberyard had been productive once. Gevar had been able to strike a deal with the sorcerers here. If Gevar had been able to do it, then Red could too.

"Yin," Red called, waving him over. "What have you discovered here?"

Yin stared with his usual intensity, his voice low but firm as he said, "No threats. Only discarded personal items."

Aly followed Red to one of the wooden buildings. The glass was still intact, but the door was hanging open, as if people had fled and not bothered to close the door behind them. There were rusted saws in the middle of the yard, and grass grew in the places where feet had once fallen. Aly recast her protective spells over the entire group. She had promised them safe arrival at the camp and safety while here; she would uphold her end of the bargain. As long as they stayed within her shields, they would be safe. The two cooks began unloading the food and carting it off toward what had once been the kitchen hut.

Red stepped up to the building, then cast a glance towards her.

"It's okay," she said. "There's no one here."

Inside the building, there were two rows of bunk beds with wooden frames and thin mattresses. Aly pressed her hands against one of them. It crunched. "Hey," she said with a smile, "this is a step up from sleeping on the floor."

Red snorted, looking around the shadowy space. "What happened here?" He kicked through a dark pile on the floor, only to find a discarded pair of pants. "I heard about it, but I was young. I didn't care. I didn't know that I would ever have to come here."

With a thought, Aly lit the lamps in the building. "I can feel it," Aly said, aware now of something she'd missed when searching out Truthwells. "A trace of magic." She tried to pinpoint where it came from, but it was *everywhere*. Not a Well, but more like vestiges of a spell—one that left her skin tingling. She'd never felt magic like that before. She only ever felt the sources of magic. "Magic made these men leave."

Red nodded, a strange expression on his face. "What can you see?"

She shook her head. "Not see. Feel. It's strange. It's like there's still a spell at work here."

Red knocked into the edge of a bunk. "Anything harmful?"

He'd nearly died of a death curse; she couldn't blame him for being afraid of magic. "No. At least, I'm not sure yet."

"That's comforting."

"I'm here. I'll keep you safe."

After a moment, he nodded once. They poked around the bunk house, discovering both mold and mice.

"This is a journal," Aly said, lifting a small book.

"Interesting." Red stepped close to her, tilting his head to look at the text. "Handwriting is awful," he said.

Aly squinted at the text. "I think it says ... '*The distant screams have returned. The men are restless. We didn't cut trees yesterday, hoping the sounds would go away. But this morning, before we began sawing, they started again.*' That's it. That's the last thing that's written in here."

"That's not creepy at all," said Red, running a hand through his hair.

Aly closed the journal. "I think you should wear it." She nodded at his head. "I know you brought it."

Red sighed. "I know you do, but I want these men to feel comfortable around me."

"Yes, but they need a leader. You *are* trying to convince them that you should be their king." She propped one hand on her hip. "If you're their best friend right now, and then you place the crown on your head later, they will feel betrayed. Better that you befriend them with the crown on."

Her king stared down at her. He lifted a hand to her cheek and tilted his forehead down to meet hers. Heat blossomed up her entire body. For a moment her magic shields flickered as her mind focused completely on Red.

"No," she said, jerking away from his touch. "I'm sorry, but it distracts me. *You* distract me. And we need my magic to remain...focused."

He stiffened and took a step back. "I understand. Does this mean I shouldn't ever...?" He stuffed his hands in his pockets.

She wanted him to lean down and kiss her—she wanted it more than anything else; but if they all died in some catastrophic accident up here, then it wouldn't matter. She had to keep them safe, and the number of spells needed to protect this many people required that she keep at least part of her mind always focused on delivering magic to the appropriate spells. If she let the spells go, they would be at risk.

Red was waiting for an answer, for her to tell him it was okay to touch her, to be near her like this. She swallowed. The closer he got to her, the more she let him in, the harder it became for her to turn him away. It had been easier when he was farther away, when he'd acted less interested. She could focus entirely on her magic and on her role as his Protector.

This was why sovereigns and sorcerers were not meant to be together.

He smiled a mischievous smile as she struggled with what to say. He stepped up close to her, hands still in his pockets. "What about this?" His face hovered just above hers, his chest so close to hers that she could feel the static between their clothes.

"This isn't much better," she said, swallowing.

At the bunkhouse entrance, a man cleared his throat. "Sorry," Amos Johnson said, popping into the dim space. Aly and Red hopped apart from each other, blush creeping up Aly's neck. "You should see this, sir."

"I think they should see this too." Red pointed at the journal in Aly's hands. She passed it to him and followed him out of the bunkhouse, pulling her mask down over her eyes as she stepped into the sunlight.

Outside, the men were gathered around an object in the grass. They parted as Red approached. One man was squatting on the ground. "Look at this," he said.

In the grass lay a partial skeleton, half-covered with dirt. Red squatted down beside the man. "What is it?"

"It's not human. Most of the bones have been picked clean."

"But there's this." One of the men lifted a skull. It was small, narrow, and pointed almost like a deer's, but at the nose, two antlers curved up like that of a hog. On top of the head, there were stubs where antlers might have been broken off.

"What is that?" asked Red, standing.

"That's what we're wondering," said the man holding it.

Aly remembered his name was Reuben. She cleared her throat

and all the men glanced at her. "The magic of these sorcerers... it's not quite like the Canyon, but I imagine they could have done some strange things here, including, perhaps, changing the animals."

The men exchanged horrified looks. Reuben stepped back with a slight shiver. "Are we talking woodwolves and foxbloods?"

"I'm sure those animals are already here," Aly said, causing another rustle in her audience. "But they've come from the Canyon. I think the creatures like this deer, or whatever this is, could be a biproduct of the Zealots' magic." The men coughed. Hands slid into and out of pockets. These men were afraid. "There could be just the one. It's not like woodwolves and foxbloods, which can breed. However, I think we should be willing to expect almost anything here."

A moment passed as the crowd of men considered what they'd walked into. A forest where never-before-seen creatures could walk out of the trees or where a mad sorcerer could come at them with unbridled magic blazing.

"My pa worked here," one of the men said, stepping forward. "Told me tales of animals with horns all over them."

Amos shook his head. "Now, don't go getting into the horned beast stories again."

"It's true. My pa saw it."

Amos huffed. "I think people see what they want to see when they're afraid."

The other man turned, puffing out his chest and drawing air for a rebuttal.

"I think he's right," Aly said, inserting herself almost between them. "Fear can taint our rationality. You are safe." She glanced at the forest. "As long as you don't go outside the borders of this camp."

Red nodded. "Until we speak with the sorcerers here, please

remain inside the camp. I cannot guarantee your safety otherwise."

The men looked uncomfortable, but nobody spoke.

Finally, Reuben asked, "The sorcerers, you're certain they'll let us be?"

Aly offered a noncommittal smile.

"What about these animals?" asked one man.

"The animals we can't control, but I can set up barriers that will dissuade them from entering the camp."

Reuben crossed his arms. "That'd be good."

She continued, "And the sorcerers...we won't wait for them to come to us. We will go to them."

The men tossed puzzled looks at Red.

He stood taller. "Aly and I are going to look for them. The rest of you, unpack your things and get settled."

Amos asked, "Will we be safe here...without you?" He looked at Aly as he spoke.

"My shields won't fail as long as you're here."

The men set about unpacking the carriages and settling the horses into the somewhat dilapidated stable. Aly walked to the edge of camp, looking at the massive stumps where the men had worked before. An old, rutted road led into the heart of the forest; it was grown over with tall grasses and wildflowers. It wasn't long before Red joined her. He wore his coronet once more.

"This way," she pointed. "They will come to us. I'm certain of it."

Red marched down the road. "I'm not afraid," he insisted, glancing back at her.

The forest blanketed the sounds of the camp as they walked farther down the logging road. To pass the time, Aly said, "I must fix those carts back there. The wheels are broken."

"One whole load had been abandoned. Did you see it?" asked Red.

"Penwater told me that those who worked here would return to Mardon full of lies, terrifying anyone who was recruited to come here. I think it was madness, as much as magic, that drove them from this place."

"Great." Red gently but swiftly swept his gaze back and forth from left to right, like a hunter on guard.

Aly sighed. Her conversation wasn't helping. "Whatever drove these men away, it didn't kill them."

"But it frightened them so terribly that no one ever returned," Red concluded.

She couldn't deny that. None of the people who once worked here had ever provided a straight answer about the events that had occurred. Of the ones who spoke of it, their stories were all different.

"We're here now," she finally said. "This will work."

"My father made it work. At least for a time. That's all we need."

They walked on in silence. The mosquitoes, held at bay by Aly's purposeful breeze, hovered in annoyance all around them. Red swatted at a spiderweb and stepped over a fallen log.

After a time, Red stopped. "If they don't like people, they wouldn't live along this road. I'll lead the way." With an inhale, he stepped off the road into the trees.

"You don't have to be the one to lead the way," she said.

"Yes, I do. I can at least remove all the spiderwebs for you." He flicked away another glistening web. "Let's try this way."

"There's magic in these woods, but I'm not sure if I can tell where it's coming from. Seems like it has lingered long after the spells were cast. I've never known magic could do that."

As they walked, the brambles thickened. Overhead, the canopy diminished the bright sun. Strange shrieking that might have been from a fox—or foxblood—sounded far off through the trees.

Soon, they came across a cabin tucked so tightly against the trees that it wasn't visible until they were upon it. It was covered in moss and the roof had caved in. Mushrooms grew along the front door frame.

"Nice place," said Red. "What is it?" he asked when Aly failed to respond.

"This place feels wrong," she whispered. "There are no Truth-wells here."

Red looked around, as if he could verify this by observation. "In what, the trees or the house?"

Aly ran her fingers along one moss-covered wall. "Even cut wood carries a vestige of its original Well. But this house..." She closed her eyes and, with her mind, searched through the forest and the space around her. As always, the energy of nature burned with multifaceted light, but it was dimmed by the close-ness of Red's luminous Well.

His light was so bright, it was like trying to see a star behind the sun. She pushed past the light of Red's Well, seeking the sources at her disposal. With concentration, she could feel the Wells of the trees, their rhythms beating softly against her consciousness. The grass swayed and even the air swirled, eddying and flowing around them in small currents. Aly's breath moved small swirls of air. As she sank into this deep awareness, she became less aware of her actual surroundings. Suddenly, beneath it all, she sensed a tiny glow from the walls of the cottage. Their Wells were so faint, it was almost as if they'd been Stripped, or nearly Stripped. What was left was infinitesimal, hardly a source to Pull from.

"Look out!" Red grabbed her arm and yanked her to him as a creature flew past them. A small squirrel landed on the forest floor and scampered off into the woods, shrieking and clicking its tongue in annoyance. "Was that squirrel trying to attack you?" he asked, his hand still holding her.

In another context, that question might have been comical.

Instead, Aly's skin prickled. "These animals...I think they've been affected by the magic here too."

"That's so creepy," Red said. "Did you see anything?" he asked.

"I feel the Wells now. It takes a little while, but I can find them. They're so faint."

This place had been affected by magic in a negative way, that much was certain. Aly had rarely seen evidence of evil magic, other than her father's own wickedness. A wave of unease crept under Aly's skin. Magic was *good*, but only when directed by truth. Lies had their own power, and their magic left a trace of bitterness and shadow in its wake.

Red poked his head inside the cabin. "Here." He pointed at the roof. "There was an explosion inside or something inside pushed its way out. It wasn't a cave-in."

She followed Red inside. Leaves and small shoot-like plants covered the cabin floor. It smelled musty and damp. Aly kicked the leaves at her feet and uncovered a bone. She gasped. It was a jawbone. A *human* jawbone. "I think," she said, trying to calm her racing heartbeat, "the sorcerer here drew too much magic into himself and...didn't..."

Red placed a hand on her upper arm, stepping close. "You don't need to say it." They backed out of the small structure. "Let's keep moving," he said.

Another half hour into the forest, they heard a human scream in the distance. They looked at each other, confirming that the other had heard the same noise.

"That journal mentioned distant screaming." Red grabbed the journal out of his pocket and flipped through it. "Yes, right here." He shut the journal with a muffled snap. "What is that?"

Aly turned toward the sound, her mind pushing outward, as far as she could, stretching over acres and acres of forest. She detected several bright Truthwells that could only be from humans. "Perhaps they know we're here."

Red fisted his hands. "The men are safe, aren't they?"

"Yes, Red, they're safe." She knew he meant well, but the question felt too much like doubt over her abilities rather than concern for the men. It sent her back to the first few conversations they'd had, when everything she said or did was anathema to Red. She shook away the feeling. She'd gained his trust, and, to her surprise, his affection too. She still didn't know how to tell him she couldn't let his affection continue. So, instead, she ignored that topic for the time being.

"We should return," he stated, already starting to march back the way they'd come.

Aly didn't argue. The men might have heard the scream as well and would be comforted knowing their Protector was there with them.

She knotted her cloak up at her waist to make traversing the brambles a little easier. As she picked her way over one particularly gnarly patch, she heard a faint *crunch* to her left.

A figure stood before them. A man. He wore only pants and had a red line painted across his torso. He held a spear in one hand and was barefoot. On his head he wore a twisted bit of cloth.

Aly's pulse thundered. She hadn't felt his Well approaching. She could sense it now, but it disturbed her that it eluded her notice. She hadn't imagined these untrained sorcerers could shroud their Wells.

"Hello," Red said in his king's voice.

"You're not welcome here," the man replied, his attention on Aly.

"We have come to speak about the lumberyard," Red announced.

The man pounded the shaft of his spear on the ground. "Silence! I speak to the woman."

Red cleared his throat, but Aly lifted a hand. "I am the Royal Sorcerer of Tandera."

"I know what you are. You are one of *them*."

Aly cooled her body temperature, then sent Red a similar spell. She set up three defensive spells in her mind, casting them without audible words.

The man continued, "Your magic is filth. Your *service* magic. It's disgusting." He spat on the ground. "How dare you pervert our gift in this way!"

In her head, she couldn't help but picture this man exploding in rage as his unbridled magic ran amok. "We have come to talk to you about resuming operations in the lumber yard. We simply need our men to be able to do their work. We will stay out of your way." She lifted two hands. "We aren't here to harm you."

The man worked his jaw a moment before responding. "You're taking our forest. How does that not harm us?"

It struck Aly then that these sorcerers lacked human Wells to Pull from. They'd never been trained to understand such magic. They pulled from the strongest sources available to them: the trees. To take their trees was to take their source of energy for their magic. She nodded. "We understand you need the trees, but so do we." Aly inhaled, deciding to take a risk. "We will repay you for the trees."

The man stamped his spear again. "You have nothing of value to offer me."

Curious, Aly asked, "Can you see him? His Well, I mean?"

With a cocked head, the man examined Red. "I see it. Flickering little thing. Why would I want anything to do with that?"

This confirmed Aly's suspicions. These sorcerers didn't—or for some reason couldn't—use human Truthwells to fuel their magic. She nodded, grateful the man couldn't sense the brilliance of Red's Well or desire to Pull all the energy from it. "You said it's a small Well." *What makes this man so blind to what is true?*

"We don't use human Wells," he said, clarifying her conjecture. "It doesn't work. It just kills them." He gripped the spear with a grunt.

Aly's breath caught. Here was a man who'd never learned to subdue the yearning inside him when Truthpulling. *It just kills them*, he'd said. Had he killed people with his misguided magic? Would he try to kill them?

"You want me to kill this lad here?" he said, eyeing Red with disdain.

"I will prevent that," Aly said.

"Think your magic can protect him? Our magic is stronger than yours. We don't limit it the way you do, pushing it down into what a book tells you."

Offense bristled under Aly's skin. "Yes, a *book* that—oh, never mind." She couldn't fight against the lies in this man's head. Not today. They needed an agreement to keep the men at the lumberyard safe. That was her aim. She might come back and fight for the truth another day. "How much would these trees be worth to you? We will pay you back. We need the lumber."

The man spat on the ground. "It cannot be as valuable to you as it is to us."

"On the contrary," Red said. "It provides homes for our people, wood for their fires."

Now the Zealot cringed, maybe at the thought of burning these trees. "We will not let them *burn*."

"Yet you use them to conjure your magic, which often kills the trees, am I right?" asked Aly.

"If magic does it, it is good," he replied.

"Okay, then if that is the case, then you believe my magic to be good." She smiled as he narrowed his eyes.

"You have made it do demeaning things."

She pressed forward. "If it's magic, is it not good?"

He shifted his weight and readjusted the cloth at his waist. "I suppose it has a goodness to it, if it is magic."

Yes. She resisted the urge to whoop or smirk. "Our men are protected by my magic. It is what I desire with my magic."

"We desire the trees," he said again.

"We do too." She stared at him hard, hoping to break his resolve. He'd admitted her magic wasn't as wicked as he perceived it to be, pinned by his own reasoning. "How can we strike a bargain with you?"

"You cannot take our sources."

Aly trembled. "There are other sources." This was dangerous territory. These sorcerers Stripped their sources. "What about the river?" It wasn't something they could use to *pay* these people, but if she redirected his attention toward another source, maybe they wouldn't miss the trees so much.

"It is heavily guarded by those who use it." He sneered and twisted the shaft of his spear.

This was new information. These wild sorcerers had a hierarchy among themselves. Those who could use the river and those who could not. She'd known they had some form of organization, but she hadn't known it revolved around their sources of magic.

Red cleared his throat. "How can we replace what we take from you?"

"There's nothing that you can give me. You're the opposite of everything magic should be."

Aly was becoming frustrated. This man's head was full of lies.

The man's spear suddenly flew from his hand and darted toward them. With a flick of a finger, the spear burst into splinters at Aly's command, its metal tip falling dully to the ground.

"You can't hurt us," she said. "You may think my magic to be less than yours, but it is actually stronger because it is controlled."

The man's face grew hot with rage, and an instant later his entire body erupted into flames.

"Toss me!" Red jumped backward.

With a phrase, Aly called water from the air and the trees and the ground beneath their feet to douse the flames on the man's body, but he had turned to ash before they could even step toward him.

"How...how is that even possible?" asked Red, staring at the steaming mound.

Still shocked, Aly's throat dried up as she tried to reply. It took several attempts to swallow before she could say, "His magic killed him." The words sounded so *wrong*. Memories pelted, unbidden, into her thoughts. Men and women in Kitrel cursing magic, eschewing it. Even her mother had distrusted magic. Experience shaped understanding, and some people's experience of magic *was* wrong. Aly had never seen such wrongness so clearly displayed until now.

She'd always thought magic itself was good, and the person employing it was either good or evil.

But this...this magic was deadly, despite the man's belief that it was *good*.

Again she tried to swallow, finding her throat as sticky as old honey. *Magic is good*, she told herself. *It is.*

Red shook his head, struggling with this tragedy before him. She briefly wondered what his internal struggle sounded like, if he, too, questioned what he knew of magic. "So, he was so angry that he burst into flames?"

Another figure suddenly stepped into the woods. Red and Aly looked up at a woman, wearing barely more than the man.

"Holy man, that," she said, looking at the steaming pile of ashes.

Aly instinctively stepped closer to Red.

His arm bumped hers. "I think I'll do the talking this time," he whispered. "They seem to hate you. A lot."

As the woman stepped toward them, her clothes morphed into something more akin to a ballgown made of leaves. The woman disregarded the movement of the leaves on her body as they gathered to her from the forest floor.

Unhindered magic, directed only by a vague thought. This

woman must have thought a dress was more appropriate for this conversation. *She thinks Red's attractive,* Aly reasoned.

He held up both hands. "We will not harm you."

At least the woman didn't carry a spear. She bent down and reached her hands into the pile of white ashes, then stood up and scattered them in the faint breeze. They fell in small, sad clumps to her feet. Her hand came away smeared with grey and white. "Holy man," she said again.

He died in a fit of rage, Aly thought. Hardly holy.

"We wish to reopen the lumberyard," Red announced, moving straight to business. The death before them didn't seem to be a sad event for this woman. If Red felt anything like what Aly felt, neither of them knew how to properly process this strange disaster. "We understand that the trees are quite valuable to you," he said. "We value them too. Is there any way we could repay you for these trees?"

Aly thought it strange he was taking the same approach she had. That conversation had ended in death.

"The trees?" the woman said, looking up, almost as if only realizing that they were standing in a forest. "Ah yes, the trees." She walked a few steps forward, ignoring them. "Hemlock will not come home. Hemlock will not come home." She said it over and over as she walked away.

Had these two Zealots been married? The histories didn't mention if the Zealots believed in marriage.

"Wait," Red said, starting after the strange woman. "What options are available to keep the sorcerers here from harming the lumberyard?"

"We don't harm it," the lady said. "You're the ones who harm it by cutting the trees down. If we remove you, we remove the problem. Like we have removed a cancer."

Red sighed. "Okay. We wish to cut trees down. We are *going* to cut trees down. My father did and you allowed it for a long time."

The woman paused and looked over her shoulder at Red. "Your father? Gevar? The man who uses a sorcerer as a tool." She shook her head, as if in pity at such a thought. "Our river keepers might be the ones you wish to speak to."

"River keepers?" Red asked.

These would be the Zealots who used the river as a source. The dead man, Hemlock, had said they guarded the river for their own use. They had to be strong enough to keep the other sorcerers away from the river.

The woman gave them a narrow gaze. "We will not give up our trees to you."

"Besides the trees, is there anything else you value?" Red asked, nearing desperation.

"Value? We value magic. You cannot give us anything," she said.

Red's jaw flexed. "Well, we value the trees too. We need them."

The woman tilted her head. "You think of them as sacred?"

"Well, I...yes," Red fumbled. Aly scowled at him but he continued. "These trees will save lives. People will survive the cold of winter. In that sense, yes, they are set apart. Sacred, as you say."

The woman fixed a wide stare on him, his words striking a chord in her. "But they are magic to us."

"They're magic to us, too," he said, emboldened. "Perhaps in a different way, but we still need them as much as you do."

"If you're telling me that you think of these trees as sacred, then maybe we might come to an agreement." Red let out a small *yes*, which seemed to pass by the woman's awareness altogether. "The sorcerers of the forest agree that the trees are sacred. None of us can harm the trees. They are what allow our magic to run free."

Now Aly coughed but said nothing.

"They will allow our people to be free as well," Red agreed, his words a bit of a stretch, but not exactly a lie, if freedom meant life and not death this winter.

As the woman tilted her head back and forth, Aly tried not to think of how Red might be examining the woman's barely covered body. She had the thin, bone-draped look of one unaccustomed to large, easy meals. "Young man has some wisdom in him," she admitted. "And who might you be?" she asked him.

Aly elbowed him and kicked her foot sideways, causing a few leaves to tumble over the toe of his boot.

"My name is Red, and I am here for the trees."

"Very well, Red. I will not harm you."

Aly's heart leapt. Red shot her a gleeful look, then turned back to the woman. "Will you tell the others not to harm us as well? You do not harm those who seek the trees, do you?"

"I cannot speak for the others."

"Will you tell them what I told you about the trees? About why we seek them?"

"Oh, if I see them, perhaps. Goodbye to you, Red, who seeks the trees. May you find your power in them."

As the woman walked away, Aly gasped at the woman's insight. The trees, in a way, were going to be his source of power.

19

RED

S weat rolled down Red's forearms. He pushed up his sleeves and regripped the axe, aware of every blister, every sore muscle. Aly's magic, rather than providing the relief of eased pain and cool breezes, upheld protective spells and constantly hunted danger. And it wouldn't help for Red to appear too soft to endure hard labor in the summer heat.

Raised in a palace, always surrounded by the luxuries of magic, Red had rarely been left to the whims of nature. There was a freeing discomfort to it, as if he were truly living for the first time in his life.

With a deep inhale, he swung the axe back and let out a grunt as the blade sunk into the massive tree trunk before him, one notch closer to the breaking point. Even the smaller spruces here measured the width of a man. Witnessing these trees crashing to the ground was a most satisfying sight, especially knowing it was his own two hands that brought down the giant.

Nearby, Aly released an angry, feminine gasp and released her axe handle, where it remained lodged in a tree only for a moment before clunking to the ground. "I'm terrible at this," she whined, wiping her forehead with the back of her hand. "Let me use magic, *please*."

Red smiled at her. She was out of her element too, and it was a strange comfort to know they were sharing this new experience, forging a bond not around magic or the running of a country, but around the blisters on their palms and the whoop of excitement when a tree came down.

"We can't use magic to solve every problem," he called over to her.

He wanted to win the crown more than he'd ever known he would, and using magic to retain it still felt a little like cheating.

"Fine," she grumbled, picking up her axe.

Veeter Yin, who'd felled a tree earlier this morning, walked up with a fresh canteen and handed it to Red. After a long drink, he wiped his mouth and thanked Yin, who marched along the line of men, offering a drink to the weary workers.

The raw spots on Red's hands stung as he swung his axe once more. *Thunk.* A great groan sounded from within the heart of the tree. *Here it comes,* he thought with a wide grin and swung again.

At the next tree, Aly sliced clean through the enormous trunk, finishing her swing with a complete spin.

Before the tree toppled, she tossed the axe aside and gripped the trunk with her palm, to make it look like she held it with nothing but brute strength. Red shook his head.

"Remember, we can't do it that way," he said, smearing sweat off his neck.

Aly rolled her eyes and tossed the carriage-sized tree aside where it landed with a victorious *whump* that shook the entire lumberyard. Every head turned toward her. A few men cheered.

"See? They approve," she said, crossing her arms.

"Well, sure. Everybody likes to be entertained." He raised a brow.

Aly threw up her hands. "Fine."

"These men don't have the luxury of magic at their disposal. They don't have that privilege. For once, neither will I."

Aly huffed but nodded. The men around them returned to work, their rhythmic chopping forming a song. She and Red sank back into the shared rhythm of swing-*thunk*, swing-*thunk*.

The heat and the tempo of the work allowed Red's mind to wander. As it had often of late, it wandered to what might happen if his Bond to Aly was severed. Would she no longer desire his company if his bright light was removed from her disposal? If Red lost his throne and she became Bound to Alexander, they wouldn't change the world much, no matter if he was a Beacon.

He swung his axe with extra effort, the *thunk* and the jolt to his muscles dispelling a little of the tension knotting in his stomach. At once, the groaning in the tree turned to a violent snapping sound. He leapt out of the way. "Timber!"

The final *snap* rent the summer day like cannon fire. Limbs cushioned the tree's fall, but it still rattled the camp as it crashed to the earth. When the silence rushed back in, Red could hear his heartbeat. This tree would help his people stay warm and sheltered this winter. In a way, he understood how the Zealots felt— the trees supplied them with something they considered invaluable. He smiled at the fallen spruce.

A new sound snapped his attention toward the forest. Aly had stopped chopping, too, her eyes fixed on the shadows under the trees.

There.

A shape was coming fast. It was definitely human.

"A Zealot," Aly said as the crashing sound of feet approached through the underbrush.

"I guess they're not all as charitable as that woman we met."

Aly rushed toward Red and stepped in front of him. Her protective spells were intact, the men were safe from any direct attacks, but the unpredictable nature of these Zealots meant that their very bodies could be weapons, if Hemlock's death was any evidence.

A woman burst into the clearing, heaving. She stopped abruptly and bent double, hands on her knees as she tried to catch her breath. The men spotted her and stopped chopping. They had their axes at the ready, from tool to weapon in a heartbeat. Yin drew a blade and darted toward his sovereign, hovering a few paces behind Red and Aly.

The woman's matted brown hair glinted red in the sunlight. Her clothes were threadbare, hardly covering her frame, much like the woman from earlier. She was short and dark and mottled with freckles. Bent over as she was, she looked almost like a child. When she glanced up at all the axes, her sunken cheeks hollowed even more as her mouth parted in shock.

"I'm not going to use magic," she declared over heavy breaths.

Aly snorted, drawing her gaze.

"I'm never doing magic again," the woman insisted.

None of the men lowered their axes. Aly held a hand backward against Red's middle. Her fingers pressed him away from the danger they didn't fully understand. These Zealots followed no rules and, thus, were unpredictable. He wished so badly it was him protecting her, rather than the other way around.

"I hate magic. I am not..." The woman swallowed and closed her eyes. Fists formed and loosened at her sides three times. "That was close."

She'd almost used magic. For some reason, she appeared relieved she hadn't.

"You're a sorcerer?" asked Aly.

Good, thought Red, *keep her talking.* Father had managed to accomplish a lot of good merely by convincing those opposed to him to talk. Might as well start with the basics. *Ask easy questions first, make them answer positively*, Gevar had advised. Aly, of course, had heard the former king's advice as well.

"Yes," the young woman said, still panting. Her clothes were handmade. They looked like they had been crafted from garments that were once much too big and looped around to fit her small frame. Then she said, "Can you keep me safe?"

Aly's shoulders twitched, likely in the same surprise he was feeling at this woman's odd request. Red shifted behind Aly.

The sorcerer clasped her hands behind her back, as if to prove that she wasn't about to conjure magic. Even as her hands moved out of sight, the ground beneath her feet began to cave in.

Cursing, she hopped aside. With a strained expression, she looked at her fingers, as if surprised they were attached to her hands. Then she stared at Aly, a wild desperation in her brown eyes. "You're a trained sorcerer, aren't you?"

Aly blinked and nodded. Poor woman wore no shoes. Her exposed legs displayed burn marks around her ankles. Her knees were brown with dirt and callouses.

The woman sighed. "My parents said it's not to be tamed, our gift. But then they killed each other with their magic. They got angry at one another and then they both—" she mimed an explosion, "—died."

Red cringed.

Aly's jaw hung open a moment. "I'm so sorry," she muttered.

"No, don't be sorry. It's what they chose." She paused a moment and crossed her arms over her chest. "Magic destroys everything here. I've heard...at least I had hoped...Can you take it from me? Can you take away my magic?" She stumbled toward Aly.

Aly held up one hand, the other still on Red. Her fingers trembled against him. "I can't take your magic from you," she said.

The woman wilted to the ground, sobbing.

Aly stepped toward her, finally dropping her hand from Red's chest. "It *is* a gift. Tell me, what is your name?"

Red was curious to see how this scene would unfold. Aly would not let any harm come to him or his men.

The woman looked up. "Naia. And it isn't a gift. It's a curse. I was hoping you could keep me safe, rid me of this festering magic." She stopped herself and looked around. "I shouldn't be here." She scrambled to her feet. "I shouldn't have come. I am endangering all of you."

"Do you wish us harm?" Aly asked.

"No."

"Then you are not a threat to us," Red inserted, finally sure of what to say. "If you do not wish us harm, then I am not afraid of you," he concluded. Possibly this woman needed his trust the way Aly did.

"You're not?" Naia scoffed. "I think maybe you should be."

"No," Red countered. "I think what you need is a teacher." He glanced at Aly with lifted brows.

Aly's face expanded with shock, then she laughed out loud. "Of course," she said, taking a moment to breathe deeply. She never broke eye contact with Red, processing what he was asking of her. She cared so much about the truth, perhaps this was one way she could fight the darkness. After a moment, she said, "Let me teach you." She turned her attention to the Zealot. "Magic can be beautiful, you know. It was meant to be."

At that, the small woman broke down in tears once more. Aly quirked her brow at Red.

"All it does is destroy," the woman sobbed. "I won't…I said I wouldn't." She started a few more sentences, finishing none of them. "I want it gone," she finally said.

Aly stepped gingerly toward the sorcerer. At first, the woman tensed and stepped backward, but as Aly continued toward her, Naia remained still, hiding her face with her hands while she cried.

"It's okay. We can teach you the truth," Aly cooed, as if calming a spooked horse.

Naia sucked in a sob-choked breath. "The only true thing I know is that magic hurts people."

Aly lowered her voice to a comforting whisper and placed a tentative hand on the woman's shoulder. "I can't take your magic from you, but I can teach you to control it. Learn with me, and see that your magic never has to harm another person."

Naia sniffed a few more times, trying to regain her composure. Red was convinced she'd dart back into the forest any moment.

Then she said, "Yes. Yes, I would like that."

20

ALY

Two weeks later on an overcast summer evening, Aly and Naia stood in the center of camp, a cloud of gnats hovering over them in a perfect dome shape, repelled by a spell. Aly had her hands up, moving in grand gestures as she explained, yet again, the best ways to concentrate while conducting magic. Naia, who'd claimed she was twenty-five despite the fact she looked barely twenty, stood with crossed arms, watching Aly with a hard expression. Her hair billowed around her tanned face in waves of rust-colored spirals.

With their labor, they'd pressed the tree line back, and Red and Seb and the other men now worked farther away from the camp buildings. Aly's shields were larger now than they'd been when they arrived. She was grateful for the added space in which Naia could practice magic without fear of catching the camp on fire or harming the men.

Aly had placed a small additional cage of magic around Naia, built to contain any spontaneous spells.

Two weeks had passed without further incident. Aly attributed this to the blessing of Theod's hand, but the men weren't so certain.

Nearby, a man yelled *timber*, and a great crack rent the air. Aly snapped to grab Naia's attention—the woman was so distractable. Naia's gaze flickered to Aly, then immediately traveled back to the falling giant.

"Another will fall in a minute, and magic takes *concentration* more than anything else," Aly said, attempting—but failing—to keep her voice the steady tone of a patient tutor. Naia's task was to push a steady breeze against the gnats in order to direct them where she wanted—a harmless spell should she fail.

Teaching Naia in the lumberyard meant that every few minutes their work was interrupted by the great boom of a tree falling. It made for a poor learning environment, considering that mastering concentration was the first step to controlling magic.

The men, impressed with Red's ability to swing an axe with the best of them, had happily agreed to Seb's recent suggestion that they at least allow their *tools* to be enchanted so as to make swifter work.

With each axe sharper, faster, and lighter in the men's hands, they tired less quickly, and each swing sunk deeper, making the work twice as fast as before.

They had felled two hundred seventy of the massive trees. They would save Mardon.

Naia chewed on the side of her tongue, an apparent concentration technique of hers. "How do you make your magic follow the commands of your hands?" asked Naia, consternation pinching her tone. They'd been practicing for hours, and the woman had a short attention span. "When I do it, they all die."

"Well, at least they're just bugs."

Naia frowned.

Compassion flooded Aly's veins. She recalled days when she herself had been afraid of her own magic, fed subtle lies from her youth about what magic was, who it was from and what it could do. Her mother had even believed some of those lies; Kassia had made sure of that. Even Aly had been affected by Kassia's lies.

The story that Aly's birth had caused her birthmother's death was likely a falsehood crafted to weaken Aly's magic from infancy. Aly had believed it her whole life, exactly as Kassia had planned.

Aly could see why Naia distrusted magic. Many didn't understand magic for what it was. They lacked access to the *Verad* to know truth from error. They had to rely on experience.

"It takes a lot of practice," Aly said for the dozenth time. "You need to trust that your thoughts are not all bad." At Naia's scoff, she added, "Not *all* bad. Not if you control them with truth."

Naia had seen pain, and Aly sensed the woman had harmed either herself or someone else with her magic, something she would likely never speak of. Aly didn't need to know what Naia had done. What mattered was where she was heading now.

Naia rubbed her face with both hands. "I don't know the book like you do. I can't even read."

"No, but you will. Nothing will keep you from learning, if you *want* to."

Looking up, Naia's brown eyes narrowed. "There's too much to learn. This isn't fun." She waved a hand, and a blast of lightning exploded against Aly's magical shield, ricocheting back at them so that they both flinched. "Sorry!" blurted Naia.

Aly pinched a glowing ember from her hair and sighed. It was possible that Naia was merely a Comforter—though the name felt odd applied to one such as her. So far, Naia had only made things hotter or colder, to extreme degrees. She was having trouble with subtlety.

"This isn't about fun," Aly argued, as if speaking to a child. Naia was older, but she'd lived in the forest, without an ounce of instruction, discipline, or love. She had more to learn than controlling her magic. She was as wild as the deer that roamed nightly around their camp. "It's about survival. If you don't learn to control your magic, you will one day harm, or possibly kill, yourself or someone you care about."

Naia growled, likely at the uncomfortable memory of her parents' deaths. The fists at her sides signaled magic might burst forth any moment.

It did not.

Instead, her fists relaxed and she said, "I care for no one, and no one cares for me."

"Now, *that* is a lie, Naia," Aly said. "We care about you. All of us." She swept a hand out at the men working along the edge of camp. "They're all cheering for you."

Naia glanced along the line of men swinging axes. It was drawing close to meal time, and the scent of roasting meat was already on the air.

"They don't trust me," she muttered, voice thick with emotion.

Aly's brows rose. "See Red, over there? He didn't trust me at first either. Trust comes with time. It doesn't mean they don't want you to succeed. They, too, work toward a goal here. We're all pushing each other on toward our goals."

A massive tree crashed to the ground at the far edge of camp. The men clapped and hollered. She smiled in the darkening space. This place had felt like exile when they'd arrived, but it had been good for her and Red.

The laughter around the dinner table here had been therapeutic, a contrast to the silence of her shrouded self these past years and the quiet days of hiding in Mardon with Red, always ducking away from watching eyes. Though she and Naia were the only two women present, these men laughed with them as easily as they did the other lumberjacks—occasionally throwing out a comment that made Aly blush crimson and made Red use his kingly voice to reprimand them.

She swelled with pride as the men stood straighter when he walked by. He had done what he'd intended and won the loyalty of these men. She only hoped it would be enough to secure his crown for the upcoming coronation. Two dozen lumberjacks weren't exactly the pulse of Mardon—or Tandera. The invitations had been sent. The meals ordered. The entire city would witness the crowning of a man in two weeks. Which man, Aly wasn't yet certain.

Now she wished she could steal a little of the mad hope Red carried around with him.

She spotted him near Seb, watching one final tree crash to the ground before work would end for the evening. Red was attractive this way, axe propped on the ground at his side, red hair clinging to his forehead. Red's skin was dusted with more freckles than he'd ever had. His initial sunburn had peeled away, leaving behind a ruddier complexion. He looked stronger, more alive.

Red slapped Seb on the back, and they walked toward the bath house. As they passed Aly and Naia, Red called out, "We're headed in."

Aly nodded. She turned back to Naia and said, "Today, you will help me."

Seb heard her, because he nudged Red's arm with the back of his hand, eyes fixed on the women. "Hey, check this out."

Red and Seb stopped to watch. At the end of each day, Aly collected the trees with her magic, stacked them in a neat pile, and saved the men—and the horses—hours of backbreaking work. What a tedious place this would be without a sorcerer.

Aly stepped up to one felled tree and lifted her hands.

Her words muffled on the breeze, but as she spoke, the tree before her rose noisily off the ground, twigs and branches snapping, falling to the earth. Several limbs remained impaled in the dirt like daggers after the great crash. The entire camp stopped to watch this part.

The massive tree moved through the air, over the edge of camp, and down onto a space cleared for the timber. Everyone cheered.

Now Aly held a hand out to Naia, who pursed her lips in

defiance. Aly beckoned her with several encouraging motions and whispered words.

With a sigh, Naia lifted and lowered her hands several times. The men all gathered near, watching the two women. Several of them placed quick bets. Seb badgered Red to place one too, but Red ignored his friend as Naia began to shout her spell.

The words stumbled off her tongue like a child just learning to speak. She was using the phrases of the *Verad*, but it sounded more like she was speaking a foreign language. Aly kept a warm smile on her face, careful to encourage in every possible way, even in observation. Naia needed to see success or she was likely to give up.

But if she couldn't lift this tree this time, Aly might surrender to the reality that her protégé was not a Protector and would focus instead on honing her ability as a Comforter.

The tree Naia sought to move obeyed. It rolled a few times and lifted off the ground, one end then the other. Cheers erupted along the line of spectators. Aly let out a small *whoop* of excitement.

Then, without warning, the branches of the tree froze in a sudden frost, and the severed end of the trunk erupted in flames.

Naia yelped in surprise and dropped the tree. It crashed down with force, its frozen branches shattering like icicles, flying in all directions. Aly shouted a spell, and all the dart-like twigs halted in the air, tinkling to the ground like a thousand tiny bells.

"Oy," Seb said, a hand on his forehead. "That was close."

Naia cupped her hands to her face and ran toward their bunkhouse.

Aly sighed and let the woman go. "But that was the best she's done yet. She *lifted* it."

As the men disappeared to clean up for dinner, Aly moved the rest of the trees, one at a time, to a huge pile at the edge of camp. It was nearly dark now, and the smell of herbed venison filled the air. Everyone bathed and headed for the mess hall.

On the way, Aly spotted Red coming out of the men's bunk house. Her hair was down and clean, voluminous with the humid night air. Per her advice, he wore his coronet for the evening meal.

He flashed her a smile.

She looked down, surprised at the sparks in his expression. "Hello."

"Hello, beautiful."

She blinked quickly at him then looked away, fighting a sudden sweat. "Naia did well today, don't you think?"

"You call that well?"

"She lifted the tree! It was her first time using magic for something *productive* instead of destructive. It was a huge win for her!

"If you say so."

Aly elbowed him, and he grinned at her playfulness. "She's so new at this. She didn't even know what the *Verad* was until two weeks ago. She's been so reluctant to try anything, afraid her magic will go awry."

"Like it did tonight?"

"Yes." Aly paused, her face sad. "I am proud of her. Despite what it looked like, that was a big step forward for her. It takes so much time to master the art of Truthpulling."

"You did it in, what, three months?"

In the dim light, Aly blushed at his words. "Not everyone learns that fast."

He reached for her, brushing her cheek with his knuckles. "But you did."

Her veins caught fire as he stepped closer. At this, she smirked and tossed his hand away. "She's so similar to me. I used to be like that, afraid of my magic. When Grey—" she stopped herself to check Red's expression, "—found me and offered me his own Truthwell to train, everything changed. When I first touched his Well and drew from it, it was like I had found what I'd always been missing. Magic had been there, but had been incomplete, as if I were only able to grab the fringe of it. When I finally knew what it was to dive into a human Well, it was like I knew magic was good, and that I was meant to use it."

Red stuck his hands in his pockets as they walked across the darkening space towards the mess hall. Every time she mentioned Grey, he retreated like this. "What is Naia Pulling from?"

"Right now, the trees. They are strong sources. I haven't been able to teach her to Pull from several things at once yet. That's trickier. But once she begins Pulling from people, she won't have to worry about that."

"People?" Red paused outside the bright, loud mess hall, where most of the men already sat.

"She's not only a Comforter. She's definitely strong enough to be a Master. She needs a lot of training—a *lot*—I grant, but I know she can use the Wells of people. It will be hard for me to keep her from Pulling from them once she realizes she can." She looked at her feet. "The draw of human Wells is, well, impossible to ignore."

He touched her fingers, pulling them up and into his own. "Like me. I'm impossible to ignore, right?" He lifted his brows, inviting her to deny or confirm his words.

She snorted. "You're ridiculous, you know that?" With a teasing shake of her head, she pulled her hand free. She thought she saw a flash of concern in his eyes.

Veeter Yin stood outside the dining hall in what had become his regular post of duty during mealtime. No matter how often Red implored him to join them at the table, he insisted on standing watch outside until Red exited the building. Red and Aly nodded at him as they walked in to the dining hall together.

"Will she come eat?" Red asked, jerking his head back toward the women's bunk house.

"If she can complete a spell I left for her to try, she'll come eat. And if she doesn't—she's pretty determined now; I don't think she will care about food if she didn't succeed with the spell. After she saw what her magic could do this afternoon, she's ready to try more. She wants to see success."

Red squinted before stepping up to the table. "Will she set anything on fire? Should we trust her to use magic alone?"

"It's trust she needs." Aly took her seat. "I think she gets tired of me watching her all the time. She needs this, and I do trust her. I've got her *contained*, so to speak. She can't hurt herself or anyone else, though I suppose she could burn a hole in the floor of our bunk house." Aly shrugged this option away and slid down the wooden bench with as much grace as she could.

Red took his seat across from her. There were no chairs at the head of the table.

"The king joins us!" announced Bruce, a short yet incredibly strong man. He stood, as did everyone else. When Red settled on the bench, the men returned to their seats and slammed their fists to the table. It was their strange, rather enjoyable way of greeting him. It wasn't all ostentatious bows and hand flourishes; it was something the men had invented and felt very *real*.

Seb hammered the table with the rest of them, a bright smile on his face.

A young man with a dark beard stepped through the doorway and took his seat beside Red. Into Red's mind, Aly said, *Reuben would train with Naia, I think. He looks at her every chance he can get. I bet he'll say yes.*

Red stared at Aly as he couldn't very well crane his neck and stare at Reuben. Aly smirked. *Trust me, okay?*

"What have we got tonight?" Reuben said as he slumped down on the bench.

A man near the kitchen walked toward them with a sloshing pitcher of ale. "Shut up and eat what you're given," said the man as he poured drinks.

Aly leaned forward, an eagerness in her eyes. "Reuben, I was wondering if you'd be interested..."

A sound shook the table. Outside, a loud *crack* split the silence of the night.

"Was that a tree?" Amos asked, half standing.

Aly's awareness burst outward like water from a broken dam. She'd let her mind focus on Red...

Men swung their legs over the bench and hurried toward the door, Reuben darting out first. Red slid out and walked behind them. Before they reached the entrance, a sickening *flump* filled the mess hall, and Reuben flopped forward, dead.

21

RED

Someone shouted.

Panic surged through the men. Some scattered out into the night and others back into the mess hall. Aly leaped in front of Red, a sparkling shield of magic descending through the air at her command.

"Stay in here," she barked before darting out into the night.

Red ignored her command and ran toward Reuben.

Aly danced over the ground, into the darkness. He knelt down and, with Bruce's help, hauled Reuben's body back inside the mess hall. They laid him carefully on the table, and the cook immediately began examining a strange burn-like wound on the man's abdomen.

Red stepped away, back outside. Aly was out there. Yin had disappeared, toward the fight no doubt.

Flashes lit the night. At least six figures stood at the edge of the woods. Atop every stack of felled trees, flames burned. Red's chest crushed at the sight.

Men scampered across the open space, trying to find shelter, unsure where the threat was coming from or how to hide from it. Aly screamed her magic into the air, great waves of glittering light arcing up before her as she cast more shields. Beside her stood Naia.

Naia's hands moved as if she were fighting an invisible foe. She was throwing magic around like darts, and Red hoped she wasn't a danger to Aly, standing so near.

All their work was burning. Aly was too busy with the Zealots to put out the flames. Even if every man filled a bucket and tossed it on the trees, it would do little good against that inferno.

"Naia!" Red shouted. He ran across the lawn, keeping low to the ground. "Naia," he hissed from behind the men's bunkhouse. She whipped her head around. He pointed at the burning trees. "Can you save them?"

Without answer, she grabbed her skirts and ran toward the nearest blaze. He nodded at her and turned his attention to Aly. The sorcerers were converging on her.

Red took the moment to dart into his bunkhouse. He fumbled in the darkness for a few seconds as his eyes adjusted. Then he found his gun before returning to the night air.

Where's Seb? He didn't have time to worry. Peeking around the edge of the building, Red scanned the yard. These Zealots wore clothes that matched the forest, and they were hard to see. Only when spells flashed could he make out their forms.

Aly was safe. She couldn't be hurt by these people with their untrained magic, but he didn't know about the other men. Somehow, these Zealots had slipped past Aly's defenses.

He had to protect his men. If they lost the wood, so be it. They'd already lost one man…they could not lose any more.

He aimed his gun in the direction he'd last spotted a Zealot. Movement caught his eye and he fired. The movement didn't stop. He fired again.

"Red!" Aly, breathless, ran up to him.

"Are you hurt?"

"No, but we must get out of here."

"The men," he said, turning toward the mess hall. He still hadn't seen Yin again either.

"I've got them." Aly hissed another spell into the air, a sizzle sounding somewhere at the edge of the forest. He had no idea what she was doing, but the intensity in her eyes told him it was merciless.

"I'll help," he said, grabbing her arm. They took off toward the mess hall. Aly looped her arms around him and soared backward with him over the ground. *Not fair.*

She launched another attack spell. This one hummed with electricity and sparked in the air. She cringed and dropped to the ground, bending over to rest her hands on her knees.

"You all right?"

"It's not me. It's...Reuben," she said after closing her eyes briefly. "His Truthwell just went dark."

"How many?" asked Red.

"Three."

The weight of her words hit like three heavy trees falling on his chest. Three dead men. The rest were fleeing out the front gate. "Get us out of here," he said.

As they ran toward the gate, he glanced back at the burning woodpiles. One seemed to have stopped burning. Naia must have put one of the fires out. Whether some of the wood was salvageable, he didn't know. They might not have the chance to find out.

He spotted the flash of a curved blade and knew Yin was fighting a Zealot near one of the massive fires.

Aly cast an arm toward the flames. With a great hiss, another giant pile ceased burning. Billowing smoke obscured their view of the forest.

"It's done, Aly. It can all burn now. We can't save that wood."

She gripped his arm and, with the strength his energy provided, she lifted him into the air once more and swung his body around so that she carried him chest to chest over the ground. It was an odd sensation, to be this close to her. He could feel her heart hammering inside of her. But this was no intimate moment. Terror pumped in his veins, and he could see it on her face as well.

This was how they'd risen from the Canyon. She'd held him then too, even when she'd feared her magic was breaking.

He'd be dead without her.

Alyana Barron, you're the strongest woman I know. The strangeness of the flight, the closeness of their faces, and the danger of the moment kept him from speaking those words aloud.

She muttered, "Aloft fly the ones who find the way of truth." They rose higher in the air. As they left the camp, she swept the ground with a spell that raked all shrubs, grass, trees, and even the burning piles of timber out of their path and left nothing behind. Soon, a wall of flaming debris stood between them and the attacking Zealots. She touched down on the ground, releasing Red immediately and whirling back toward the lumberyard.

"They won't come after us," she declared. At those words, she collapsed.

Red dropped to the ground beside her. "Aly?" He pressed his hand to her back. She wept into the soil. "Aly, are you okay? It's over now."

Magic didn't drain her, so this was something else.

"Reuben," she whispered between sobs. "Mauri. George. They didn't make it."

"You defended us. It's not your fault." *She didn't say Seb's name.* Amos and Yin were also absent from her list of the dead.

"I was supposed to keep you all alive!" She slammed a fist into the dirt. "My magic was...I was distracted." She sat bolt upright, glaring at Red. "You! I got distracted by *you*, and people died!"

He recoiled. "Are you saying their deaths are somehow my fault?"

She pressed two dirty hands to her face. "No," she moaned.

"But I can't do this, Red. I can't...let you do this. It's what I want." Her eyes peeked out between her fingers. "Desperately. But I hate myself for even saying that." Her legs kicked against the ground, tantrum-like. "Those men are dead."

He stared at the distant flames for several minutes. She was right. He hated himself for agreeing with her. Being with Aly was a danger not only to themselves, but to any who relied on her magic. It wasn't fair. It wasn't *okay*. He needed her, and she'd admitted she wanted him.

Theod, why does life have to be like this?

When he'd said he was irresistible, he'd meant it as a joke. It had led to three men's deaths.

His throat tightened. "Seb?" He needed her to confirm he was alive.

She shook her head. "He's alive. Somewhere over there." She pointed off to the left. "Oh! Naia!" She hopped up and spun around.

"I'm here," Naia said, her shadow emerging into the dim glow of Aly's distant, flaming wall. "I can't fly like you." She placed her hands on her knees and heaved air. She must be fast, considering how far she'd run from camp.

Aly swept Naia into a tight hug. "I'm so sorry," Aly said, as if somehow what had happened was her fault.

"What are we going to do now?" asked Naia. She glanced at Red and added, "My king." She offered a small, unpracticed curtsey. "I'm coming with you. Wherever you're going, I'm coming. I will not stay here."

"Sure. You can come with us," Aly said, answering before Red could form a response. They couldn't leave Naia here, but he disliked the idea of an untrained sorcerer tagging along with them.

Them. What was to become of Aly and him? He'd lost three men tonight. He needed to mourn them. He needed to recognize that their work these past weeks, along with his hopes of helping Mardon, had all burned up.

Aly. He needed Aly.

Toss all the rules. Toss all the stupid reasons they weren't supposed to be together.

He ran both hands through his hair, where, shockingly, his coronet still rested. He snatched it off his head and stared at it for a moment. The metal felt cool in his hands, glinting dully. It represented the expectations his father had held for him, the strife since his father's death, and his own failures in trying to retain his crown. He tossed it out into the night with a grunt.

"What are you doing?" Aly asked.

"It's over, Aly. All of it." *Mardon won't see any of the ways I've tried to help. No one will care.*

Off to the left, Seb hollered as he crashed toward them like a bull through the tall grasses. Relief washed over Red at his friend's voice.

Aly lifted her chin in an apparent debate with herself, then sighed and reached out her arm. In a moment, his coronet soared back into view and settled again on his head. "Do *not* give up," she demanded.

"What use is it to return to Mardon now? I have nothing to bring." His stomach growled, an insult to the more important matters they now faced.

Aly looked at Naia, then back to Red before saying, "You have a throne to win."

ALY

Dust swirled at Aly's skirt hem, and clouds of gnats hovered over the sunbaked road. Her skin burned with heat, exacerbated by her dancing nerves and the rhythm of her furious heart. She pushed a breeze against their little band of exiles, which did little other than keep her hair out of her eyes.

They marched toward Mardon with nothing more than a dream and a feeble plan.

Beside her, Red stared toward his city, his fortress, his home. His shoulders slumped despite the fierceness in his eyes and the doggedness in his steps. By day's end they would reach Mardon.

A stripe of green hugged the banks of the Cresen to their left. The return was slow and arduous without all their horses, many of which had spooked and run off the night of the attack. The carriages had all burned, along with everything of value at the camp.

The men walked behind Red, as if following their general. They'd secured a wagon from a farmer near the Crescent Forest for what little they could salvage from the camp. It also carried the bodies of the three men they'd lost. Aly's magic preserved them against the summer heat and the flies, but it couldn't preserve the families from the pain heading their way.

News of the disaster in the lumberyard had traveled faster than their feet could carry them. Though few lived near the Crescent Forest, Alexander had eyes and ears waiting in the nearest large town, Excheter. Sorcerers there had sent word back to Mardon that the attempt had failed and ended in tragedy.

Now, Red walked toward a city that had demanded he not return. The men walking with him were not headed toward welcome but war, their lots cast with his.

A warning from Alexander's sorcerer—a person they had yet to identify—had come to Aly as they'd left Excheter. *If he returns, he will be killed, as will any who try to protect him.*

A bold threat coming from a man not yet crowned.

The threat was meant for Aly as well, though it amused her that Alexander would threaten her when he hoped to claim her as his own sorcerer, should the coronation proceed as planned.

Aly's heart ached with the thought of it. Red's Well swirled tumultuously beside her. She had Pulled from it all day and night, her magic welded to his being in the masterful way Theod himself had designed, the way that kept sorcerers from containing all power within themselves. The thought of severing her Binding to him made her hands shake.

Who am I without him?

Red coughed, startling her out of her troubled reverie. He was more than his light, more than the power he provided her. He was so much more.

Images flooded her mind: Red swinging an axe, Red losing himself in the music of a piano sonata, fists pounding the table at his arrival, his kiss, the way he'd honored her in all their hours alone.

He must have sensed her gaze or the direction of her thoughts, because he reached out his hand and clasped hers, linking his fingers through her own—all without turning his head.

She pressed her eyes shut and squeezed his fingers.

Words were difficult, but she wanted to speak with him before they arrived at the city. They needed to discuss what they were facing as neither had said a word about it on the return journey.

What if Alexander takes the crown? What if— She stopped herself. She tugged on Red's hand as she paused on the road.

"What?" he asked, puzzled.

Everyone on the road behind them stopped too.

Aly flicked a glance at Seb and jerked her chin in the direction they'd been traveling.

"All right, everyone, keep walking," Seb announced, whirling an arm through the air. He nodded at Aly and led everyone down the road. Yin looked reluctant to put any distance between him and his king again, but he obeyed.

When the men reached a little distance ahead, Aly wrapped her shroud around Red and herself and let go of his hand.

"What is it?" he asked again, eyes wild with worry. They hadn't said much aside from small talk since leaving Excheter.

"The coronation is in two days," she said, by way of preface. They both knew this, but she had to broach the subject they'd been avoiding.

Red shrugged and huffed out a hot breath. "Alexander can't expect me not to at least show up. If he thinks he can kill me with you by my side, he's downright mad."

His words gave her pause, though she couldn't quite pinpoint why. "True. I won't let him hurt you. He must know that." Then, she blinked as his statement echoed in her head and with it, clarity. A new thought formed as she turned in a slow circle, a potter crafting a jug with tentative hands, spinning and watching a shape emerge. "Wait, *that's* it. Don't you see? Alexander *is* mad."

"You don't say?"

Aly pursed her lips. "He's not thinking straight. As in, I think he's potentially compromised his ability to Bind." There it was, the thought she'd been grasping for, the thing she'd been missing and now saw plain as day.

Red's brows rose, his mouth twisting in confusion.

"See," she said, stepping forward, "if he's been lying, he won't be able to Bind at all." An unexpected laugh burst from her lips. "What's odd is that he should know this. He's likely read the Binding ritual, and he must know that to Bind with the one sworn to protect the crown, he must have *a clear conscience and a sound mind*, as the vows state."

Red scratched his chin. "Is lying and being an idiot the same thing?"

She slapped his shoulder. "No, but I bet that he had something to do with that rotten seed. And I wouldn't be surprised if somehow he set those sorcerers on us at the lumberyard. It was too well timed, too perfectly aligned with what he wanted."

Red sighed and turned away, hands raking his sweat-darkened hair. "No one could prove that."

Aly bit her lip, knowing he was right but not wanting to give up on this new idea. "If we can prove Alexander was lying, he won't be *able* to Bind. Then, it would be obvious how awful he is and how silly this whole thing has been, and the people would want you anyway!" Her words piled up on top of themselves as she spilled over with excitement.

Red kept his hands on his head for a quiet moment. Aly swatted a nosy bee away from her dingy blue dress.

He turned to her. "If he's really a liar, and you really think he won't be able to Bind, then why are we afraid at all?" A mischievous smile curled one side of his mouth. "All this time, we've been giving him more things to lie about. If in two days he's standing at the head of the cathedral, hand on the *Verad*, trying to Bind with you, and it doesn't work, everyone will know it." He smiled up at the cloudless sky. "He'll be exposed in front of the entire nobility, the priesthood, and the royal family." Now he looked at her with wild, fierce eyes, and her insides caught fire. "Thank Theod you remembered what those vows said, because I forgot."

She smiled back. "I don't know why I didn't think of it sooner."

"You thought of it in time, that's all that matters." He smiled with a flicker of mad hope. Then he blinked and his expression hardened. "Aly, you need to go to the coronation, no matter what happens between now and then." He reached for her shoulders with both hands. "No matter what happens to me, you go and you show the world that he's a fraud."

He marched off toward his men, a new energy in his step.

She cupped her neck with her fingers and smiled at his back. Maybe she wouldn't have to lose him after all.

Mardon's skyline hugged the horizon, its spires and smokestacks stabbing dark fingers into the swelling light of dawn. Aly's white cloak whipped around her as she drove a fierce wind toward the city, carrying with it a handful of spells. She'd never cast magic this far.

Tell me where my enemies are, she commanded her magic. Her ability to see Truthwells told her a small army waited for them at Mardon's entry points. Groups of men stood in perfect formation along each of the main roads into the city.

Alexander was ready for their return.

But more than the location of the soldiers, Aly needed to know where the sorcerers hid among Alexander's men. Weapons were of little use in a battle of magic, but they could kill Red and his men if she was distracted by fighting other Masters.

Her spell couldn't pick out the Truthwells of sorcerers, but she'd crafted the spell to pinpoint their Master's rings, the ones they all wore that were held together by magic. That magic would leave a tiny signature, as long as the rings were consuming energy.

One, two, three, four, five. She counted as her spell identified the rings of five different Masters. The spell wouldn't search the entire city, only among the soldiers. Alexander likely had all his defenses lined up, ready to fight. He wanted to present his strongest showing. No sense hiding his Masters deep within the city, as Aly would have recommended.

Five Masters. She swallowed. That was more sorcerers than she'd ever fought. Naia paced nervously in the field behind them, her hands wringing, her gaze flying toward the city every few seconds. Her magic might help, but it could just as likely go awry right when they needed it.

She needs our trust, Aly reasoned.

Aly sent another spell toward the city, a protective spell for Isabelle, Elise, and Carolyn, wherever they travelled. The palace had its enchantments, but should Alexander kick the women to the streets, they would remain safe from most other spells cast, at least.

Elise, despite her actions toward Seb, did not deserve to die in the crossfire of a sorcerers' war.

Naia questioned Aly from nearby. "How do you make the magic flow so far in one direction?"

Aly lowered her hands and the breeze stilled. The calm summer morning hummed with the song of birds and the buzz of insects. Grasses poked against Aly's long cloak, snagging the fabric.

Red and Seb and the other men stood in a line facing the sunrise over the city of Mardon.

Aly smiled at Naia. "I send it with the breeze. My mind can picture the breeze flooding the streets, and I imagine my magic floating on that breeze. It helps." She touched Naia's arm. "Magic is most controlled when our thoughts are most disciplined." It was a line from the *Canticles of Magic,* one Ondorian had often brought up in her early days of learning the *Verad.* "Images can help us solidify our ideas," she added. "Theod gifted us with the truth to control our magic, but he also gave us imagination as well."

Naia smiled and nodded.

Now Aly turned around and met Red's waiting gaze. Alexander had warned them not to return without wood. Somehow, the man had known they would return empty-handed. If Aly were the betting type, she'd wager Alexander was behind the loss of wood, unlikely as it appeared.

"He has the city blockaded."

The men grunted, but they'd expected this.

"How many Masters?" Red cut straight to the heart of the problem.

"Five," she muttered, eyes down.

"Oy!" yelled Seb. He rubbed his hands up and down his temples and stomped around the field in small circles. He, too, had been warned against returning.

If Seb set foot in Mardon, Alexander had promised to make a public display of him, first with lashing in the city square—an antiquated and brutally excessive punishment—followed by stripping him of his title and banishing him from Mardon once again.

Aly wanted to rip the mustache right off Alexander's face. From here.

The thought made her lip quirk in amusement.

"What will you do, sir?" asked Amos Johnson. These men hadn't left Red's side. Amos, as well as the other men, were dirty, sore from travel, and tired. They were in no fit state to fight, yet they carried their shoulders high and their hopes higher. But what was a dozen men against an army?

Red stared at the city for several minutes, the rising sunlight blazing off his hair, his coronet, then, finally his face. He blinked and looked at Amos. "I will return. I do not ask you to accompany me. In fact, I wish you all to remain here, where it is safe."

Amos's stubbly face sagged a moment. He was the oldest in the group, and he'd become somewhat of a spokesman for the other lumberjacks. Then he pulled off his hat and saluted. The other men mirrored his action. A warmth blossomed inside of Aly at their respect for Red.

Yin however, stepped forward. "I will not leave your side, my king." He'd incurred a severe burn on his hands and part of his neck from one Zealot's erratic magic. Aly had healed him, but his skin remained a shade pinker where the strange magic had touched him.

Red nodded at him.

Seb beat his fist against his chest twice. "I'll also go."

"No," Red countered.

"It's not exactly your choice, mate."

Red frowned. Elise had pushed this awful fate on Red's best friend. Certainly, she'd been threatened, coerced, or otherwise blackmailed into it. Nothing else made sense.

"What good will your presence do?" Red asked his friend. "Stay away from the city until this is over."

"I'm no coward. I want Alexander to see my face when I laugh at him and his stupid edicts." Seb marched forward, crushing wildflowers with each step.

Red glanced at Aly. She supposed it was now or never. They had to return to the city, one way or another. Coronation was tomorrow. The city needed to see Red's determination, if nothing else. They wouldn't know of his attempts to fix the food shortage. They wouldn't know of his attempts to bring wood to rebuild the city. They wouldn't know of how he'd lived like a vagabond for weeks, gaining firsthand knowledge of what it felt like to have nothing or to perform backbreaking physical labor. They wouldn't know any of this.

They would only know that he hadn't given up.

But to the people, would that appear like entitlement? Red wanted the throne because he wanted to *lead* Tandera, to nurture her and protect her, not because he wanted her riches or her power or the deference of a multitude. Aly pressed her fingers to her lips as she watched Red stare out at his city. He was not the boy who'd barged into her room the morning Gevar had died.

He was a king.

To Naia, she whispered, "Keep them safe," and stepped toward Red.

He flashed a smile, saluted his men, and rushed toward his city with all the fury of a summer storm.

Aly stalked beside Red, Seb, and Veeter Yin on the road. No carriages travelled the path at this early hour. The thumping of their feet on the packed dirt became a steady rhythm, their own battle drum.

"I can't fight them all," she whispered to her companions. They had to know this, but she didn't want them overestimating her ability.

"Just keep us alive," Red answered, eyes fixed forward.

A crier spotted them and, before they'd passed the first home on the outskirts of the capital, soldiers fanned out across the road ahead.

"Here we go," said Seb.

With one more small spell, Aly cast off all the dirt from their clothes and hair—as best she could. The effect was small but pronounced. She glanced sideways, noting how Red's coronet caught the morning light.

"Halt!" A soldier stepped forward. "Do not approach, or we have orders to attack."

Attack? Alexander was out of his mind. He'd gone too far in this. His claims against Red's character had worked well enough, why bother with this show of force? It made him appear afraid.

Aly's body trembled as she waited for Red's next move. She was electric, her magic ready to explode in a hundred directions, with a dozen ready spells.

Faces appeared in windows. *Good, they need to see this.* They'd see four people standing up to an army. They'd see Alexander's injustice, Red's courage.

"That's it," she mumbled. *Come and see your king.*

Red lifted his voice. "I wish to speak with Alexander."

The soldiers ignored him.

They might have to wait a long time. Aly had sworn she wouldn't help him win back his throne with magic, but she would keep Red upright, preventing him from weakening, even if they stood out here for hours or even into the night. Her magic could at least do that.

Alexander did make them wait.

While they did, every so often, Red would repeat his request. Still, the soldiers ignored him, standing still as the morning warmed to an uncomfortable degree.

Aly walked around, her cloak and mask the only movement on the street. Occasionally she would disappear and reappear a few steps later. She wanted the watching eyes to have something to look at or they might grow bored and turn away. Eventually, she began crafting creatures from the dust, swooping her arms in large gestures, raking clouds of grayish dirt into the air and forming them to her heart's desire. People watching from windows began to clap.

Excellent, keep watching. She wasn't helping Red regain his throne in this way, but she was ensuring people witnessed what was happening here.

By midmorning, citizens trickled into the streets, then swarmed. They squished into the spaces between buildings and peered out of upstairs windows.

Aly smiled to herself. Now what would Alexander do? He couldn't fire on them or attack at all, not with so many witnesses. He would have to listen to Red's request.

As noon approached, Alexander finally appeared.

Dressed in king's attire, complete with ostentatious crown, he stepped between the lines of soldiers and onto the street. "You should not have returned."

Red stood straighter. "This is my city. My country. I shall travel where I will, when I will."

Alexander *hmphed*. "You think so, but I wear this." He pointed at his crown.

"Stolen crowns do not make a man a king."

"I have as much royal blood in my veins as you," quipped Alexander. "The difference is, I have not been corrupted by the Deep. You are poison for Tandera, and I the antidote." He pranced back and forth before his armed men like a pony on parade. A pony with a long, grey mustache.

Aly sneered at him, but it did no good. She couldn't fight this man until Red gave the command. Instead, she pressed her awareness around Alexander's Truthwell. As she expected, it swirled with black streaks and pockets of shadow. He was full of lies.

Red's Well, in comparison, had few shadows snaking among the million points of dazzling light. She'd almost lost him once to the darkness. She would not lose him now to this liar.

Almost as soon as she'd finished this thought, Red stepped forward and drew his ash blade. Instantly, twenty rifles trained on him. Aly's blood turned to ice.

"I do not want to fight," he yelled over the growing hubbub in the crowd. "I want the people to choose their king." He set the blade on the cobblestones where it glowed innocently.

Aly deflated. He was too good for them. For all of them.

Alexander burst out laughing. "Choose? What a notion!" When he recovered, he turned to his men. "Hear that? This madman wants the *throne* of this nation to be determined by no more than the choice of the people. That is an insult to Theod! He alone chooses sovereigns." Several people in the crowd grunted their agreement.

Well, when you say it like that, Aly grumbled to herself. Alexander was a skilled manipulator. A white cloak hovered just behind the line of soldiers. She'd not noticed it until now. His personal Protector, then. The mask was hard to see, but it looked a bit like a wolf.

Alexander swung back around, arms lifted. "A man without reason cannot rule. Surely you all see this."

Hypocrite, grumbled Aly.

He blazed on. "Prince Frederick was corrupted in that Canyon, and his rationality is breaking down. It is what I have been telling you this whole summer."

The crowd shifted. Tension mounted, and Aly could see Wells swirling with the battle between truth and lies. Every person was a mixture of the truth and the lies they'd believed their entire lives. Theod's light within them was often buried under years of darkness. Aly closed her eyes, trying to feel the way the people were leaning.

Shadows swarmed inside of every Well, including Red's and Seb's. To have shadows was to be human, for it meant there was a capacity to believe a lie. She sighed. The light around her was beautiful, perhaps even more so because of the way it swirled among the darkness.

When she opened her eyes, the faces around her were frowning. Her muscles tensed. These people, though she'd wanted them present, were not looking upon them with favor. She stepped backward, shocked.

See the truth, she begged them, internally.

But they saw what they'd been told to see. A lunatic trying to face an army on his own.

Before it happened, she sensed it.

A spell leaked through the air toward them. She stopped it with a word. Then, from five—no *six*—directions at once, spells flew at them.

Her arms whirled like a windmill as she tried to stop each spell as it reached for them. Her shield broke most of them, but some were designed to puncture shields, while others were less obvious. Some were the spells of Comforters, freezing spells or burning spells—an odd addition to the more sophisticated magic of the Masters.

Red, Seb, and Yin watched her, but they could do nothing.

Alexander's mouth flattened, then turned down, as Aly battered away every spell hurtled at them. The spells were so numerous that a powder-like cloud of pale light surrounded Red, Aly, and Seb. Despite the hot afternoon, an icy breeze now whirled around them from all the magic in the air.

"Take it!" screamed Alexander after another minute. "Take his crown!"

Aly spun, danced, leapt, and slashed, her movements mirroring her magic as she directed spells with her hands. Her cloak rippled and snapped; her braid waved like a snake.

After a moment, Alexander lifted a hand. The oncoming spells stopped.

"Very well," Alexander said. "Fire."

23

RED

At the sound of two dozen rifles discharging, Red's body lurched, but he managed to keep his hands clasped behind his back, turning only his face away. All that practice shooting at Aly had calmed his knee-jerk response to gunfire.

A flash of white light blinded him. In the instant it dimmed, he found himself on the ground, wrists sore from colliding with the cobbled road.

Before he could gather himself enough to stand, the ground fell away beneath him, Mardon shrinking so fast it made his stomach lurch and he feared he would wretch down upon the men who'd just shot at him.

Seb's hollering screams drew his attention, but, unaccustomed to being shoved like a ragdoll through the air, Red couldn't find the coordination to look over at Seb.

"You all right?" he shouted.

Seb's only response was a higher-pitched scream.

They crashed onto a rooftop crisscrossed with hanging sheets and underclothes. The fabric whipped in the wind made by their arrival, a dozen ethereal banners waving at them.

Red took a moment to ensure his head was no longer spinning and his last meal wasn't about to reconstitute itself. When he stood, a whistling sound drew his eye upward.

Aly slammed down beside him, landing with barely a bend in her knees, like she arrived this way to all important occasions. Her cloak settled around her, but the hair around her face remained wind-tossed. Her eyes held a deadly ferocity.

She marched past him and yanked Seb up from where he was sniveling like a lost child.

"Never do that again," Seb choked, pressing both hands to his stomach.

"What? Save your life?" Aly nodded. "Got it."

"Aly, thank you," Red said, his anger at Alexander tempered by his total admiration for Aly. "Where are we?" He gazed out over the rooftops. The cathedral's spire was to his right. The roads here appeared narrow, and judging by the laundry all around them, there were no Comforters living in this neighborhood. "Where is Yin?" His heart shrank.

"He and I had a deal." At Red's surprised expression, she added, "I deposited him just inside the city, to throw off the search for you. He'll be fine. He's enchanted. And to answer your other question, we're in the Creaks. Best place to hide." She winked at Red.

Seb looked at Aly and Red. "Won't his sorcerers find us?"

Aly peered over the edge of the building, looked left and right, then whirled back around. "Yes. They will eventually find us. I only hope to hide us until the coronation. I got us into the city, at least."

Seb nodded exaggeratedly. "Yes, you did. If that's how the birds feel every day, I'd hate to be one."

"One more day," Red muttered, ignoring Seb.

Red's future with Aly and the fate of Tandera, including Red's dream to close the Canyon once and for all, would be decided tomorrow.

I wish I could have brought those trees home, he thought for the hundredth time. He would have to save Tandera once he was officially crowned. Until then, all he could do was wait.

Aly stepped to the edge of the building, her feet never wavering on the small bricks. "This is where Amos' family lives. They will shelter you. I will work on sneaking the rest of the men into the city. Not sure Alexander's sorcerers will allow any others to fly in, so I'll need to get creative. My protective spells won't falter, even when I'm away." She lifted a hand. "I'll be back by nightfall." And she leaped off the building.

Amos stared at Red across his small sitting room, where Amos' wife and children huddled in the corner on their bed, pretending to play a game of jacks. The two children kept covering yawns and glancing up at Red, Aly, and Seb, eyes wide with curiosity, despite their mother's swats and admonitions to let the people talk. The children seemed delighted to be up so late.

"Sire," said Amos. "We have men. Two hundred. Ready to fight for you."

It took Red a moment to comprehend his words. Amos waggled his bushy brows. There was a twinkle of rebellion in his eyes. His chin was freshly shaven, his hair combed. He wore a vest.

"Looking sharp, Amos," Red said, glancing around, as if these two hundred men would come slinking out of the woodwork.

"Well, they ain't here, sir." Amos took off his hat, clutched it at his chest.

"Where did you find two hundred men on such short notice?" They'd been in Mardon a matter of hours.

Amos grinned. "You did. When you spoke to the people on the street that day after church. People 'round here talked about it for weeks. When you came to the lumberyard, people heard 'bout that. People even heard 'bout that load of rotten seed that was tossed in the burn pile outside the city. And we told them about the wood." He leaned forward. "People *know* what you been doing, sire. They know, and they're with you."

For a moment, Red stared at Amos. His gaze drifted to Amos' wife and children. The people of Mardon—at least some of them —knew what he'd attempted for them. And they didn't care that he'd failed—they cared that he'd tried.

"We will fight, Your Majesty."

Pride swelled in Red's heart. "Thank you, brother, but I don't anticipate a fight."

Seb shook his head. "You should. If she's right," he pointed at Aly, "Alexander will be left looking like a fool in that gaudy coronation crown, and I doubt he'll simply hand it to you and say, 'My apologies, here you go.'" Seb used his best Alexander-impersonation that made the children laugh.

Aly uncrossed her arms under her cloak, which stood out against the dim interior of Amos' home. "I think it would be wise to have your men present," she agreed.

Amos slapped his knee. "We gonna fight, sir, one way or another. They'll see the end of our pistols sooner or later. It's been a long time coming, this wretched summer."

Maybe they were right, but Red hoped this would end without bloodshed. Aly had to be correct about the Binding— Alexander was the one not fit to rule. Power hungry did not equate to madness, but there was something off in the way Alexander had plotted this coup and in the way he'd snatched up so much loyalty and admiration from citizens who only months ago had wept at Gevar's funeral and celebrated at Red's Accession Ball.

"Two hundred, you say?" Red asked.

Amos grinned, then saluted. "Started gathering the moment we sent word you'd returned. Want to meet them?"

~

The room above Everett Street was cramped and hot with so many men—and one woman, as Naia stood among them, arms crossed and face downcast—crammed in the tiny space. It was the nicest and most accommodating headquarters Amos and his fellows could find. Yin stood against the wall to the right, his arms crossed, his face as stern as ever. Among the gathered faces, three masks peered back. Three more sorcerers.

Most of the two hundred soldiers recruited by Amos and his friends couldn't fit in this room but they were all hidden away in rooms on this street or the next. It was the best they could do on short notice. Dawn was only hours away.

Two doors down stood the empty building Red and Aly had occupied that night he'd kissed her.

His insides blazed with anticipation as he took a seat in a single wooden chair in the center of one wall. All other furniture had been removed from the apartment to make room for this improvised meeting space.

The men saluted and muttered excitedly among themselves. Red scanned the faces. His men from the Crescent Forest, every last one of them, as well as faces he didn't recognize, watched him with admiration, waiting for his first words as their commander.

This was foolishness, but it had a flare of mad hope to it—and that was Red's specialty.

He grinned and stood. No leader should sit at a moment like this. He'd never commanded troops before. He'd barely even paid attention in military history lessons, but he'd watched his father closely over the years. Gevar always stood when addressing a crowd, no matter how small.

"Men," he began, "thank you for coming."

"Long live the king!" someone shouted.

Red nodded. "Thank you, but we should wait until after coronation to make those declarations."

"You're our king!"

He paused, trying to memorize every man's features. He wanted to *know* these men, the ones he'd never met, the ones who didn't know him but wanted to fight for him. But no king could know every one of his soldiers. It was an honor to know strangers would take up arms with him—for him. "Tomorrow will be an interesting day," he said. "I do not expect any bloodshed." A few murmurs. "But I will *not* sit idly by while a liar takes the throne and—" he cleared his throat, "—the Royal Sorcerer." He glanced at Aly. "But when he tries to Bind with Aly, with the Royal Sorcerer," he added for the group's benefit, "he will not be able to if he has acquired the throne by lying."

"Won't work if he been lying?" shouted one man. "Guess we know how that'n will turn out."

Laughter shuffled through the cramped space.

Red looked over at Aly. "I am not willing to give up. Not the throne, not the Royal Sorcerer." A few men whistled. Red's cheeks burned, but he pressed on. It was time the world knew how he felt about Aly, rumors be tossed. "If it comes to a fight, know that I go to this fight not merely for the promise of a throne that once was mine, but for the promise of remaining beside the woman I love."

The whoops and hollers of Seb and the other men dissolved as he met Aly's wide-eyed stare. In her face was the future he wanted, the world he needed, and the stability he craved.

Aly's eyes remained wide as coins, her cheeks redder than his own, but a small, astonished smile curled one corner of her lips.

"All right," he grunted, steeling his swirling nerves and turning back to the men and Naia. "We need to plan our course of action for tomorrow, examining all possible scenarios. Alexander has at least six sorcerers fighting with him, not to mention the regiment." He pinched his fingers over his nose, wiping away sweat.

"But we have her," said one man, pointing at Aly.

Aly's voice was small but carried to every ear. "I serve the crown. Whomever wears it tomorrow will be the person I'm Bound to protect."

"You mean you could be fighting *against* us if Alexander wins?" said another young man.

Aly cringed and peered at Red. "My vows bid me protect the one to whom I am Bound. I will not harm you, if it comes to that."

The crowd shuffled and murmured, but Red lifted his hands. "She is no threat to any of you. And I will not lose her." He smiled again at her and she nodded back.

They talked strategy until every face dripped sweat and the moon cast shadows on the floor. By dawn, they had a plan.

Most of the soldiers returned home to their families, but Red had designated twenty men as leaders among the rest, and to these men he now looked. "I think it will work." It was a mad hope, but he was okay with that—it was becoming his style. "Today, we will see whom Theod has chosen to lead this nation."

24

ELISE

The entire palace buzzed with the news of Red's return. In the Rose Room, the morning meal had been served, but Elise was not interested in food. To keep up her charade, she nibbled on a piece of buttered bread, lifting silent prayers to a god she wasn't sure would listen to her after what she'd done.

Carolyn sipped her tea with a brooding expression, not trying to hide her discomfort.

Lady Alexander sat at the head of the small table, the mother hen among all those courting favor with the usurper, soon to be king, if her brother failed to magically sway the entire nobility and the army back to his good graces.

"Elise, darling," cooed Lady Alexander, "What do you make of your brother's return?"

Elise had steeled herself for these comments as she'd dressed this morning. "He is a fool to return, my lady." *And he'd be a fool not to, as you well know.*

Alexander's attack on her brother wasn't her fault either, but she carried the weight of her betrayal like a fifty-pound sack of flour hung around her neck. She'd committed to her role as informant, but she'd never assumed people would actually be hurt.

How wrong she'd been.

The food tasted rotten, from the smoked ham to the poached eggs to the lemon cakes. All Elise could think about was whether her brother was alive or dead. And Seb, what would happen to him?

At the meal's conclusion, an envelope was presented to Lady Alexander.

"Ah," said the gray-haired woman. Her thick neck glimmered with diamonds. "It appears that before the coronation, there is to be a flogging in the square."

Several women gasped in surprise. Elise's fork paused over her plate as fear lurched through her veins. She hoped her reaction was no more or less noticeable than the reactions of shock from the other women.

Lady Alexander curled a thin smile at Elise. "Sebastian Thorin has been discovered."

Elise's stomach flipped, but she covered her discomfort by patting her mouth with her napkin and setting it gingerly aside. Her hands broke into a sweat. *At least he's not dead.* The thought brought only little comfort.

Carolyn tilted her head as the servants cleared the last of the plates. "A flogging seems an odd prelude to a coronation, do you agree?"

Lady Alexander painted a measured smile across her thin, wrinkling lips. "I believe it is meant to set a precedent."

"But my brother is not fool enough to show himself today, surely?" Elise pressed, digging for information. Pulling secrets from Lady Alexander was like pulling feathers from a down pillow—they poked out everywhere and slid out with little effort.

Lady Alexander clicked her tongue as the women began to rise. "Your brother, it appears, has gathered a pathetic little army of commoners to attend today's coronation. That is how Sebastian was discovered—he was leading a group of these men through the streets." She rose last. "Come, my dears, we must watch this demonstration." She smiled at the ladies, as if her sparkling presence were enough to lighten the dour mood. "In support of our new sovereign."

Elise stood beside Lady Alexander at the edge of Mardon's largest square, the cathedral's spire pointing directly at the sun. A dark-robed priest stood on the top step, arms crossed in disapproval. He was the fill-in for Arthur Ondorian, who'd apparently disappeared on an oddly timed leave of absence. A huge crowd murmured all around, coaxed to the scene by Alexander's threats.

A post had been erected in the center of the square. Seb stood shirtless with hands bound above his head.

The whip snapped the air, then a loud *pop* signaled that the first lash had been dealt. Elise cringed and looked away, an acceptable action for a lady, thus one she didn't need to hide. Seb made no noise, but his body collapsed against the post.

Carolyn sobbed quietly a few feet away. She'd not spoken to Elise since they'd left the dining room. Elise kept her gaze from wandering to her sister and mother. What had become of Red and Aly? What was her brother thinking bringing a small army against Tandera's military?

"Poor soul," whispered Lady Alexander, no sympathy in her tone. She pressed a handkerchief to her mouth, possibly to block the scent of the sweaty crowd. "Does it pain you to watch?"

Elise wanted to vomit onto the pavement beneath her feet as another lash cracked through the stillness and rocked Seb's body. "No." The lie went down like a piece of broken glass.

He was only to receive five lashes. She could endure it. He

would live. He would heal. Grey had warned her that this job would break her.

She had to believe it was worth it, to have gained the trust of her enemy. Now that she'd gained the Alexanders' favor, she sensed a new direction for her future as an informant—one in which she might not be heading for Refere after all. Her new goal was to bring ruin upon this loathsome family who'd hurt the people she cared about most.

With an inhale, she braced herself to watch the final lash. Blood sparkled in the bright sun. Her insides ached.

The whip cracked. Seb's groan reached her ears and she nearly fainted. She hoped her face remained unaltered.

Someone walked up and untied Seb's hands. He collapsed to the makeshift platform with a *thunk*, his head landing with his gaze toward her.

She looked away. "A pitiful sight indeed," she said.

As Lady Alexander led her away, Elise caught sight of Weston Grey watching her from among the crowd. He stood beside some of Alexander's most trusted men. He was playing this game too. Did the remorse ever dissipate? Did the self-hatred eventually harden one's heart enough that betrayal no longer hurt?

Would she end up like him, calloused and unfeeling?

As the crowd began to move into the cathedral for the coronation, he gave her the most imperceptible nod of approval.

The cathedral was bursting with people crammed into every pew. White cloaks and elaborate masks dotted the crowd. Princess Redonna of Virienne was led in toward a front row seat. Elise knew who would enter next.

King Lordan of Refere pranced into the nave like some grand peacock. His bright blue suit and sash of silken ivory glared among the pale summer hues of the crowd's attire. Elise, from her seat on the third row beside a large woman in a feathered hat, did not so much as look his way as he passed and took his seat among the most honored guests.

Her heart twanged. She hated him more than ever for still affecting her. Perhaps a stone heart would be beneficial.

Once all the important guests had taken their seats, the ceremony began. Elise's thigh pressed against the woman beside her. Sunlight streamed through stained glass onto the altar where the priest stood, waiting to make Benedict Alexander the King of Tandera. Only four months ago, Red had said these same vows in the temporary Accession Council. Coronations were grand events that required months of coordination. In those months, so much had changed.

Her brother should have been the one standing up there, reciting the vows of sovereignty. Ondorian possibly couldn't stomach the idea of coronating Alexander; perhaps that was why he'd disappeared and an unknown priest was conducting the ceremony.

The crowd rose as Benedict Alexander entered the narthex and began his march toward the altar, a train the length of the nave in his wake.

A weight pressed on Elise's chest. The tall ceilings and the magic of many Comforters were not enough to stave off her rising temperature and shortness of breath. The woman beside her offered her a handheld fan. Elise shook her head.

Every time Elise blinked, she saw Seb's bleeding body lying on the platform in the square. If Red showed up with his miniature army, what would happen? Part of her wanted him to swoop in and declare victory, Aly by his side, but another part of her knew Alexander was not giving this up without a fight. She didn't want to see any more blood.

Elise didn't hear a word of the ceremony, not until everything went quiet.

She snapped to attention when the woman beside her leaned over and whispered with giddy anticipation, "The Binding."

Alexander had a sorcerer. He had several, actually. Who would he Bind to? What would become of Aly? Would she and Red simply be able to disappear together? Perhaps that was best. A smile of relief flitted across her face. Possibly something good would come of this after all.

Then the woman elbowed Elise and craned her neck toward the back of the cathedral. Everyone else turned as well, and between the hats and the flowers and the six-foot candelabra lining the aisle, Elise could barely make out what drew people's eyes.

Then she saw her.

From the end of the aisle, dressed in a white cloak, walked Aly.

25

ALY

The cathedral door closed with a soft *thud* behind Aly, hitting her like a train at full speed. She was walking toward Red's redemption, his exoneration, but somehow this felt like a betrayal.

From his place among the throngs outside the cathedral, Red was shrouded and clad in the finest suit Aly's magic could produce. He waited for her to give him the mental command to enter the cathedral. She would wait until the Binding with Alexander had proven him a fraud.

Alexander's mustachioed face flashed a victory smile that reminded Aly of the Canyon's dark depths. His Truthwell was ribboned with black, hungry lines, like ink twisting through water. She smiled right back. He was in for a surprise.

She concentrated on the golden tips of the feathers protruding from her phoenix mask and created the illusion of fire. The crowd *oohed*.

With each step, her heartrate intensified. She'd practiced leveling her emotions, controlling her thoughts, but today they were wild horses, untamable.

Breathe, she told herself as she stepped up to the altar. Ondorian was not present. *Where was he?* Instead, a thin, freckled priest stood holding the *Verad*. His eyes widened as she looked at him.

The priest's throat bobbed before he spoke, and he had to restart to make his voice loud enough. "Ah, the vows of the Binding secure the protection of our sovereign." He angled toward Aly. She did not have to say her vows again, as her word when she'd taken this job six years ago was binding and could not be said again. Aly bowed slightly to the priest.

Theod, help us.

This was it.

She recalled, briefly, what it had been like to Bind to Red—the informality of doing it in the palace yard, the humiliating way she'd fallen into him, overcome with the way his light crashed into her. When she'd Bound to Gevar, she'd anticipated a future of doing the same with Red. She'd not assumed it would happen when he was so young, or that Binding her magic to him would eventually bind her heart as well.

Alexander said his vows with a fierce clarity, never wavering, even on the words *clear conscience and sound mind.*

As each word reverberated against the arched ceiling, Aly's muscled tightened, her smile cinching into a tight-lipped grimace.

She felt it before it truly started, a tiny sensation in the back of her throat, as if she needed to cough. Then, her entire body heated like a blast furnace, her fingers tingling and her mind swelling with the reality of Alexander's Truthwell beside her.

Her magic was *changing.* She could do nothing to stop it— bound as it was by her vows to serve the crown of Tandera.

Aly gasped, doubling over, as her magic lifted from Red's Well—a ripping and tearing that brought bile to her mouth—and instantly clung to Alexander's. She stared at him, his lips curling into a satisfied grin, even as his body shook and his skin radiated light.

His Well, while still bright in places, swirled with darkness.

How? How had this happened?

She wanted to fall to her knees and beg Theod to intervene, but it was his words that secured the vows of the Binding.

The crowd had risen, and were chanting *long live the king.* Aly's heart threatened to damage her chest. She could not control her heaved breaths or her flittering gaze as she desperately looked over her shoulder at the door.

She hadn't called him.

Will he come?

Can he save me?

There had been a time when she couldn't speak to him. He'd come that time, and he had saved her then. But this time, there wasn't much he could do.

She'd been so certain Alexander's lies would prevent him from Binding. *How can he possibly be of sound mind and a clear conscience?*

Theod, what is this? she begged, staring at the rose window set into the wall above the cathedral doors.

She missed the remaining words of the ceremony. Her mind reached for Red. His Well, bright as ever, remained stationary outside in the square. He was waiting for her word. She pressed a hand to her mouth and forced down her scream.

What have I done?

Slowly, Aly turned toward Alexander. He nodded at her and the organ began to play. It was over, the coronation concluded.

Red would know it was over now. He would wonder why she hadn't spoken to him. He would—

The cathedral door burst open—as much as a heavy wooden door could *burst.*

Aly spun, and her heart leapt.

Red marched down the aisle, fists swinging. People started shouting and pointing.

"Why?" he shouted, voice, eyes, and intent only for Aly.

The pained look on his face broke her and she stumbled toward him.

"Stop him," Alexander said calmly.

At once, three white-cloaked figures surrounded Red. He pushed against them violently, landing at least one punch, but then his body went rigid and he ceased struggling.

"Don't hurt him!" Aly shouted. The sorcerers did not obey her.

Alexander lifted a hand to silence the growing murmurs. "I told you he was dangerous. Now, remove yourself peaceably, or I will be forced to—"

The rose window above the cathedral entrance exploded inward, spewing fine glass shards across the vaulted space. Aly yelped a quick spell that turned the glass into falling sand. Everyone ducked, screamed, and bumped into each other in the tight spaces between pews. Sorcerers hovered near the walls, stopping the frightened crowd from jostling toward the exits.

In the round space where the window had been, a figure appeared, wild hair billowing across a face obscured by the sunlight behind it.

"Naia?" Aly had been there when they'd planned this, but they'd not planned Naia entering through the window. She'd finally mastered the spell to fly, then, or perhaps to climb with only her fingertips and toes.

Aly smiled at Naia's accomplishment, then gasped as she recalled what came next in that particular version of their plans.

Screams outside in the square filtered through the now open window. The crowd inside hushed into a terrified silence.

"It won't work!" Aly shouted to Naia. *This* plan, the one where Naia distracted the crowd and the sorcerers with her explosive theatrics, was only supposed to happen if they feared Aly needed a moment to escape. The men would be approaching the cathedral now, weapons at the ready.

Aly couldn't leave. Not now. Her magic was Bound to

Alexander's Well, and she was sworn to protect him at all costs. She pressed her hands to her mouth.

A *clang* sounded at the end of aisle as Red's coronet fell to the stones beneath his head.

Red, still bound and bespelled by his captors, could say nothing. He stared up at Naia, head lolling backward at his awkward angle.

"Ah, finally," said Alexander. "Retrieve that crown," he commanded Aly.

"I will do no such thing."

He raised his bushy brows. "Defy me again, and I will have my other sorcerers torture him," he muttered so only she could hear.

The coronet lifted from the stone and soared through the air to Aly's lifted palm. She clutched it with a white-knuckled fist.

Red coughed and choked on words his frozen tongue couldn't say. This wasn't fair.

Her rage surged like a river after snowmelt. Without warning, the coronet in her hand burst into a cloud of golden dust, sparkling in the diffused light from the colored windows and flaming candles.

Aly yelped in surprise. She hadn't done accidental magic in a long time. Above, where Naia perched, a faint cackle of laughter flowed down.

Angry at Alexander, Aly spat a quiet spell toward the men holding Red. They each stumbled forward, two of them clunked heads, and Red's body fell to the floor. In an instant, he scrambled up and raced the aisle toward Aly.

"Go!" she commanded him, knowing he was racing toward a battle he couldn't win, a future she'd destroyed without meaning to.

He did not stop. Her heart lifted and sank so fast she nearly heaved. With a hand raised toward him, she slowed his progress, pain in her every muscle, every muttered word. She gave a slight shake of her head and nudged him toward the exit. He had to go. Turn his men away. Avoid a fight.

A pounding at the door signaled Red's men had arrived. Aly pressed her eyes shut.

The remaining sorcerers and a handful of uniformed soldiers tramped toward the cathedral doors. Aly prayed the men wouldn't attack. If Red could speak to them, he'd call them off; she knew he would. This was a misunderstanding. Naia had misread Aly's stillness.

Red stared back at Aly, his eyes full of fire that crackled with both anger and confusion. The anger she sensed was not for her, but for Alexander. Even now, he believed in her.

"Armed men," shouted a soldier.

Alexander lifted the hand that wasn't holding the royal scepter. Silence fell inside the nave. His mouth opened, but he hesitated, as if rethinking what he'd planned to say. Alexander's Truthwell flickered with the tongue of a hungry shadow.

Aly recognized the concentration on his face, the way his eyes danced as if he were hearing an invisible figure speak to him. *He's listening to something—no, someone.*

Someone was speaking to his mind with magic.

Only sorcerers could communicate silently with each other or with the person to whom they were Bound. That meant someone *else* was also Bound to Alexander.

No king should have two Royal Sorcerers.

Aly's senses leaped to the sorcerers in the room, but before she could discover who else was Pulling from Alexander, one phrase shattered her concentration.

The king said, "Eliminate them."

2 6

RED

The ache inside Red's bones slowed his movements and clouded his mind. The absence of her magic was like the absence of oxygen in his lungs, and all he could do was gasp and wait for its return.

Or was that his heart crushing under the knowledge that she'd betrayed him?

No, she wouldn't. The truth was hidden in her masked face, and he needed to know what it was. Lies wove clever webs, and in moments of distress, the mind more easily fell into those traps. He would not doubt Aly, not now, not after everything.

Alexander's three sorcerers grabbed him again and dragged him away from the cathedral doors, where his men were assembled, ready to attack. If he couldn't call his men off, they would fight to reach him.

This had not gone according to plan.

And now Aly wouldn't be protecting him when the bullets began to fly.

His limbs were frozen by a spell, and only his eyes could resist. Moving him this way was more humiliating than floating him along with their magic. The faces he passed looked on him with pity or arrogance. He closed his eyes, unable to bear their gazes and their scorn and the realization that he'd failed.

He'd failed Tandera. He'd lost Aly.

She was Bound to Alexander now—Bound to protect him no matter the threat, even if the threat were Red.

The anger inside of Red's chest begged him to attack, to command his men to overtake the cathedral and claim his crown by force. But this was not the way to win a crown, and his small band of men would be nothing against the army, against *Aly*.

As he was hurled out a side door adjacent to the altar, his last sight was of Aly's white cloak and black phoenix mask, not watching him, but frantically scanning the cathedral, as if suddenly there was something more important than what might possibly be the last moment he'd ever see her.

The door closed and gunfire split the day. His heart snapped like a piece of dry bread.

Unsure if anyone could hear him, Red shouted, "To me!"

He ran, but his movements compared to the rapid gunfire were slow and miserable. By the time he'd rounded the wall of buttresses, the masses—panicked and crazed—fled toward the side streets, but some had not made it.

Blood trickled onto pale stones in the bright sun.

Red screamed, "Cease fire!"

No one heard.

He drew his pistol and fired into the air. It was lost in the sound of a small battle. His men stumbled toward the cathedral, others lay lifeless. Seb was nowhere in sight. Flashes lit the inside of the dark cathedral, as if a battle of magic was taking place within.

Red took aim at a red-clad soldier and fired. The man spun away and out of view. Red had to make this stop. He would fight his way to the front and call his men off.

At the sound of gunfire from behind, Yin discovered Red's

presence and ran to him, immediately taking up a protective position in front of his king.

Two white cloaks soared out of the shattered rose window, apparently entangled in their own struggle. One of them had a whirl of dark brown hair.

"Aly!"

Of course she didn't hear, and he didn't expect her to.

A massive *boom* pulsed outward from the soaring figures and shook the square. Everyone paused.

Beside the cathedral, the façade of the great university library cracked and crumbled to the pavement, the angelic statues holding up the entrance falling prostrate before whatever force had brought them down.

As the dust billowed out from the crash, Red yelled once more, "Cease fire!"

This time, his men heard. They lifted their weapons to the sky, but as they did, the soldiers again took aim and fired.

Yin's body jerked sideways.

"No!" Red raced to catch Yin as he fell. "I said *cease fire!*"

The soldiers faltered, as if wanting to heed his command, but their king stood behind them and they obeyed Alexander now. They kept their guns trained on the retreating men but did not shoot again, now that they were certain their enemies had stopped firing at them.

Red choked back a sob as he looked at Yin's half-lidded eyes. "Stay with me."

Yin wheezed. "The phoenix will rise again." He took a shallow breath. "Rise with her."

Veeter Yin's eyes drifted shut.

Red couldn't bear to look down. He lowered Yin's head to the pavement and fisted his hands. All around him were more faces of men who would not be returning home, of men who'd died for him. All for nothing. He was still crownless, and Aly was Bound to Alexander.

Grey emerged from behind the soldiers, a pistol level at Red and his men.

Ah, so you are a traitor. Red didn't have much disappointment left in him.

The soldiers and Grey picked their way over the dozen or so fallen bodies and pressed Red's band of men away from the cathedral, toward the crumbled face of the library. The angelic faces that once peered down from the façade now, with broken noses, lay staring up at the sky as if wishing they could truly fly. The cobblestones had buckled in places from the impact of large stones, and in one hole lay a splayed copy of a leatherbound book, too dirty to tell which one. Much of their history, their art, had been destroyed in that strange blast.

Grey made his way forward until the barrel of his pistol pointed directly at Red's forehead. Red ground his teeth as he stared at the face of a man he'd trusted.

A strange muting fell around Red, and before he could process that he'd been shrouded, Grey whispered, without moving his lips at all, "With you."

Red narrowed his gaze. *What is Grey's game?*

"I wanted to know you could fight. That you *would* fight. For the crown. For her," Grey said, again not moving his lips. He flicked his pistol as if directing Red where to go, but Red noticed on the side of the gun a small slivered moon. "Waxing crescent, when you're ready."

The sounds around them returned.

As Red stepped backward over a fallen stone that might have once been an angel's ear, Alexander appeared at the cathedral's doors. His crown glittered in the sunlight. As if to make a point, he still held the ornamental royal scepter in his hand. *Aly is the scepter. He's holding that to remind me who she now serves.*

Red thought of the palace. Of his rooms. Of the hall that led to the sorcerer's chamber. Of her soot-stained fireplace and the twisting iron staircase he'd once climbed.

Nothing had been as he'd imagined. His assumptions had all turned out wrong. Even his assumptions about himself, that he could somehow turn himself into a good leader and take up his father's mantle, and carry on.

The palace, and all that went in it, belonged to Alexander. *Aly* belonged to his enemy.

She doesn't belong to anyone, he chided himself. But her magic *did*, and it was Alexander's to command. Her heart, on the other hand, he wasn't sure.

He'd hoped she loved him. What did that matter now?

His pulse thundered so fast his fingers throbbed. Wreckage he couldn't explain cluttered his mind, his chest, and his lungs. Men had died here, and he would have to bury them. Their deaths were his fault.

Yin and the other men had given their lives for something they believed in—a Tandera that didn't exist anymore.

Alexander called for silence. No one was talking, but everyone stilled and listened. From across the square, a white cloak arrowed toward them like a bird swooping to her master's arm. Aly, mask removed, dropped to the stones beside Alexander, her hair wild, her cheeks enflamed.

She scanned the faces until she found Red's. Her jaw was hard, her eyes angrier than he'd ever seen them. She was dangerous in this moment.

Alexander nodded condescendingly at her. Red almost laughed at how pathetic the man in the crown was next to Aly. He'd been that man once. He'd been so arrogant and foolish when he'd first met Aly.

She was the real power in Tandera.

As Alexander began to speak, Aly strode forward into the rubble-strewn space between the soldiers and Red's men, effectually silencing the new king. Alexander attempted to stop her. Fool.

She lifted both arms and dropped them toward the pavement.

Silence descended as heavy as the statues beside them. Grey stepped away, backing behind Alexander's soldiers and slipping away, unseen. Red kept his eyes on Aly.

"I will speak to him," she said, her words carrying over her shoulder to the king she now served. Her gaze remained fixed on Red. She looked at him like he was the sun on a distant mountainside—lovely and unreachable. The look surprised him. A moment ago she'd been as frightening as a coiled viper.

When she was only a few steps away, she hissed, "It's Kassia!" Her chest heaved with her breaths. "He wasn't lying—but she was."

Red's brain, still rattled by what had happened, tried to process her words. "What? Kassia?"

"She's been manipulating him. She was the one who did all the lying. Not him. At least not so much that he couldn't Bind. I am so sorry."

She reached for him, and he caught her hand in his, pulling her to him. His mind reeled with the truth even as his heart leapt to the heavens.

"Kassia is a sorcerer. Comforter, I think. Not strong, but clever. She resisted, but only with simple spells. I chased her away," Aly pointed up at the sky, "but my magic bid me return to Alexander since the idiot was approaching gunfire. She did all of this, Red. Every bit of it." Aly hung her head but Red lifted it with a finger. Tears leaked down the sides of her cheeks.

He leaned down and, between fast breaths, kissed her. "I will come with you."

Again, she shook her head. "He won't allow that."

"I haven't given up this fight. If I must conquer the entire world to have you, I will do it."

She leaned into him. "I know. But enough men have died. Besides, I can still see your light." She traced the side of his face with a finger.

"Then let my light guide you. Come back to me."

Behind them, Alexander called out for Aly to return to him.

Ignoring Alexander, she smiled weakly at Red's word. "I don't know why this happened or how, but I will remove Kassia as a threat, and when I do, I will find you."

"Until then, I will fight my way to you, no matter who stands in my way." He kissed her again, this time not allowing their hurry to interfere.

Aly wiped a tear from her eye. "It was always her plan, to separate us. She fears what we can do—or could do, before."

Red did not want to let her go. He wanted to hold her forever. Instead, he tilted his forehead against hers and whispered, "We will still do it, Aly, I promise." With a final breath, he released her and as she stepped away, he said, "I will not stop until this is over."

Aly walked backward, her feet never stumbling over debris, her stare not breaking from Red's as she moved to stand beside her sovereign. Theod had placed her there beside Alexander, and for whatever reason, the Maker had removed Red from beside her.

The shuffling noises of his men and the moaning of the injured returned as Aly's shroud lifted.

Alexander shoved the scepter at Aly and stepped forward. "You and your men are to be sentenced as traitors."

Red's stomach dropped. The punishment for traitors was death.

"I. Beg. Mercy," Aly said, her voice firm and unwavering. She punctuated each word with a small *thunk* of the scepter on the stone, as if reminding him who had the real power in this conversation.

Alexander peered back at Aly a moment, as if debating within himself whether or not he would risk offending her. "Fine," he barked, turning back to Red. "Though I do not see how this is a much better fate, I assign you to a post at Caridan. We are in need of men at the Canyon's edge. Take your band of traitors with you." He flourished a hand, as if entertained.

The men beside Red stiffened and grunted.

"We will go, Your Majesty," whispered Amos. "We're with you to the death, sire."

Red nodded, his eyes still on Aly. If his purpose was to fight against the Canyon, going to Caridan might not be such a bad start. Though without Aly, his chances of survival were much slimmer.

Aly shoved past Alexander and lifted the scepter, swirling it in the air around and above her like a circus performer might whirl a baton. Alexander shrieked his disapproval, but Red merely laughed. What was she up to now?

The pale stone dust on the ground swirled up like a small tornado, then lifted from the pavement and hovered in the air before Aly's face. With another flourish of the scepter, the dust took shape.

Aly snatched a small, simple band from the air and held it up for all to see. "He may not wear the golden crown of Tandera anymore," she called to Red over the open, sunlit space. "So here is a crown made out of Tandera's dust." She tossed him the crown.

He caught it amid the uproarious cheers of his men. *Long live the king*, they shouted as he placed the coronet on his head, staring in awe at Aly, who smiled back at him with the hint of promise in her eye.

"Long live the king," Aly said, and slammed the scepter sideways into Alexander's midsection.

The usurper king scrambled to remain standing and keep hold of the scepter, hands fumbling the heavy staff. Several people snickered. Naia cackled from somewhere behind Red.

As Aly turned away, she disappeared from view, stepping once more into the shadows. He wanted to hear her voice in his head, but he had to trust her now without being able to see or hear her.

Blind faith.

Mad hope.

He smiled, then turned to his men with a sobered expression. "To the Canyon," he declared.

ALSO BY C. F. E. BLACK

Scepter and Crown series:

Shield of Shadow

Blade of Ash

Scepter of Fire - coming soon!

Other titles:

The Veritas Project

To read Lord Weston Grey's backstory, sign up to be a reader VIP at

vip.cfeblack.com/join

If you enjoyed this book, please consider leaving a review. It helps more than you know.

ACKNOWLEDGMENTS

This book enters the world with the help and elbow grease of so many people and the grace of the good Lord.

First, to my family. Will, you have given me my dream. From that first gift card you gave me to get coffee while doing this crazy thing called NaNoWriMo, I knew you were someone who would support my dreams. Thanks for letting me write 2,667 words of a really bad fantasy novel each day while you had to study for things like differential equations. You are my favorite, and you tolerate my weird writer brain, even when I act like a dragon who lives in a pool.

To my boys. My sunshines. My heart. I hope you read and enjoy this book one day. Thanks for the naps that made this book possible.

To Mom, I will always need your ceaseless cheerleading. Thank you for loving my stories. To Dad, the world's best dev editor, thank you for reading the sketchy version of this book and fixing Elise, as well as basically everything else in this book.

To Hannah, this book might have come out next year (or never) without you. You gifted me my sanity during the sleepless months with a newborn and the precious gift of time.

To my street team, you people are amazing! Your encouragement and enthusiasm mean so much, and you deserve all the chocolate and sparkly things for all your help.

To Anshul, Laura, Jade, Anais, and Cissie, thank you for taking care of my heart while it was in your hands. You guys were magnificent beta readers. Thank you especially to Jade, for helping me see the ending this book needed.

To Monica, thank you for weeding out my boring verbs and sentence fragments, and for reminding me I forgot a character!

To Damian, thanks for the best cover yet.

To everyone who has shared or posted about Crown of Dust, thank you! It means the world.

To my Bright Fantasy crew and fellow authors, you are truly shining lights in my life. Thank you, Sarah Wilson, Constance Lopez, and Anastasis Blythe!

Constance, you have helped and encouraged me more than you know.

Sarah, you are an answer to prayer, and I am so privileged to call you friend.

Alisha Klapheke, thank you for your continued support.

To my Worlds of Wonder authors and readers, thank you for celebrating Crown of Dust with me.

As always, soli Deo gloria.

ABOUT THE AUTHOR

C. F. E. Black loves to get swept away in books, both reading and writing them. Fantasy and science fiction have been her bread and butter since childhood, and she can't imagine life without her beloved fictional worlds. She lives in beautiful north Alabama with her superhero husband, sons, and fur-family. Connect with her and find free stories at www.cfeblack.com.

IT ALL ENDS...

READ THE EPIC CONCLUSION TO THE SCEPTER AND CROWN SERIES,
SCEPTER OF FIRE, COMING SPRING 2023

Printed in the USA
CPSIA information can be obtained
at www.ICGtesting.com
LVHW041931250823
756325LV00008B/11/J